ROD I

The Year 1070
~Survival~

The Harrying of the North Series

Hindrelag Books

THE YEAR 1070
~SURVIVAL~

This is a work of fiction. Names, characters, organisations, places, events and incidents are either a product of the author's imagination or are used fictitiously.

For Judith, Lara, Clarissa and all who encouraged me...
...a tale woven around the edges of our distant family history.

To Anne,

With grateful thanks.

Rod x

Jan 17.

Contents

Author's Note

My motivation for writing the tale of Hravn and Ealdgith was a desire to leave something for my family's future generations that brings to life an early and easily forgotten period in our past. My parents' families, the Flints, Martins, Wilsons, Mattinsons, Pattinsons, Curwens et al can trace their lineage through 1000 years of life in Cumbria and the Borders, as far back as the nobility of the pre-Norman north, and through Gospatrick to Earl Uhtred of Northumberland and King Ethelred 2nd of England.

Modern Western societies are increasingly equal and diverse in their social attitudes. The Anglo-Saxon and Norse societies of pre-Norman England had evolved from pre-Roman Germanic cultures and followed an Orthodox English Christianity. They were more equal in their attitude to women, and their legal status, than the strongly Catholic, constraining and more misogynistic society that developed under the Normans. I wanted my two heroes to reflect all that is good about today's society whilst remaining true to their own time.

I live in Richmondshire and chose to use the traumatic time of the Harrying of the North as a vehicle for the tale. The geography speaks for itself; these are the places I have known and loved all my life.

I would like to thank all those who have supported and encouraged me, particularly in the laborious task of proof reading and for helping ensure that the story is understandable to all. In particular, my wife Judith for her support and encouragement; my mother Clarissa, herself a true Cumbrian and incredible font of family history; my daughter Lara, always full of enthusiasm for the tale and in some little way a role-model for Ealdgith; my brother Paul and his meticulous attention to detail; my niece Bella Haynes for her advice as one who is of an age with Ealdgith and last, but not least, my good friend Anne Wicks and her teacher's eye.

My thanks are also due to Andy Thursfield for his graphic design and art work, and to Kathleen Herbert whose book, 'Spellcraft – Old English Heroic Legends', recounts the tale of Hildegyd and Waldere.

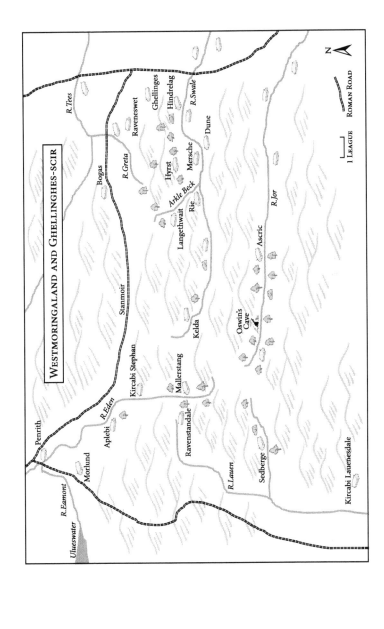

WESTMORINGALAND AND GHELLINGHES-SCIR

Place Names

Place names are those shown in the Oxford Dictionary of English Place-Names. I have used the name for the date nearest to 1070. Where a similar name has several spellings, I have chosen a common one in order to avoid confusion. Places that existed in 1070 but aren't listed retain their present name.

Aplebi. Appleby in Westmoreland. Village where apple trees grow.
Ascric. Askrigg. Ash-tree ridge.
Bebbanburge. Bamburgh. Stronghold of a Queen called Bebbe.
Bogas. Bowes. The river bends.
Carleol. Carlisle. Celtic; fortified town at a place belonging to Luguvalos.
Cumbraland. Cumberland. Region of the Cumbrian Britons.
Daltun. Dalton. Village in a valley.
Dune. Downholme. Place in the hills.
Dyflin. Dublin. Norse, derived from Gaelic 'Dubh Linn', meaning 'black pool'.
Esebi. Easby. Village of a man named Esi.
Euruic. York. From Celtic; probably meaning yew tree estate.
Gales. Gayles. Place at the ravines.
Ghellinges. Gilling West. Capital of the Wapentake of Ghelliges-scir.
Ghellinges-scir. Approximates to Richmondshire. North Yorkshire local government district embracing Swaledale, Arkengarthdale and Wensleydale.
Grinton. Grinton. Green farmstead.

Hagustaldes-ham. Hexham. The warrior's homestead.

Haugr-Gils. Howgills. Hills and narrow valleys.

Hep. Shap. Heap of stones.

Hindrelag. Richmond. English name before 1070. Origin not known.

Hudreswelle. Hudswell. Place at a spring of a man named Hud.

Hyrst. Hurst. Place at the wooded hill.

Jor. River Ure. Origin not known.

Kelda. Keld. The spring by the apple tree.

Kircabi Lauenesdale. Kirkby Lonsdale. Village with a church in the valley of the Lune.

Kircabi Stephan. Kirkby Stephen. Village with the church of St. Stephen.

Kircabi Thore. Kirkby Thore. Village with a church in the manor of Thore.

Langethwait. Langthwaite. Long clearing.

Loncastre. Lancaster. Fort on the River Lune (meaning: healthy).

Lundenburh. London. Celtic; place belonging to Londinos.

Marige. Marrick. Boundary ridge.

Mersche. Marske. Place at the marsh.

Meuhaker. Muker. Narrow cultivated spot.

Morlund. Morland. Grove in the moor.

Penrith. Penrith. Chief ford.

Ravenstandale. Ravenstonedale. Valley of the raven stone.

Raveneswet. Ravensworth. Ford of a man called Hrafn.

Richemund. Richmond. Norman name after 1070; meaning strong hill.

Rie. Reeth. Place at the stream.

Ripum. Ripon. Territory belonging to the tribe called Hrype.

Stanmoir. Stainmore. Rocky or stony moor.
Sedberge. Sedburgh. Flat topped hill.
Swale. River Swale. Old English 'Sualuae',
meaning rapid and liable to deluge.
Ulueswater. Ullswater. Lake of a man called
Ulfr.
Westmoringaland. Westmorland. District of
the people living west of the moors (Pennines).

Principle Characters

Ealdgith's Family

Thor. Father. Thegn of fourteen manors including the manor of Hindrelag.
Aebbe. Mother.
Earl Uhtred. Earl Uhtred The Bold of Northumbria. Great grandfather. Killed in 1016. Ealdgith's grandmother, Ecgthryth, was his first wife.
Earl Gospatrick. Earl of Northumbria 1067-69 and 1070-72. Grandson of Earl Uhtred and his third wife, Aelfgifu. Aelfgifu was the daughter of King Ethelred 2nd of England. He is Ealdgith's second cousin.
Gospatrick. Ealdgith's uncle. Brother of Thor. Thegn of nine manors.

Hravn's Family

Ask. Also known as The Bear. Norse heritage. Holds the manor of Raveneswet for Thorfinnr.
Hild. Ask's English wife. Sister to Thor.
Freya. Ask's Norse mistress. Hravn's mother.
Bron. Ask's mother, Hravn's grandmother. Cumbrian.
Rhiannon. Bron's sister.

The Pendragons

Uther. Head of the Pendragon family.
Urien. Pendragon's youngest and only surviving son.
Owain. Urien's son.

Nudd. Pendragon's grandson.
Math. Nudd's younger brother.
Beli. Nudd's son. Same age as Owain.
Bran. Pendragon's great grandson. Orphaned.

Others

Brother Oswin. Monk and former soldier.
Gunnar. Lord of the manor of Morlund. Norse.
Brother Patrick. Priest to the manor of
Morlund. Cumbrian.

The Harrying of the North

The Year 1070
~Survival~

Aefter Yule

Chapter 1

Pulling her cloak close Ealdgith squeezed her thighs against the fell pony's bare back, drawing warmth into her chilled core.   They'd turned around. The day was a failure; Sköll and Hati were lost on the wild high moor. A leaden haze filled the dale's head, black clouds loomed towards them from the west and a wet, possibly snowy, return home heralded trouble from her mother.   It was already late in the Aefter Yule day and home would be an hour away by the time they crossed the river Swale at the ford near Hindreslag and climbed around to the top of the cliffs north of the river.

"No!"   Hravn's scream caught in his throat before he choked it off.   He had sensed the danger before he'd seen it.   The strong wind, ripping the last of the dead leaves off the birch trees, had not quite muffled the screams. Screams of terror and pain.   The screams of men, women, children, animals. The sky, still blue to the East, was strangely yellow. He knew what was happening. He'd been warned weeks ago that it would happen – but he had pushed the thought of it away. He knew instinctively that his life, their lives, would never be the same again.

Hravn quickly slipped off the fell pony and, tethering it by the muddy track, motioned Ealdgith to do the same. Crouching below the scrubby line of gorse in front they left the cover of the birch thicket that had sheltered them from sight. They froze. The village of Hudreswell was one of her father's manors. It was only three fields away, but the peaceful cluster of thatched houses that they'd passed that morning was gone. In its place burned wooden skeletons. Smoke billowed away from them, eastward. Flames driven by the wind, ripping through the thatch and wood, were catching on the adjacent hay ricks and whirling into an inferno in the wind. Four armed men dressed in chainmail walked from house to house torching the thatch roofs. Four others, mounted and similarly dressed, stood guard in pairs at either end of the village whilst four more penned a dozen women and girls a short distance away from the flames. Bodies of men, boys and younger children lay where they had been slain as they left the houses and workshops. Animals too. Hravn could see that the destruction had been sudden and total – just as it had been foretold.

The horsemen to the left of the village started, their horses rearing up then moving forward at a gallop. Three figures had suddenly burst from the end house just as the flames in the thatch caught. A man and a woman moved quickly, an elder man lagged behind, limping. Theirs' was a forlorn hope. They could not out run the horsemen, the first of whom drew his sword and swinging it in a lazy, forceful, arc as he urged his horse forward struck the old man from behind on the base of the neck. Blood spurted from the semi severed head of the twitching body. The younger man turned, throwing himself behind the girl, taking the full blow of the sword frontally. The second horseman had ridden past the men and turning in front of the running girl grabbed her collar and used her momentum to hoist her over his saddle. It was over in seconds. She was dropped, sack-like, by the group of huddled women.

Hravn was numb. He felt sick, wanting his father; he would know what to do. But he knew that, just as a rabbit frozen in fear by a stalking stoat will surely die, he could not risk being afraid. He thought, too, of Ealdgith. He suspected he knew the fate of the penned women. Did she? He reached to touch her shoulder, maybe reassure her. Ealdgith was too rigid to respond. Turning to her he saw the tears below her wet green eyes, her half open mouth, her lower lip trembling. Her gaze was not towards the women or the fallen bodies; it was through and beyond the smoke to the hill across the valley. Her home, the hall at Hindrelag Manor on the high bluff above the Swale, was burning. The Normans had arrived.

3

"Come Edie, come now." He called her by her affectionate name, his voice strangely controlled, soft, insistent in her ear. "Maybe your folks saw them coming and fled north. Ghellinges is stronger, it's the capital of Ghellinges-scir, and everyone should be safe there. Earl Edwin will surely hold the Normans off. Come, we'll try to cross the river at Grinton and get to Ghellinges by way of Raveneswet. It will be long after dark by the time we get there, but the ponies are sure footed enough." Ealdgith nodded, too numb to speak. She followed Hravn as they reclaimed their ponies and led them quietly back though the birch copse before mounting and galloping west across the high moor, knowing that in the dead ground they were safe from view.

Riding into the wind they again heard screams that heralded death and destruction. Dune, a cluster of houses below the high moor, was on their way to the Swale crossing at Grinton. Dropping to the ground just short of the hillcrest they crawled to the edge. They could see Dune clearly a furlong away, lower down across the wild heather and scrub that bordered the high moor. A body of armed men, similar to those at Hudreswell, were clearing the wattle and thatch houses of their occupants, clubbing and beating them with their swords, forcing them all into the largest of the buildings. Cattle and pigs were stampeding in disarray; those that came close to the men were brutally hacked. A last stray child of six or seven was thrown into the larger building. Two men held those inside back at spear point, as the doors were slammed shut and a cart of hay pushed across to block the exit. Even a furlong away the screaming was intense. The armed men paused as a mounted man, obviously in charge, came from the back of the building. Hravn focussed on the shield slung over the man's shoulder. He'd seen those black and white chequered colours before, but where?

Taking a torch from one of the armed men the leader looked around the group, fixing their gaze and gaining their consent to his action. He then deliberately tossed the burning brand onto the thatch.

Hravn and Ealdgith couldn't watch. They clung to each other and sobbed, their shaking bodies covered by the fading purple of the heather as the wind blew the sound of the screams over them.

The screaming stopped. Hravn raised his head cautiously. The men had gone. Smoking wooden frames and piles of flame-licked ash were all that remained. All the animals had gone too; he could hear their distressed cries in the valley bottom. A smell of roast meat, reminiscent of feasts in his father's hall drifted over them. He felt nauseous.

"Edie, we can't go home now" he said slowly, hushed. Black columns of smoke were rising from behind the fells north of the Swale. It wasn't the random smoke of a heath fire. Instead, the pattern of the columns mapped the pattern of the life they knew. The manors of

Ghellinges, Raveneswet, Gales, Daltun and many more were all in flames.

Hravn had heard their uncle, Lord Gospatrick, warn about harrying when he had returned from the autumn rising against the Normans and spoken to the local thegns in the hall that belonged to Ealdgith's father, Thor. Now he knew what harrying was.

He remembered too where he had seen those colours before. The black and white check was the sign for Count Alan Rufus of Brittany, the King's kinsman and companion. Lord Gospatrick had one of Count Alan's knights with him as his hostage when he fled north, defeated.

Chapter 2

The first rain roused them from a numb stupor. Fine drops, mixed with wet snow, blew in on the wind. "We have to find shelter" Ealdgith's voice was strangely shaky and younger sounding than that of a 14-year-old. "There's the shepherd's hut we passed earlier, I'm sure we'd be safe there." Hravn nodded, not yet trusting himself to speak. He could tell from the clouds that were now almost overhead that they had little time if they were to stay reasonably dry. They certainly couldn't risk being soaked and exposed overnight on the high moor. "We'll back track and loop around, we can't be seen if we go that way" he shouted as he ran back to the ponies. Ealdgith followed, mounted and chased after Hravn at a gallop.

They reined the ponies to a halt in a small clearing in a birch wood just as the larger drops began to fall, darkening the soft purple and green colours of their cloaks. The shepherd's hut was in a clearing in a wood that was at the top of the fell separating the valleys of the Jor and the Swale.

The hut was old; a low dry stone wall circle topped by a turf-covered cone of birch poles. Tying the ponies under the shelter of a tree, they ducked under the low door. It was dry inside, but dark. A little light came through the door and from a hole at the apex of the roof. Dry ferns piled to one side would provide bedding, and a stack of dry kindling and wood stood by the small central hearth.

Now that they were busy, they felt better and set to instinctively. Hravn kindled a fire from the flint and steel he kept in a leather pouch and Ealdgith pooled their remaining crusted bread, small lump of ewe's cheese and dry mutton to form a meal. "I've no appetite, but we're going to have to eat. Here take this," she sighed, passing Hravn a portion of their food.

Later, as smoke drifted up through the hole in the roof and occasional raindrops fell sizzling on the fire, the cousins lay back on the dry ferns, wrapped their cloaks close around themselves and cuddled together thinking through the shock of the last few hours.

The day had started so well. They'd set out early. Hravn was desperate to find Sköll and Hati, the two young Irish wolfhounds that they'd raised to be hunting hounds.

Hravn and Ealdgith shared Sköll and Hati; the hounds were the focus of their lives. Two summers ago, Hravn had accompanied his father on a hunt to find a notorious wolf that was attacking flocks along the edge of the Arkengarthdale forest. Hravn's hound, Loki, had caught the scent and taken off in pursuit. They hadn't seen the wolf but after a search they had found Loki's body, his throat torn out. For Hravn it was a bitter lesson in the danger of wolves. Hravn's father, Ask, could see how upset his son was. Even though Hravn had fought back his tears it was obvious that the loss of Loki really affected him. That autumn Ask had returned from a visit to the market at Kircabi Stephan with two Irish wolfhound cubs, both male, one for Hravn and one for Ealdgith. Ask was rather fond of Ealdgith. She was obviously closer to Hravn than any of his son's half-sisters, so he tended to indulge his niece just as he did Hravn.

Last week, on the eve of the Yuletide feast, they'd taken the hounds, who were now over a year old and almost fully grown, to the moors south of the Swale. It was new ground for them and an adventure for Ealdgith and him. It ended in failure and they had returned grudgingly at dusk without Sköll and Hati.

It now looked as if they had lost their hounds, as well as their homes, and families.

The day after the Yuletide feast that had heralded the start of the year 1070 Hravn's father, Norse thegn of the manor of Raveneswet, had forbidden Hravn to go south of the Swale because of the threat that the Normans would come seeking revenge for the latest rising against their rule. They had heard at Yuletide that the King was at Euruic for the Christmas festival. This was proof that he wasn't going to let matters in the North rest as they were. Ask was sure that the broad and fertile dale of the Jor was going to be ravaged but he was hopeful that the narrow, more defensible, dales to the north would escape. He also thought that King William would wait until the worst of the winter was over before leading his troops into the North; but he didn't want to risk Hravn and Ealdgith straying too far from the safety of the many, local, small manors.

Ealdgith, Hravn's cousin by marriage and only six months younger, was his closet friend. The youngest of a brother and twin sisters she was of little interest to her father, Thor. Ealdgith was a boy at heart, she played instead with Hravn.

Thor's sister, Hild, was married to Ask. When Hild failed to bear him a son Ask had taken a Norse mistress, Freya. Freya was Hravn's mother; who named him for his black inquisitive eyes. He was brought up by his mother and was indulged by his father who considered him his heir. Although Hravn's father was a thegn, he was of a lesser status than Ealdgith's father. He held only one manor, Raveneswet, and his lord was Thorfinnr who held all the Norse manors in the enclave in the valley of the Greta, just north of the river Swale.

Hravn and Ealdgith slept, their bodies exhausted by their reaction to the adrenalin surge of the past few hours. Hravn roused sometime later. The fire had burnt out and the rain appeared to have stopped. Taking care to leave Ealdgith asleep he headed carefully towards the dull light of the low door and ducked outside. The clouds had cleared causing the temperature to drop suddenly – that must have woken him. Frost was forming, turning the grass and dead bracken crisp beneath his feet. He shivered.

From the vantage at the top of the fell he knew that in the star light he should be able to see along the length of both dales. What he saw confirmed his fears. Instead of the normal black quiet of the country night a dozen or more patches of light glowed in the valley bottoms to the north and south. The light was from the remains of villages that still burned despite the overnight soaking, testament to the intensity of the fires that had consumed them. It was testament too of how the Normans despised them all: Saxon, Norse and Dane.

"Edie" Hravn gently shook Ealdgith's shoulder. She woke quickly, reassured by Hravn's silhouette in the half-light. "We can't stay here, the Bastard's men have attacked the Jor villages too, they're on both sides of us now. The only thing we can do is to keep going west and hide in the forest at head of the Jor. We might be able to find my grandmother's people."

"Who?" Ealdgith was confused. Hravn continued to explain. "My father's mother, Bron, was from the Cumbri, across the far fells. She taught me their tongue, or some of it anyway. Cumbraland was never the English king's land, its sworn to the King of Scotland. The Bastard's men won't go there". Hravn continued to abuse their oppressors, questioning the legitimacy of their new King in the way that the men of the North did.

"I know, I suppose there's not much else we can do" Ealdgith sighed. "But why is it all happening? It's wrong! My father's people, my people, all killed, their homes and crops burned. Why? It's hateful!"

Hravn knew why. "We knew it was going to happen, we all did. We just didn't want to believe it. You were there in the hall with your uncle and Earl Edwin when he said that if his kinsman, Earl Gospatrick, and the rightful heir to England's throne, the Atheling Edgar, failed in their rising against the so-called King then we would all be at risk. The Normans are cruel, they'll burn and ravage. Grind us all down and make us respect them. Respect!" He spat "How? Not after this!"

"So" Hravn continued "We run, we hide and we stay alive. We'll find sanctuary somewhere. I don't know where but we'll keep going 'til we do. I know little of the Cumbri, but I know something of your family's history and their links to the old King Ethelred and I am sure we will have a chance. Earl Gospatrick is a Prince of the Cumbri as well as the Lord of the North. He has lands both sides of the border. If he escapes the King, I'm sure he will return to Cumbraland. Earl Gospatrick's father, Prince Maldred, was from the Cumbri. The Earl's mother is called Ealdgith, the same as you, and her mother was Aelgifu. Aelgifu was King Ethelred's daughter. Her husband, the Earl's grandfather, was Lord Uhtred the Bold of Northumberland; Aelgifu was his third wife."

12

"Edie, you are kin to Earl Gospatrick too. Your great grandmother was Lord Uhtred's first wife, Ecgthyth. That's why your uncle is also called Gospatrick. It's a family name. If we can gain sanctuary with the Earl we will be safe, but Cumbraland is a dangerous place. I know that my grandmother had to flee her lands because of strife in Cumbraland. She says the border there is wild and that men live beyond the law. She had a hard time. Her family held land at Ravenstandale. One day their manor was raided by a warlord called Pendragon and they were sold into slavery. Thank God that she was away at market in Kircabi Stephan at the time and managed to flee across the border into Swaledale after she returned home and discovered what had happened. That's when my grandfather met her."

Ealdgith didn't look convinced. She was confused by the sudden burst of family history and the fact that there were two Gospatricks, or were there three? It didn't much matter; it was more than she could take in at the moment. But she knew that they had no alternative plan, so she just nodded and changed the subject "What about Sköll and Hati? Can we still try and find them? They would help protect us, and they can't survive for long without us." Hravn sucked his lip "No", he said hesitantly "We can't risk calling them with the hunting horn anymore. We'll be heard and give ourselves away. I guess they are something else we've lost."

"We'll need food too, and blankets" Ealdgith started to tick items off on her fingers.

13

"Something to cook with, knives, flasks, even some more clothes." She was more confident when thinking for herself. "I know what we can do," interrupted Hravn, "We'll go back to the houses at Dune. They weren't burned so we might find something there."

"I, I can't" stammered Ealdgith "I just can't. It's too…". Her voice tailed off as Hravn said softly, "I know what you mean, I'll go. You stay close by and keep watch from the ridge line."

At first light Hravn led the fell ponies cautiously down from the scrub. He had found the nearest point to the dead village and spent a few minutes checking that it was deserted. The low sun threw dark shadows behind all the buildings and he peered intently. There was no sign of life, neither human nor animal; though the stench of burned flesh still hung over the village. Thankfully, there was no movement in the valley either and no signs of any soldiers. Ealdgith crouched in a gap in the scrub watching him intently.

Keeping well clear of the smoking ruin, and using the buildings to screen him from the valley below, Hravn tethered the ponies by the entrance to one of the larger houses before edging open the door. Taking a few moments for his eyes to accustom to the gloom, he searched methodically for what they needed and quickly made a small pile by the door. They were riding the ponies bare backed and he needed to sling small sacks together, tying them so that they would hang comfortably across both flanks of each pony without slipping off. He worked his way through his mental list. Bread, cheese, a flagon to hold spring water, tinder, kindling, blankets, some spare clothing if it was suitable. He realised that they would be limited by how much the ponies could carry and that Ealdgith and he would have to walk much of the way if they weren't to overburden them.

The more that Hravn thought about it the more he realised the size of the challenge ahead. They would need to be as self-sufficient as possible if they were going to cope alone in the wild border lands. That morning he'd also seen the white reflection of the snow that now lay all along the fells that formed the border. Yesterday's bad weather had brought the first winter snow; they would have to choose their way with even more care.

They would also need coin to pay their way and some means of defending themselves. Ealdgith and he carried bows that they used for hunting with the wolfhounds. Hravn also had a seax of his own that his father had given him. The seax was a short sword, with a broad two-foot blade, that marked his freeborn status. His seax was razor sharp and the heavy blade was ideal for close fighting where slashing and stabbing were what counted. If he had a sword, he could also use the seax in his left hand instead of a shield to parry an opponent's sword. Hravn's father had given him the seax a summer ago when he had proved that he was capable of using it in training. The blade of Hravn's seax was engraved with runes in a traditional curse on all enemies and inlaid with intricate patterns in copper and silver, beaten into both sides of the blade. They would need more than just the long seax and bows and Ealdgith would need to be able to defend herself or, at the very least, deter someone from attacking her.

There was a collection of utensils by the hearth and Hravn took a couple of small copper pots, a beaker and two silver handled eating knives or small seax. He also found a rather longer seax with a delicately patterned bone handle and fine twelve-inch blade that had probably belonged to the mistress of the house. The seax was a work of art. Hravn could tell by the way that the now slim blade had been honed down to a fine razor-like edge that it must be very old. The blade fitted into a leather sheath suspended from a fine leather belt that was entwined with gold thread. He would give this to Ealdgith; it would show her status as a freeborn woman of some wealth. The belt had been repaired and adjusted several times and Hravn was sure that he could move the buckle and adjust the belt to fit Ealdgith's slim waist. He hoped that a display of status might just help protect her in the days ahead. The seax would certainly help defend her.

Once Hravn had found all the food and utensils they needed, he wrapped them in bundles and secured them to the ponies. He then went looking for coins and weapons. He had a boyish knack for hiding things and enjoyed the challenge of searching. By the time he had checked the third house he had a mixed handful of silver and cut pennies that he collected in a leather pouch.

Then Hravn hit lucky. The last house stood slightly apart from the others and someone of importance and status seemed to have lived there, probably the reeve. It must have been rent collection time because several small pouches of silver pennies were laid out on the table. He weighed them in his hand, maybe fifty coins in all? They would need to hide these carefully in their kit and about their bodies. The coins had been due to be paid to Ealdgith's father as rent from the manor. Hravn felt no guilt in taking them.

Several spears of varying lengths were propped in a corner. Hravn took two, each about six feet long with an iron head on an ash shaft. The shaft butts were capped with iron and the heads were inlaid with bronze and silver patterns in a Danish style. He knew that as well as doubling up as good walking staffs the spears would further display their free-born status.

Hravn knew that neither they, nor their ponies, could carry more than he had gathered. He led them briskly back up the hill, re-joining Ealdgith at the gap in the scrub. He continued further up in to the birch thicket before stopping to show her what he had and give her the decorated seax. Her eyes widened as she realised its significance. They had both stepped into adulthood. The seax appealed to her boyish side too. "I'll be a Valkyrie, a shield maiden to guard your back" she quipped, only half in jest.

"Come on, let's go," she urged. "It's time for us to move on."

Hravn had an instinctive understanding of the lie of the land. His Norse and Cumbric blood-line hefted him to the fells and dales as effectively as the Herdwick sheep that his forefathers had introduced across the Northern uplands.

They walked, leading their fell ponies. Hravn's was brown and Ealdgith's a lighter bay.

It was hard to tell the cousins apart at a distance. When they had set out the day before Ealdgith had dressed for winter on the moor and wore some of her elder brother's old clothes; both wore leather boots, stockings bound with leather and cloth, thigh length trousers, a linen tunic with a wool over tunic and a woollen cloak clasped at the shoulder with a silver brooch of Norse design. Neither covered their head. Hravn's hair was worn long in the Norse fashion and was as black as his eyes, another sign of the Cumbric blood of his grandmother, and the reason for him being given the Norse name of the raven. He was stocky for a boy a month shy of fifteen, not yet tall but starting to grow quickly.

Ealdgith was tall for her fourteen and a half years and certainly as tall as her stockier cousin. She was slim and lithe and her long fair hair showed her Saxon heritage. It was unbraided and pulled through a ring at the back of her head. As they walked across the moor Ealdgith was very conscious of the seax hanging from her belt. It was a very physical symbol of the many ways in which she was suddenly moving into womanhood. It gave her confidence, although she was daunted by the thought of what womanhood meant.

The purple, green and russet weave of their cloaks blended quickly with the dull heather, dying bracken and rough upland grass as they wound their way around limestone outcrops, taking care not to expose themselves on a skyline.

Down to their right, a little further up the valley, fresh smoke rose from Marige, another of Ealdgith's Uncle Gospatrick's manors. Rie was burning too. They didn't speak. There was no need.

Chapter 3

Ealdgith and Hravn walked slowly, but with determination. The lie of the land forced them progressively to the south, away from Swaledale, and as the spur of the high moor rose and broadened they were lost in their own small world of wild heather. Although they couldn't see down into either valley they could see behind, across the broad Jorvale, to the far moors by the coast where the grey summits were now topped with white. As the day progressed more and more plumes of smoke rose across the vale, rising lazily and merging into a dark blue pall. If they needed a further reminder of the destruction of their world, then this was it.

Ealdgith was learning not to view life with the optimism of a child. It was obvious from the density of the smoke that crops as well as villages were being burnt. They had seen animals slaughtered at Hudreswell and she knew that they were now being slaughtered in the valleys below. With the onset of winter, and the destruction of all the barns and the animals, there would be no food and no shelter. If anyone did survive, just as she had, how would they cope? They would be imprisoned in a desolate, freezing wasteland and unable to walk out because the distances were just too great.

The thought of what could happen to them chilled her. She thanked God that they had a small supply of food and were hopefully beyond the edge of the terrible destruction. She thanked God too that she was with Hravn. She trusted him like a brother and knew that he would succeed in finding his grandmother's people; but who were they and what would they be like?

Hravn's thoughts were of the threat posed by marauding wolves. An encounter with a wild boar was less likely than a wolf at these heights but he knew a boar would be a serious threat if they were cornered in one of the many steep, narrow, wooded valleys that they were constantly forced to cross. Hravn was determined to keep their route well above the inhabited valley sides but low enough to have a ready supply of fresh water from the many springs that flowed from the limestone. He knew also that they would need shelter at night. It was early in Aefter Yule and the temperature would fall rapidly to freezing, with the cold seeping down from the snow-covered moor above them.

They spent their first evening sheltering under a limestone ledge that jutted above a broad bluff at the head of a little valley. They couldn't see down into the broader valley of the Jor below. Hravn chose the most discreet place, where an old rowan tree shielded the view of the valley, and moved some small boulders to build a fire place that would not allow any flames to be seen. Whilst he did this, Ealdgith scanned the valley for sign of life. It was still. He waited until the sun sank behind the high ground before lighting a small fire, making sure that tell-tale smoke wouldn't be seen in daylight. Huddling together, they eked out a small meal before falling into a cold and fitful sleep until dawn.

Ealdgith woke first. The fire had long since burned out and she could not risk relighting it. At least it was dry and the day was still, heralding winter sunshine. Her fingers were numb with cold and she blew on them and sucked them; life returning to them with a painful tingle. As she scrutinised the valley opposite the sun's early rays caught a movement at the base of the limestone cliff on the far side, a half furlong away. She froze, then relaxed as she realised that the movement was from a murder of crows, hovering above an object at the base of the cliff. Intrigued, she shook Hravn. "Do you see?" she questioned, pointing. He roused on his elbow, still stiff from the cold and hard ground. "See! Do you think we should take a look? Something has been killed, the crows are after carrion. If it is fresh, we might be able to take some and cook it." Hravn was unsure. "Possibly," he hesitated, "but only if it's very fresh". "Come on then..." They left the ponies tethered by the rowan and ran, following the contour of the cliff around to the far side of the valley.

A small fawn, a roe deer, lay by the cliff. It was not yet stiff and must have been killed at first light. Hravn dashed forward. His sudden delight tempered by caution. He wasn't delighted by the chance of fresh meat, although that would be very welcome. His delight was at how the fawn had been killed. It had been attacked by the throat and its head nearly severed, large parts of its chest and haunch had been ripped away. Could this mean that Sköll and Hati had done this? Were they nearby? Surely this was the work of either a wolf or a large dog? Then he saw the paw prints in the mud. His heart leapt. He dared to hope. The print was from the large pad of a wolfhound.

"Keep a look out Edie, it's just possible Sköll and Hati have been here, but if they haven't then we're stealing a wolf's breakfast, and that's not a good idea," he added with a wry smile. Ealdgith paused and looked up. She felt very vulnerable and longed for the reassuring touch of Hati's nuzzle against her hand. "May be, just may be, we could try calling them?" she urged. "We are a long way from the valley and surely the sound of the horn won't carry that far. Even if it does, no one would know where the sound came from". Hravn hesitated, mentally tossing the consequences; they would risk a lot but they could gain a lot too. "Let's try," he decided at last.

Hravn grasped the horn that was slung around his neck and hung under his right shoulder. It was a work of art and his prized possession, even more precious than his long seax. The horn was another present from his indulgent father. It was made of white ivory with the rim and mouthpiece trimmed in ornate silver. His father said that the ivory came from one of the sea monsters that his Norse kinsfolk hunted on the far northern coasts. He placed the horn to his lips and blew a quick three-note call. They listened, waited! Hravn blew again, louder this time. A couple of seconds passed, and then... a long howl replied from above the cliffs. A second, slightly higher pitched howl, followed the first.

Hravn and Ealdgith jumped up, looked at each other and then jumped up and down and embraced grinning widely. Hravn blew the horn again, more softly this time, and seconds later a rustle of the trees on the side of the cliff heralded two grey bodies that threw themselves at the cousins, their noses nuzzling their hands. Ealdgith threw her arms around Hati's neck and hugged him. She loved Hati, just as Hati loved his mistress. Her warm tears dripped onto Hati's furry neck. As Ealdgith hugged Hati, Hravn rolled on the turf shaking Sköll in a mock fight. The four were reunited and Hravn and Ealdgith at last felt that maybe they could survive. This must be a good omen.

They had named their hounds after two characters from the tales of Hravn's Norse heritage. Hati and Sköll were evil wargs that chased the sun and the moon. Cunning and strong they succeeded in their quest, just as Hravn and Ealdgith hoped their two wolfhounds would succeed as hunters of wolves. The names worked too: short, sharp and easily distinguishable by the hounds when shouted as a command. Both wolfhounds had grown quickly and were now heavier than either of the cousins. Hati was taller than Ealdgith's waist.

"We can't play here all day," Hravn teased Ealdgith. "We'll need to make use of the fawn as well. We should let the hounds eat their fill and then cook the rest now before moving on. I think we can risk a small fire. There's so much smoke in the air now that it probably won't be noticed." Ealdgith agreed. She was so relieved to have Hati back that her nausea had gone; she was ravenous.

They ran back to the rowan tree, where Hravn quickly restarted the fire with a little of his kindling and Ealdgith began skinning the fawn with one of the eating seax. The hounds hovered about her, expectantly. Her mouth watered in anticipation just as much as their jaws drooled

The meal over and the fire stamped out they finally got under way quite late in the morning. Hravn let the hounds run ahead, though Hati kept circling back to nuzzle Ealdgith's hand. The ponies followed closely, carrying their loads.

Ealdgith almost skipped along. Hati's return restored her confidence and lifted her spirits. Where they skirted around patches of snow she scooped it up and threw snow balls for Hati to chase. She aimed the odd one at Hravn's neck as he walked ahead, sensing out the driest track to follow through the peaty bogs and marshy grassland that formed this part of the moor.

Although Hravn had managed to shrug off some of his gloom he couldn't find it in himself to play snow balls. He knew they had to find shelter again before the failing afternoon light disappeared and he scanned the middle distance repeatedly for somewhere that might provide some cover. He was concerned that as the day had progressed the sky had become increasingly overcast and the clouds were darkening into a heavy yellowy grey. He worried about more snow.

As they wound their way across the moor Hravn wondered about Ealdgith. She'd always been his closest friend and companion. He had never really thought about her as a girl. He supposed that because she was the daughter of a high born thegn who held several manors, she would always be required to marry a husband of status. She was already of marriageable age and he knew that the day must come sooner rather than later. He knew that Ealdgith had never thought of life like that. He just supposed that it was inevitable that she must marry to suit her father's wishes. Yet whenever he thought of his own adult future, which wasn't very often, Ealdgith was always there as part of it. All that had now changed. Their lives were here and now. Their futures would be driven by Wyrd, one of the three goddesses of fate, and what little they could do to influence her. He knew that their lives were going to be much interwoven; it couldn't be otherwise if they were to survive in the unknown lands ahead of them. He knew too that he now had to care for Ealdgith, and he was happier for it. The latent deep affection for her that he had subconsciously bottled up suddenly surfaced and he felt awed at the responsibility. He smiled as he walked. Turning quickly, he caught the snowball she had aimed at him and threw it back in her face, laughing.

A little later, seeing a reflection of light ahead, but lower down the fellside, he called back, "Come on! I'll race you, we can camp by the tarn." The hounds won. Hravn and Ealdgith came in together whilst the two ponies ambled stolidly behind, unfazed by the momentary madness. The cousins collapsed, panting, on the grassy bank of the tarn that was sheltered by a small mixed wood of rowan, birch and pine.

"This will be brilliant," Hravn shouted cheerfully, relieved not to be caught out on the exposed moor. "We can camp under the shelter of the giant holly that's growing out of yon outcrop. There's enough dead wood under the pines for a fire and we can water the horses in the tarn."

"I'll get the wood," volunteered Ealdgith. "You sort out the bedding and some food."

They relaxed in the half-light, sitting on boulders by the fire and soaking the warmth into their bodies. Hravn spoke first, "Edie, I think we are going to make it. I don't know why or how, but I just feel that we will."

"I know" she said softly. "I know we will, just so long as we stay together."

The snow came just after dark. They used one of the blankets to extend the cover provided by the holly and sheltered the ponies as close by as possible. The hounds curled up with them under the holly, their warmth a welcome price to pay for a restless night.

Hravn lay awake for a while in the half light of dawn. The silence was overwhelming. Raising himself up, he saw that the world around them had changed. Deep snow covered the ground away from the cover of the trees, their boughs bending under the weight of the snow. A light mist cut visibility to a furlong at the most.

Chapter 4

The change in the weather was not welcome.
Hravn knew immediately that they wouldn't be
able to continue following the lower edge of the
high moor to the head of the dale. The snow
would hide the rocky and boggy ground. There
would be no tracks to follow and they would be
at risk of breaking an ankle or losing direction
altogether. It would also be far too cold for
them to survive overnight. This meant that they
would have to go down into the valley bottom
and risk facing discovery by the Normans. He
was sure that the soldiers would clear the valley
at least as far as the wild Mallerstang Forest.
Even the thought of moving down into the valley
bottom worried him. He didn't know the area
this far south west of Raveneswet and he had no
idea of the lie of the land other than that the
valley head was filled by the wild forest.

The snow was about a hand's width deep, which
meant that it was probably thinner in the valley
bottom. They would be able to move alright but
they would leave tracks, which added to Hravn's
concern. The hounds on the other hand loved
the snow. It was their first experience of it, and
after a first few tentative steps on the new cold,
soft land they dug into it, and rolled and jumped
all over it until they were called to heel.

After a quick cold breakfast, they packed the blanket and headed down the fellside. Hravn angled their route across the fall of the land, trying to keep some height as long as possible. As the mist thinned gradually, they were able to see across the white expanse of the valley; a small world locked in upon itself. The snow threw the features of the terrain into sharp relief, with the black silhouettes of trees and occasional buildings making a stark contrast against the white.

"Look Edie that must be the River Jor and where you can just see a dark smudge must be where the wild forest starts. That's Mallerstang Forest, it has to be. I think there is a settlement just inside it. You can see where there is a clearing beyond the first trees, and there's hearth smoke too."

"There is certainly one this side of the trees," Ealdgith pointed. "See that low ridge with the line of trees on it? There are buildings just this side of it."

Hravn nodded. "Mmm, and a track that links the two I think. We'd have to cross the river. Can you see where the track cuts across it? I wonder if it's a bridge or a ford?"

"Do you think it would be guarded?" Ealdgith worried.

They stood looking, thinking. Hravn weighed up the risks. "Let's try and miss the first village and then see if we can find a way through into the forest without crossing the river. We might be able to miss both villages if we are lucky. I just hope we are."

Hravn continued to lead, angling their route carefully down across the slope of the valley side and aiming for the northern edge of the forest where it touched a limestone cliff. It wasn't easy going; the fall of the slope was getting steeper. "We can't get across that, Hravn." Edith called ahead, dispirited. They were dropping into a small steep valley that ran below the cliff and cut across the front of the forest. It was becoming obvious that a beck, swollen by winter rain, ran down the valley.

"It's no good" he agreed. "We'll have to follow the beck down and see where we can get across." The line of the beck lay between the forest and the first of the two settlements.

The low ridge with the line of ash trees hid them from the village. "Stay here Edie, I'll see if there is anyone about before we go further." Hravn handed his pony's bridle to Ealdgith and made his way up to the top of the ridge. Shielding his head behind the trunk of a tree, he peered around to have a closer look at the village. He'd been right to be cautious. The Normans had been there too. Half a dozen snow covered bodies lay contorted by the track that led towards the Jor. He slid back down from the ridge. "Edie, it's not good, they've been here too. There are bodies by the track, but no sign of anyone in the buildings. It must have been yesterday or the day before because they are

31

covered by last night's snow. There is no sign of burning though so I wonder if they were cut down whilst fleeing. Maybe others managed to escape to the manor in the forest?"

"If the Normans are still nearby, or if they've moved into the forest to sack the next manor, we are going to risk getting caught in the open. We're going to have to move quickly. Why don't we ride? I'm sure the ponies would cope for a short distance" Ealdgith suggested, rising to the challenge posed by the new threat.

"You're right. If we go at a quick trot the ponies should still be able to keep their footing on the track. The snow's not as deep here."

They mounted, headed their ponies out of the little valley and trotted down the track feeling suddenly very exposed and vulnerable. The Jor was crossed by a wide ford, where they dismounted and led the ponies cautiously across through shin deep freezing water. Their feet numbed quickly and Ealdgith knew that they would have to stop and dry them before very long; it was just another problem for them to overcome. Remounting, they could see where the track entered the forest a furlong away; the trees marking a forbidding black line against the white snow and grey mist. "Let's go for it." Hravn called to Ealdgith. Digging his heels into the pony's flank, he urged him into a gallop towards the sinister gap ahead, reassured that there were no tracks in the snow. The hounds followed.

They eased up as they entered the gap in the trees, cautiously walking the ponies along the forest track. The stillness was even more foreboding, the trees crowding in as they rode abreast. The hounds lagged behind, distracted by the scent of a deer at the forest edge.

"Edie, I think we should see if we can find a track to the right, we…." Hravn was cut short. A rope jerked taut across their path at chest height, the sound cracking through the still air like a whip lash.

"Hold there! Sit still!" The harsh command froze them both. Hravn's half drawn seax remained in its scabbard. "Now turn, slowly! No tricks!"

Their way ahead was blocked by the rope and they slowly wheeled the ponies to face two men. Hravn immediately saw them for who they were, churls; low born freemen who were using the shelter of the forest for robbery. They were no doubt capitalising on the chaos in the valley and preying on those who might try to escape the devastation in the dale behind.

The men, although roughly dressed, were well armed. Each held a long seax pointing directly at Hravn and Ealdgith's stomachs, blocking their way and deterring any thought of their riding out of the trap.

The taller of the two was badly scarred on his right cheek; he appeared to be in charge. "Now lad, we mean you no harm. We've had good pickings from the likes of you; these Normans have been good for us for once. We'll take what you have in those bags and let you go on your way, if you cooperate that is." "Not until the girl has given us payment too…" the second sneered, letting the true meaning of their intention sink home. Ealdgith's mouth clenched. She stared at him in disgust, horrified by the sight of his face; one eye stared back at her, the other was a sightless white ball.

Hravn knew he would have to fight. He would risk all to save Ealdgith from their assault. He just needed to create a distraction in order to draw his seax and place himself between the men and Ealdgith. "We'll cooperate," he said slowly. As he spoke Hravn was looking past the men at Hati and Sköll. The hounds had sensed the threat and were stalking along the edge of the track, their heads down and hackles raised, their eyes fixed on the backs of the two men. Hravn refocused his eyes on Scar Face, not wanting to give any indication that they weren't alone. Ealdgith slowly moved her right hand onto her seax. Her hands and her seax were covered by her cloak. She slowly released the thong that bound the seax in its scabbard and began to draw it. She would stab through her cloak at the stomach of the first man to come near her.

Maintaining eye contact Hravn said "I'll dismount and empty the sacks for you".

"Slowly. Keep your hand clear of that pretty seax – not that you'll have it much longer," cautioned Scar Face.

Sköll pounced just as Hravn swung his leg over the pony's back to stand in front of Scar Face. Scar Face pitched forward, the hound's fangs crushing his neck and pinning him face down on the track. One Eye turned to face the sudden threat as Hati caught him full in the face taking him down onto the track, his head hitting the ground with a loud hollow thud. The hounds pinned their prey down, growling.

Hravn kicked the weapons out of the men's reach before drawing his own seax and bending down to check them. One Eye was dead, probably from a combination of the blow to the back of his head and the laceration of his throat. "Come off, Hati, come off!" he commanded. He didn't want either dog getting too much of a taste for human blood. "Sköll, Off!" The wolfhound pulled back, growling, his muzzle still close to Scar Face's head. Hravn knelt down, checking for vital signs. Scar Face was unconscious, not breathing but he did have a faint erratic pulse. The back of his neck was bleeding profusely.

"He's finished," Hravn said to Ealdgith, who was still sitting on her pony, stunned by the pace of events. "Come, help me search them!" His tone was hard, urgent; he knew he had to jolt her into action. "He's going to bleed out. Don't have any sympathy for him."

"Sympathy!" spat Ealdgith. "Sympathy – those bastards were..."

"I know," Hravn interrupted gently; "I know." He stood up and held her as she slipped off the pony.

Ealdgith shivered and slowly began to cry. It was more than just a reaction to the violence and threat to her safety; it was an expression of grief for all she had lost. He held her, stroking her hair, the shared affection calming them both.

Sköll prowled around the two bodies, prepared to pounce if there was a movement – there wasn't. Hati nuzzled against Ealdgith's waist. She stopped sobbing and bent down to hold his great head and stare into his dark eyes, thanking him for what he had just done for her, as he licked her tears away.

Ealdgith stood up with a sudden resolve "I'll take one of their weapons. Choose the lightest for me. I'll cut my hair too, to be like yours. The more I look like a boy the safer I'm going to be. I'm going to have to learn how to defend myself too. It'll be better for us both if I can." She paused, adding almost to herself, "No man will ever do to me what those...bastards, threatened."

Hravn quickly checked the two bodies. Scar Face had been honest when he said that they'd had 'good pickings' from refugees. He had a large leather pouch around his waist, holding many gold, silver and copper coins. Hravn took the gold and silver, they would surely need it in the future. He was less concerned about the slivers of heavy copper coin. Hravn rolled the bodies off the track and took the two long seax, unbuckled the harness and scabbards from the bodies and then tied both to the ponies. He would choose one for Ealdgith later, the other he would use for chopping wood; it would save blunting his own blade. He felt no emotion about the churls' deaths. If anything, he felt a quiet confidence that he and Ealdgith had survived and that he had held his nerve. Hravn had passed his own initiation test; he was no longer a boy. Finally, almost as if he was packing up a camp site, he coiled up the rope that had been used to trap them – he might find a use for that too.

"It must be late, we'll have to get going" Hravn urged Ealdgith, and then pausing to look at the sky, he realised that the sun's dull glow through the mist was still high in the north east. "Sorry Edie, we've more time than I thought. It feels like an age but really we were only stopped for minutes, not hours."

"Let's just get away from here," prompted Ealdgith. "I fear we're going to have to go close by the houses we saw".

"No" Hravn countered, "look yonder, where the main track bends to the left there is a narrow one heading straight on. We might just be in luck. We'll stay on the ponies, go in single file and keep the hounds close by. Take your spear in your hand as well. We'll go as quickly as we can."

They moved on at a brisk canter. After a furlong or so the narrow track led to an opening to the side of a largish settlement in a clearing in the forest. They could see that the main track, the one they had originally been following, became the main street of the settlement. There was a large crowd building something at the point where the track left the forest. Hravn realised that it was a barricade and assumed that the manor had been forewarned and were planning to protect themselves. If they blocked the track where it entered the clearing, perhaps they could stop the Normans destroying their houses.

"Oy! You lad! Get down there and work on the barricade – now!" Three men were stripping wood from a derelict house on the edge of the village. One of them gestured to Hravn. "There's no point in running, the Bastard's men will have us all if we don't hold them here." The gruff urgency of his voice spurred them on, and they swerved away instinctively, not wanting to be drawn into any further violence. The ponies' hooves slipped on the icy stones of the track as they galloped around the village before regaining the main track up the hill away from the village. They didn't look back.

It was obvious from the many footprints in the snow that others had been fleeing the village ahead of them. They kept going, pushing the ponies hard, but they tired quickly.

Five minutes later the track split and they reined to a halt. The footprints all led away from them, along the main track. "There must be another settlement up that way." Hravn panted, out of breath after their frantic gallop.

"I think we need to keep clear of settlements that might still be ravaged by the Normans. There could be more like Scar Face and One Eye about." Ealdgith was adamant that she was going to avoid other people.

Hravn agreed. "I think we should head down here to the right. It leads down into the valley bottom. I think we'll cross the river again if we follow it". Ealdgith nodded, as winded as her pony.

Still riding, they moved at a walking pace. The track wound down through the trees to a point where the river was wide and slow flowing, but there was no obvious ford. "Do you think we can cross? If it's wide, it might not be too deep," suggested Ealdgith.

"You could be right. Hold him whilst I take a look." Hravn tossed his reins to Ealdgith as he slid off his pony. Using his spear as a staff, he began to probe his way over the river bed. "By Hodhr its cold!" He exclaimed, cursing the Norse god of winter.

Ealdgith was right, the slow flowing Jor wasn't deep at that point. Hravn found a route across and then, choosing a prominent tree on each bank as a leading mark to show the way, he waded back to Ealdgith, gathered the ponies and led them all across. There was no track on this, the north side of the river.

"We're going to have to dry our boots out soon. Our feet will rot if they stay like this for long." Ealdgith warned Hravn.

"I know, we should be safer on this side of the river and away from the tracks. We just need to find somewhere with some decent shelter." The forest was more open on the north side of the river. The woodland was a mix of stunted oaks, rowan, ash, birch and thickets of willows by the river bank. Whilst parts of the forest were dense others appeared to have been cleared in the past and had only re-grown recently. Hravn took a route slightly above the river, where it was drier, and they wound their way through the more open parts of the wood, keeping the river on their left and the high ground to the right.

Hravn was lost in his own thoughts for a couple of minutes before calling back. "Edie, we don't just need to dry out. We've been on the run for three days now. We need to take stock of what we are going to do, how much food we have and to graze the ponies properly. I think we need to find somewhere to shelter for tonight and rest up tomorrow before we move on. We don't really know where we are and I think we need to make a proper plan."

Chapter 5

"Sköll! Kill! Hati Go!" Hravn called both hounds to take up the chase of two roe deer that Sköll had just startled. The deer ran but had barely managed twenty paces before the two heavy hounds pulled them, kicking, to the forest floor. Hravn dismounted and ran up, quickly cutting the throat of each deer.

He slung the carcasses over the back of his pony and he and Ealdgith then led both ponies on foot further into the wood.

"How about sheltering under there?" Ealdgith pointed to a fallen oak tree. The old tree lay against its neighbour, the trunk creating a natural roof line.

"Good choice. I'll cut some branches off those pines to make a roof and walls."

The two cousins were now settling into a familiar routine, making a camp together. Hravn chose the lighter of the long seax for Ealdgith's personal use and used the other to chop pine branches which he then wove against the trunk of the fallen oak to form a wind and waterproof screen. It provided good camouflage too.

Ealdgith used her eating seax to cut open the deer, gutting and skinning them. She wondered to herself whether she could have gutted One Eye as easily? She decided that she could.

Whilst Ealdgith fed the rougher parts of the deer to the hounds Hravn took the rope that he had saved from their ambush, slung it over the fallen oak and hoisted the carcasses high above the ground, protecting the meat from hungry mouths whilst the juices dripped out.

"I'll go and graze the ponies by the river" Hravn called to Ealdgith, leaving her to gather wood and set a fire at the entrance to their shelter. Ealdgith instructed Hati to stay with her whilst Hravn led the ponies down to a stand of willow that overhung the river. He knew that the fell ponies were very partial to willow, which was just as well because there was little else for them to eat. The ponies quickly reached up to pull at the dry leaves that drooped from the pendulous willow branches. Once they had exhausted the leaves the ponies used their teeth to strip the bark from the trees. Hravn knew that the ponies were content and wouldn't wander far, so he returned to help Ealdgith, and crouched down to put a brotherly arm around her shoulder as she struck sparks from steel and flint to light the dry kindling at the base of the fire.

With the light starting to fade they lay on the ground under the shelter, their blanket over them, and stared at the embers of the fire. Sköll and Hati prowled around outside for a while, alert to the many unseen scents of the forest.

"I think we need to rest tomorrow," suggested Hravn. "We've pushed the ponies hard today and only Wyrd can tell how long we're going to have to keep going like this. It's going to get harder when we cross the high ground."

Ealdgith agreed. "I think you're right. I don't mind walking but we're always going to need to find food and shelter. We'll certainly need a good few days' food in reserve if we are to go over the fells. Have you any idea of a route?"

Hravn sucked his lower lip in thought. "Look, Edie, whatever we do, we both have to be happy with it. We do have options."

"Such as?" Ealdgith shrugged. "They seem pretty thin to me".

"I guess they are," Hravn continued, "but we still have them. We could stay here, in the forest. I know it's rough but we are good at living like this. We have the shelter of the forest, there's plenty of fuel for a fire and we will always be able to hunt for food. It would be far easier than going over the tops, especially if winter really bites. We could stay 'til Lencten and either move on or see if there is anything for us to go back to. It's something we have to think about."

Ealdgith shook her head. "I know you're right, we could do that, but after what's happened today, who else do you think will be sharing the forest with us? We are bound to attract attention. There will be more refugees and they'll be in a worse state than us. They will be desperate and there will be others preying on them. I'd die rather than submit to men like those this morning and the Normans would be no better. I saw what they intended for the women of Hudreswell. The forest is tempting, but it's no place for us. Besides, we only have these clothes. We'll be in rags by the summer and how could we find your family looking like beggars? We're growing, you especially. If you end up like your father, you'll be out of those clothes in a twelve month."

Hravn nodded, he couldn't argue. Ask was known fondly by his people as 'The Bear'. It was recognition of his build and strength as much as his nature; calm and purposeful until roused, then his anger could flash.

"We've got to keep going," Ealdgith insisted, "no matter how difficult the conditions. We should stay in the forest as long as possible and try to keep ahead of any others. We have to find your grandmother's people, or a sanctuary somewhere else, and then see if we can get word about what has happened at home. We might still be able to go back if anyone has survived and if the Normans have gone again. All I know is that we can't stay here now."

"Aye, I agree. I just needed to know what you really think." Hravn smiled.

"Thank you, I do trust you, I trust you in everything." Ealdgith smiled back, the warmth in her green eyes reflecting the firelight, "Look, what do you know about the land ahead?"

"All I know is that the valleys of the Greta, the Swale and the Jor lie alongside each other and point east and west, and we are still heading west along the Jor. There is high ground in between each of the valleys and it leads up to the high fells that are the border with Cumbraland. It's a bit like the back of your hand, the valleys are the gaps between your fingers and your knuckles form the spine of mountains that shield Cumbraland. I used to go to Kircabi Stephan, which is just into the land of the Cumbri, with my father. We usually went along the old stone road that follows the Greta and over the pass to Kircabi Stephan. It's the way the armies go when they raid each other. I can remember the lie of the land and where the ridges and peaks are. If I pretend I'm a bird looking down from high up I can picture the way the valleys and ridges link together. It's just a gift I seem to have."

Hravn continued "There is another way that goes along Swaledale and over the top. It's much higher and wilder and is slow going but there are more settlements along the dale. My father took me that way once. All this is now to our north. The western half of the Jor's dale is filled by the Mallerstang forest, which is where we are now. I think we will have to follow the Jor to its source and then head up and along the spine to the right. If we can find a river or a valley that drops down towards the north or west, we will be sure to find the Cumbri. I know it's not much of a plan, but it's the best I can think of at the moment."

"I'm happy with that," Ealdgith reassured him, "but we'll need to build up a stock of meat before we leave the forest, and cook it so that we can eat it cold if need be. The weather is so cold that it won't go off and the hounds can eat it too. The ponies will be alright; they could stay out all winter on the tops if they had to."

"It sounds like a plan to me." Hravn sat up. "All we need to do now is to turn you into a boy and teach you to use a seax" he joked. "We'll call you Eadmund too, instead of Ealdgith. After all, Edie is short for both and I won't get confused."

Ealdgith kicked him playfully. "It won't be easy you know". She was suddenly serious. "I'm slim enough to get away with it now, all wrapped up in the winter, but it will be very difficult to carry it off for long if we are around people, you must know that?"

"Mmm, I guess so" Hravn agreed with a sigh, "but you do need to be able to hold a seax and the more we can stop you looking like a girl the safer you will be. Come on, it's time to lose your beautiful locks!" He made as if to draw his long seax, but switched hands and drew his much smaller knife-like one instead. Kneeling by her as she sat by the fire, he cut Ealdgith's hair carefully into a bob.

Ealdgith wasn't too worried about losing her long hair. It would be much easier to look after whilst they lived rough, although she knew that without long hair, it would be hard to show her status as a well-born young lady when she needed to revert to her real self.

Hravn, on the other hand, felt strangely moved by the experience. He tenderly kissed the top of Ealdgith's head when he finished, whispering "There you are, Edie, my special Valkyrie."

Chapter 6

"Edie, what do you think? I fear that we're lost."

Ealdgith and Hravn had rested for a day, preparing a large reserve of meat and gathering as many of the remaining edible nuts that they could find: hazel and, as a last resort because they were so bitter, beech. They had repacked their kit as efficiently as possible and, most importantly, stitched the best part of their gold into two new cloth collars for Hati and Sköll. This would be the safest place to hide it in the event of another attack upon them.

They had then set off early the next morning, slowly making their way westward, hugging the northern edge of the forest. The going was heavy and tiring, snaking around dense thickets and rocky outcrops, and they were very relieved when the early evening gloom forced them to stop for the night. They had camped on a small hill that over looked the valley. The hill top was clear save for a few beech trees that gave some shelter; and there was grass too for the ponies that they could reach by scraping away the thin layer of snow.

The forest dropped away from the camp into the valley bottom. In the distance across the valley they had seen the lights and smoke from a small village. The chimney smoke and the few lights had been a reassurance that the Normans hadn't forced their way into the forest. Neither of them had wanted to change their plans and risk going there.

The weather had remained stable. Shallow snow still covered the valley and fells and the cloud hugged the top of the valley, enclosing them in a quiet grey and white world. As the light had faded, the cloud had lifted to reveal that they were in a circle of fells. "Edie, look!" Hravn called gleefully. "We're at the head of the dale at last. See there, around to the right" Hravn pointed to a break in the skyline to the right of the dale head. "I'm sure that will be our way into Cumbraland."

By dawn everything had changed. The cloud had closed in, mist filled the valley and soft snow fell. They were wrapped in a silent white world of their own. Hravn was still confident that by following a route that kept the valley bottom on their left and the high ground on their right he could find the pass over to Cumbraland. "I'm sure there will be a beck that runs down into the Jor. If we follow it up, it will lead us to the pass," he had said as they set off.

For once his confidence had been misplaced. "I can't work out the route, Edie. Look, there's a new river in front. We must be coming to the end of the valley, or maybe there's a new valley coming in from our right. I can't see across to the other side in all this gloom."

"I don't want to attempt crossing that anyway. I can't see the bank for the snow and we've no idea how deep it is". Ealdgith erred on the side of caution. "I think it would be best to follow the valley upstream. We might find out if this really is the end of the Jor's dale or if it isn't, we could probably cross higher up where the river is smaller."

They turned north. Ploughing their legs through the snow they led the ponies whilst keeping an eye on the river to their left and the limestone cliff to their right. The valley quickly narrowed and deepened, and a high cliff on the far side of the river loomed out of the mist.

"Hravn! Stop, listen, what's that? It's getting closer!" They paused, peering into the gloom ahead, the ponies' ears pricked up too. A rushing, roaring, slapping sound echoed between the cliffs.

"Stay here, Edie, with Hati and the ponies. It sounds like falling water, a lot of it. "No" Ealdgith countered, "I'll follow at a distance. We mustn't lose sight of each other in the mist."

Hravn and Sköll moved off. Ealdgith watched them almost fade into the mist before following a half furlong behind.

Hravn stopped, then waved to Ealdgith to join him, calling "It's a waterfall, and a little tarn. It's really quite beautiful and safe." As he shouted, Sköll suddenly ran forward, growling, his hackles rising.

"Whoa boy! Steady! Stay back!" A voice called from beyond the beck that ran out of the tarn. It was loud but calm and authoritative, cautioning Sköll who slowed to a halt. Then, addressing Hravn, the voice added "Come forward brother, there is no danger here. Come, join me. I am Brother Oswin, all are welcome here." Hravn called Sköll to heel and slowly walked forward, his hand covering the hilt of his seax. He relaxed as Brother Oswin stepped forward, reaching towards him with a handshake and a broad welcoming smile on his face. "Welcome to my cell." He was tall but slightly stooped. Long grey hair that hung below his tonsured scalp contrasted with his ruddy face. He wore a rough grey wool cloak and breeches with cloths bound around his feet.

"There are two of us." Hravn gestured to Ealdgith as she emerged from the mist leading the ponies. "My cousin, Eadmund. We've fled the Norman destruction of all the manors in the Vale of Euruic".

"Come, brothers, I have warmth and shelter here. Tell me about it for it is news to me, as it is many months since I had a visitor."

When Hravn had first seen the little lake his focus had been drawn to the tall spout of water that poured into it from a cleft high in the cliff that blocked the head of the little valley. He could just see the top of the waterfall through the mist. It was almost as if it was falling from heaven itself. He now saw that there was a small rise to the left of the tarn and that there was a narrow cleft in the cliff a few feet above the ground. It was tall and narrow, but wide enough for a man to pass through. A small fire burned in a hearth to the side of the entrance.

"Come, leave your ponies, they won't stray. Bring your hounds, they are more than welcome if they will risk the dark." With that, Oswin turned and nimbly stepped up to the cleft and disappeared into the cave. Hravn turned to Ealdgith, shrugged and then followed Oswin. She called the dogs and followed too.

The narrow cleft opened into a chamber the size of a small house. Several tallow and reed lights burned throwing light that reflected off the white of the limestone walls. It was lighter than Hravn had expected. It was warmer too, certainly warmer than the chill damp air outside. The floor of the cave was gravel and dry earth.

"Take a seat." Oswin gestured to the several stubby logs that served that purpose, "or perch on a ledge, I'm not house proud." The cousins looked at each other, grinned and sat down. Oswin was so reassuringly calm and friendly that the nagging doubt and uncertainty that had haunted their last few days suddenly disappeared.

Oswin perched on a ledge. "Before you tell me your story, let me tell you something of mine. I'm sure you're wondering just what you've stumbled into."

They were looking around the cave and as their eyes became accustomed to the light they began to notice very rudimentary signs of a home; deer skins folded in a corner by a bed of dry ferns, a further stack of dry ferns in another corner, a small collection of cooking pots and wooden bowls on a rock shelf; a staff and a seax propped against the rock and a rough-hewn wooden cross standing on a ledge flanked by two tallow candles. Oswin's cell was his home and also his sanctuary.

"You may have heard of Cnut. He was King a long time ago, before your fathers were born I'd wager. Cnut was a Dane, as am I, and I was his man. As a young man, a very young man," Oswin looked directly at Hravn "I served Cnut as a soldier, first in his campaign against the Scots, then against the Swedes and after that the Russe. My travels took me as far as Byzantium and the bright world of the East."

Ealdgith and Hravn sat captivated by Oswin's obvious age, his manner of story-telling and by the tale itself. What was he, a king's soldier or a king's champion perhaps, doing here in a hole in a frozen mountain?

Oswin paused, sensing the impact of his story on the two young cousins.

"There is a lot I could, perhaps should, tell you; another day maybe. Let's just say that as a soldier I saw and did many things that I came to regret. One day I awoke and knew that I could be a soldier no more, not in a martial way. If I were to be a soldier it could only be as a soldier of our Lord, as a soldier of Christ."

"I returned to these shores but I didn't go home. Instead, having landed in the port of Lundenburh, I made my way slowly north to the monastery at Ripum. That is where I took my vows and also the name of our Saint, Oswin. Sadly, I could never quite accept the ordered world of the cloister. It was too comfortable, too predictable. I did try. For many years, I tried, but I still yearned for the hard unpredictable life of a soldier; a life where I could live by my wits alone. So, with my prior's blessing, I left the life of the cloister and made my life in the wild forest, in God's world, with His creatures, and His peace and understanding."

Oswin paused, the cousins stayed silent, staring at the reflection of the candles in his intense blue eyes.

"Now, do please tell me of this destruction of our World by the Normans. It grieves me greatly to hear of it and I fear for my brothers at Ripum. It is many months since I had a visitor, and then only from the little manor of Appersett, across the valley. It is a year or more since a traveller came by with news of the wider world about us."

Ealdgith and Hravn looked at each other, and then Hravn spoke first. He spoke honestly but cautiously, referring to Ealdgith as Edie, but not as he or she. He explained who they were, their parents and relationships and their position in the community. Oswin's eyes widened in surprise as Hravn explained about the uprising, Earl Gospatrick's role in support of the Atheling and his links to Ealdgith's family. He nodded in understanding and support. Hravn went on to explain why they had been on the high moor on the day of the harrying, what they had seen and why they had fled.

As Hravn paused to collect his thoughts before continuing their story, Oswin interrupted asking Ealdgith "Brother Edie, how do you feel too?"

Oswin had seen Ealdgith's gaze become fixed and introspective as Hravn recounted their tale. Ealdgith drew breath and Hravn nodded slightly as she said quietly "I'm Ealdgith, not Eadmund. I saw what the Normans were doing to the women at Hudreswell and I've been threatened with the same once already whilst we've been in the forest. We agreed it would be safer if I pretended to be a boy, but I can't deceive you in this. Can I trust you, Brother, please?"

Oswin responded with a broad smile and he nodded assent and understanding. "Have no fear, Sister; you are wisest to do as you have done. The world you tell me of is not the world of women or of the common man anymore. You must take care, for your journey will be uncertain. We are all one, here, under God's eyes. You have my protection, of course, though I'm sure that Hravn's protection is all that you will ever need."

Ealdgith continued quickly. "Brother, this is a lot to ask you. Hravn is to teach me how to defend myself with the seax and, as a boy, I must be able to use it. As a man of God, I am sure you have forsworn the use of weapons but, as a soldier, would you be prepared to teach me? I will need all the skill I can acquire."

Taken aback, Oswin stood and paced the short strip of gravel in thought. Turning, he said softly and slowly, "Sister Ealdgith, what you ask of me is a lot. It is many years since I shared my life with others and many more since I raised a weapon against another. But I know the sort of world in which you both must now live. It is a world I thought never to see again. I hope it will still pass me by, but you cannot escape it, not for long I fear. Yes, I will teach you. I will teach you both because I am sure there is much that Hravn has still to learn about the art of the sword."

He paused "There is though one condition. A condition that will need your word to honour. You must promise to only raise arms against another if your cause is honourable. That is, only to defend yourself and the lives of those whom you might have a duty to protect. Killing can become easy when you are accustomed to it. You must never venture along the way I did when I was young. Do you agree?"

"Yes, Brother, I promise," they said in unison, unprompted.

Oswin returned to sit on the ledge and leaned forward to peer intently at the two cousins. "There is much we need to think about. I never expected company in my life again but I rather think I will enjoy it, for a while at least; which is just as well because I could not let you go further in this weather. You have done well to get so far in your quest already, but the weather is closing in. It would be foolish indeed to leave the forest for the high tops before we see the first signs of Lencten, which means that we must share each other's company for some weeks to come."

"Thank you, Brother Oswin." Hravn leaned forward and shook Oswin's hand "Thank you."

"There is another reason for you to stay a while. If I am to teach you both, and Sister Edie in particular, how to really defend yourselves then there is more than just the use of the sword to master. There are other martial skills you need to use; the art of balance, of holding an opponent and using his weight to help throw him; how to use blows of the hand that can quickly disable, and then there are the softer skills of understanding your opponent's mind and how to control it. This will all take time and is hard and hungry work. With three mouths to feed, you will need to hunt well too to keep us all fed. If I am to spend my days teaching you both then you must also take it in turns to do the daily chores as well. It takes effort to live as humbly as this. Are we agreed?"

"We will do all you ask and more," Ealdgith promised. "What you offer is so much more than we could ever ask. I will learn, quickly, I know it and…" she paused and looked around, "with a little more light we could perhaps continue our lessons in here when it is dark outside; if you would permit that of course" she added, realising that her enthusiasm was perhaps too great an imposition upon Oswin.

"Of course, Sister, of course. This is a challenge I welcome and if I can teach you well then maybe, just maybe, you will be able to make some difference to our world in these dark times. I sense that there is a goodness and honesty in you both that will justify my faith in you. There are times when the way of peace and the word of our Lord must be pursued more forcefully than my faith teaches."

Oswin added, after a pause "I know the Normans, I fought alongside them, and against them, during my days in Byzantium. They are a Norse-Frankish race; clever but cruel and demanding, thinking all others are beneath them. Their way with women is not that of the English. They control, give no rights and demand obedience. Edie, I fear your future will not be as you once thought it would be and I will help you all I can to prepare for it."

Oswin held Ealdgith's gaze and she nodded slowly, understanding.

Chapter 7

"Right, let's start!" Oswin clapped his hands, the sound echoing around the cave. "The day is still young and there is a lot to do if you're to learn half a lifetime of skills in a few weeks."

"First, we need to get your kit under shelter. How much food do you have?"

"We hunted a couple of days ago and cooked and prepared meat from two young deer. We have a few days yet" Hravn said confidently "Sköll and Hati are our lifeline, they really know how to hunt."

"Good, good..." Oswin's mind was focussing on the many demands of running an impromptu training camp. His skills were ingrained, but rusty. If the cousins learned quickly he would, at times, be only a step or two ahead of them. It was a challenge he that he relished. "Once you've unpacked, find a training place. You'll need flat dry ground five paces by five. The stand of firs by the beck should do. Make me three wooden seax too, one each and one for me. Make them the same length and width as your seax, Hravn, but thicker so that they have some weight and strength. Make a small one too, like that very pretty seax that I see Edie has. She will need to learn how to use it properly. The skills I teach you first will be for close fighting with the seax, not the stand-off you would have with a longer proper sword. Maybe I will have time later to cover the sword with you, Hravn, but Edie needs to master the skills of self-defence as well as the seax."

"Come on then, Valkyrie." Hravn teased Ealdgith.

Oswin raised an eyebrow "Don't joke, Brother Hravn. As a servant of our Lord I couldn't agree. Valhalla is not Heaven. Edie can surely guard your back, but I pray that she will never be a shield maiden taking your soul to Valhalla." Oswin paused, then added, "I appreciate your wit and I'm sure Edie has the spirit of a Valkyrie"

"Sorry Brother Oswin, I know you're right I didn't mean…."

Oswin cut him off. "Worry not, I understand; spirit, focus and good humour are all we will need. I will train you each to play to your strengths. Hravn, you are strong and will grow in strength and stature. You will be able to use your size and weight and fight aggressively. Edie, you are light and nimble and whilst we will build up your strength, you will never match a man in size and strength. I will show you how to use your opponent's weight and speed against himself. You must learn how to fight as a pair, with you, Edie, guarding Hravn's back whilst he faces the foe."

"Let me know when you're ready, we'll have some food, then I'll see what young Hravn can really do. Now off you go!"

Later, whilst there was still light to train by, Oswin stood facing Hravn in the little training space that they had cleared under the pines. It was free of snow and dusted with dry pine needles. Ealdgith sat between Sköll and Hati, a calming hand on each of their collars, as they glared intently at Oswin wondering just what their master was doing. Hravn tossed his wooden seax from hand to hand, getting a feel for its weight and balance and then held it in a short guard, anticipating Oswin's first move. Oswin circled, watching Hravn's eyes and the tension in his muscles, as well as the tip of the seax. Hravn parried the first three of Oswin's moves, but failed to see the fourth that knocked his seax aside.

"Well done, Hravn, well done! You've good footwork, poise and anticipation, but we need to work on your speed and perception…but I don't blame you for appearing too tense in your shoulders. You have to read me, understand me, know what I'm going to do almost before I even know it myself, and then act before I can react…and when you act, it must be quick and forceful. 'Clout; don't dribble,' is what I was taught…but that's very good, and I have your measure now".

Hravn looked a little shame faced. Ealdgith tossed a fir cone at his face that he knocked away instinctively, with a smile back at her.

"Good reactions," she quipped, "but poor anticipation!" Oswin grinned; they certainly had spirit.

"Now who's going to milk the goats?" Edith and Hravn just looked at each other, "Seriously?" "Certainly, here they come" and they heard the faint tinkling of bells as six small, wiry, mottled brown and black goats jumped from ledge to ledge down the cliff by the waterfall, "They always come home to be milked at dusk" Oswin laughed at their perplexed faces "How do you think I would survive otherwise?"

After dark, milking and a simple meal, they sat around the glowing embers in the hearth outside the cave and talked long into the evening. Once Edie and Hravn had started to tell Oswin about their life in Ghellinges-scir, they couldn't stop. He mainly listened and nodded reassuringly, occasionally interjecting with a perceptive question about the politics and relationships within Edie's family in particular. They warmed to him as if he was a trusted great uncle, saying repeatedly how fortunate they had been to find him.

"You might not be so thankful after a day's training tomorrow," he teased at last. "You will need a strict regime and I promise you will be stiff this time tomorrow. I know of muscles you've never heard of, and you will discover them all in the morning with aches and pains galore."

"Now, this is what you will do. First thing every day, before you breakfast, I want you both to race from here to the training ground. Then, Edie, you will carry Hravn halfway back, over your shoulders, across the flat ground. Hravn, you will then carry Edie up the rise back here to the hearth. You will then repeat that ten times without stopping. It will warm you up and start to build up your strength and stamina. You'll find it hard at first, especially you Edie, but I have faith that you will do it."

"After you've eaten we will proceed with stretching and strengthening exercises. Your bodies are supple and still growing and it will be easier for you. This will develop your flexibility and balance and there are techniques that I learned in the East that will help. After that, I will either work with you both, and match you against each other, or I will work with one of you whilst the other does the chores for the day. We'll then do more physical training at the end of the day before you milk the goats."

Oswin grinned. "Oh, and every fifth day we'll go and hunt and gather fire wood. I rather think that will be a break you'll come to long for. Now, it's time to sleep, you'll be up again soon enough."

~~~

The next evening Hravn slumped on the ground by the hearth, "I'm whacked! Oswin's right! So much for it being easier because we're young and supple, I feel like an old man already! How do you do it, Oswin?"

Ealdgith was already sitting on a log staring at the fire. "I know, but it was fun and so enlivening. My body is so tired, but my mind is racing. What Oswin calls self-defence is such a skill and a God-send for a girl. I can certainly put you in your place," she said, slipping him a sideways smile.

"I could say that 'I could eat a horse'," quipped Hravn, "but that might not go down too well with them." He glanced over at the ponies grazing in the half light.

"Well, I'm going to crawl off to sleep," yawned Ealdgith "There's no chance of my staying awake any longer. Come on, Hati, I need a soft pillow and something to keep me warm."

"You too, Hravn, I think we all feel the day's strain. My old bones certainly do, whatever you may think of them. I'll secure things here for the night," said Oswin as he placed turfs over the fire to damp it down until the morning. "But thank you both for your efforts today, well done."

As Hravn and Ealdgith lay on the cave floor, feeling their bruises and drifting off to sleep, they each dwelt on what life with Brother Oswin might be like; neither had lived with a monk before. Hravn understood the Christian faith. His father was a convert and whilst his mother claimed to be a Christian, she still quietly followed the old Norse faith. He therefore took a very personal and pragmatic view of religion and the interaction of the different beliefs.

Ealdgith was more influenced by her parent's Christian faith, although her father often harked back to the old Saxon gods and their ways. Her time with Hravn and his mother had given her a degree of scepticism and she often inwardly challenged some of her family's assumptions. They both now realised that whilst they lived with Oswin they should respect and follow his own very strong and personal beliefs. After all, they had a great deal to learn from him and they must not jeopardise his care of them.

Chapter 8

"Yours!" Hravn hissed just loud enough for Ealdgith to hear. She tracked the roe deer with the tip of her arrow as it trotted through the trees towards the clearing in front of her. Ealdgith stood, her bow flexed ready, looking through the narrow gap between two trees, judging the speed at which the deer was moving. Having estimated her arrow's time of flight, she tracked a point where arrow and heart would meet. The deer, a buck, was moving briskly, sensitive to a disturbance behind him, but not running in fright. Once she was sure of the point at which the buck would enter the clearing she released her arrow.

The still quiet of the snowed-in forest was shattered by the unnaturally loud thwack of metal into flesh. The buck stopped, eyes wide in surprise, shock, fear; its breast bone pierced by Ealdgith's arrow. Just as it lurched forward again, fear driving it to flight, a second arrow pierced its eye sinking deep into its brain. Hravn had covered the field of fire across the other half of the clearing and had stepped forward from cover releasing his arrow the moment Ealdgith's shaft struck home.

The cousins ran to the fallen buck, clapping each other on the back in congratulation. The buck lay still. Hravn's arrow shot to the brain had killed it instantly, saving them the need to hunt for it after a death flight through the forest. He raised his horn to his lips and called the hounds to heel.

"Well done, boys, well done! Let's go and get some breakfast." Ealdgith made a fuss of the hounds as they ran into the clearing. The success was as much theirs as it was hers and Hravn's.

Hravn had woken Ealdgith very early that morning, well before first light. It was the fifth day of their training regime and therefore the day to hunt. Hravn, in particular, had looked forward to a break from the intense concentration that weapon training demanded. Ealdgith had no hesitation about her training. The skills that Oswin was teaching her were so liberating for a girl, she felt more empowered than she had ever imagined and her confidence about how she might face her future grew daily.

They had left before breakfast, taking just a handful of nuts to sustain them, and led the ponies around the western side of the cliff by the cave. Hobbling the ponies at the top of the cliff, they had slowly worked their way through the forest of beech and birch and up the steep narrow valley above the waterfall. After a couple of furlongs, as the valley broadened, Sköll had reacted to a scent upwind from them. Hravn knew that Sköll had his mark. Keeping the excited hounds close, Hravn had scouted for a clearing where they could be used to ambush a deer. Then, making sure that the hounds understood where they must direct their quarry, Hravn had set them off. They had taken a wide looping route moving silently through the undergrowth parallel to the path that its scent had indicated the deer was following. Both hounds had sensed the position of their prey before separating. Hati stayed on one side of the valley whilst Sköll pushed even further out and around to the other side of the valley. Then, working in tandem, they had moved through the undergrowth towards the deer making just enough noise to unsettle it and prompt it to backtrack the way it had come, encouraging it ever closer to the site for the ambush.

As Ealdgith ran back to bring up the ponies Hravn cut the arrows out of the buck's carcass. Ealdgith's arrow was undamaged, his own had been blunted by the impact on the skull and the shaft was cracked. He could save the arrow head but would need to work on it before fitting it to a new shaft.

Slinging the carcass over the back of Ealdgith's bay pony, they made their way back towards the cliff top and the route down to their new home, chatting cheerily as they went. "I thought my father had taught me well, he certainly thought that he had," Hravn mused, "but I realise that there is so much more to skilled sword play, and I know I've still a great deal to learn. It's not just that it is physical, but it's all the mental effort, you know, getting inside the other's mind, out thinking them, making them do what you want them to do. That's Oswin's real skill. He must have been really good in his day."

"You'll soon learn; I know you will," Ealdgith reassured him. "It won't be that easy though. I guess you might have to change how you do some things before you can progress, so that will be a challenge. But I've seen a big change in just four days. Honestly, you're good. Just like you're a good hunter. It was your plan that worked today. You trained the hounds, you've got a skill for strategy, you just need to learn how to use a few more tools – and Oswin is the one to teach you."

"Anyway," she added "It's easier for me. I'm like a clean slate, ready to be written on. It's all new and I just soak it up."

"I know," said Hravn. "You're amazing, and so fast. Like a sparrow hawk out of the sky, or a cat taking a mouse. Oswin's right; you could never face a man sword to sword but you could show enough ability to deter many who are less skilled. It's that twelve inch seax that really works for you. The way you get inside the circle of the sword is beautiful to watch and once you're there you have them every time so long as you can strike before they can hit you with the hilt – at least you have me every time!"

"That's what scares me," Ealdgith admitted. "It's fun in practice, but for real I know I'd have to follow through with a stab to the throat or stomach, and that scares me. I guess if it was me or them it would always be them," she admitted rather soberly. "Anyway, that's why I prefer to use the grabs and throws Oswin has shown me. If I can use a man's strength and weight against himself, I can hopefully wind him and disarm him. Anyway, I can certainly keep you in your place now," she teased, letting the subject drop.

"Ahoy! Oswin!" They called in cheerful unison. "We've a present for you." The cousins waved to draw Oswin's attention as they crested the cliff by the waterfall before making their way around the edge to the cave.

"You've done well, I rather thought you would," he called back. "You've got messy work ahead of you now though. That buck will take some butchering. I'll give you a hand to sling the carcass from a branch."

Oswin stood back from the carcass that he and Hravn had almost finished stripping of meat. "Hravn, something you said the other evening set me thinking whilst you were off hunting." Hravn caught Oswin's eye and paused to listen.

"You mentioned your grandmother's plight, how she'd fled Cumbraland when her family was taken by one called 'Pendragon'. I knew the name was familiar, but I couldn't recall why."

"Yes, she always said that it was he that took her family and sold them into slavery," confirmed Hravn.

"It puzzled me, although my travels took me to Scotland and all over the lands to the east I've never ventured to Cumbraland, so I couldn't understand why the name was familiar. I remember now. It's rare, very rare, for me to have someone visit here that has come from Cumbraland, but once one did, some years ago."

Hravn held Oswin's gaze, rather anticipating bad news. "He spoke of one called 'Pendragon', who controls the valley of Mallerstang, extorting money from those who travel through it. It is possible that those who took your grandmother's family still hold that area. If you are set on finding your family there, you must tread with care."

"Mmm" Hravn sucked his lip. "I see, aye, I know what you mean. From what little I know of Cumbraland its strength lies in the vale of the Eden. It's a rich land protected by the cradle of the fells. The Eden rises in the fells behind us here then runs through the valley of Mallerstang to Kircabi Stephan then beyond, north to the sea. Perforce we must go that way if we are to look for my grandmother's people."

"That's what I too fear," Oswin nodded gravely. "The forest there will no doubt be like that here. You're either forced along the line of the river or over the high tops to the side of it."

"You're right, Brother," agreed Hravn. "Edie and I planned on going over the fells, if possible, but I think that this confirms that we must delay, as you said, until spring and the thaw."

71

They both turned as Ealdgith spoke. She had approached whilst they talked and had caught the gist of the conversation. "It also means that our training here is even more important. You were right, Brother." She turned to Oswin. "My life has changed for ever and….," turning to Hravn, " …we will have a real challenge ahead. We must be prepared."

Lencten

Chapter 9

Oswin stepped down from the cave entrance and watched Hravn race Ealdgith back up the hill, neck and neck, each striving to be first. They threw themselves onto the ground at his feet, almost too winded to speak.

He looked up, breathed in deeply through his nose and smiled. "Lencten is here. You can smell it and feel it". The pale sun was warming the ground, the snow had gone from all but the highest of the fells, and the whites and yellows of the earliest flowers were just visible.

"I know, we were just saying the same," said Hravn. As he spoke, he looked across to Ealdgith and added: "We think it might be time to think about moving on."

Oswin looked from one to the other, his brow furrowed in thought then he smiled, saying slowly: "Yes, yes, you're right. It has to be. I've taught you all I can and the way over the tops should be clear now, but still cold at night I fear. If you are sure you are ready, then it is not for me to stop you. But do not rush. Let us prepare your departure well and let me be sure you are ready to face what you must. I suggest a holmganga."

"Good idea," said Hravn.

"A what?" said Ealdgith.

"Holmganga. It's a word my people use. It means fighting one to one, within rules, in a fixed place. The word really means 'going to an island', not a real one, just a special place...don't you Saxons know anything?" Hravn teased her, getting a very frosty glare in reply.

"Well, now I know," Ealdgith shook her head in sad amusement "...but yes, it's a great idea."

Oswin looked from one to the other. "Now that's settled, what I suggest is a day when, Hravn, you and I face each other with sword and seax each. That will test your skill to the limit, fighting two handed. You can attack and defend with each, as you choose. We will follow that with my sword against your seax. That will place you at a disadvantage and force you to break into my sword circle. We will finish with seax against seax, which is perhaps what you will face in a skirmish on the highway. That should be enough for us both and it will certainly be enough for my old bones in one day. Edie and I will face each other the day after. We will finish on the third day with me facing you both with a sword. Hravn, you will have your seax and Edie, you will have your short seax to guard his back."

"That sounds good to me, it's a challenge I'll enjoy. Just don't put any money on me winning all the bouts!" Hravn teased, hiding his sudden nervousness.

Oswin smiled knowingly. "And you, young Edie, we'll do something different. We'll start with seax on seax, which is the heaviest you could bear, but would be enough to deter most men. After that I will really put you to the test challenging you to break into the arc of my seax with your short seax. Men would see you as a threat with a knife like that but would assume that they have the advantage. We will finish with you facing my seax unarmed. A challenge and one you must expect. Your strength is that they won't know your real skills and will be complacent and bullying – use that against them. I will play the role in each case so you must read me as you would a stranger. Just forget that I am Brother Oswin."

"Thank you Oswin, I won't disappoint you, I know I won't." Ealdgith smiled at him.

Oswin nodded, knowing that he must let them win each of their bouts, but that they mustn't realise it. He would make them work for their victories, but wanted them to leave with the self-confidence borne of success. He knew that confidence in battle has a strength of its own. A defeat for either of them now could shatter that confidence and risk all.

He clapped his hands to instil a sense of urgency. "Anyway, that's for the morrow. Right now, you need to think about getting ready. You're going to be travelling for a while. I suggest you patch up your clothes where you can and wash everything that you won't wear. Prepare as much food as you can; winter can return with a vengeance and it's best to be prepared."

"You read my mind," said Hravn as he looked up. "Do you think we should go across the river to Appersett where the villagers might have supplies and clothing we can purchase?"

Oswin shook his head. "No, it's more likely that they would want to take what you have. They only scrape an existence at the best of times and after the ravaging lower down the dale they will no doubt have struggled to get through this winter. Best leave well alone and look to yourselves, you have all you will need."

~~~

"Watch him, Edie, watch him!" Hravn cautioned under his breath as she turned slowly, her eyes fixed on Oswin as he circled her, keeping her penned to the centre of the training ground.

It was the last of their individual bouts. Hravn had won all of his on the previous day. Oswin had pushed him hard, really hard, testing his ability to the limit. What Hravn had lacked in strength he had compensated for with speed, agility and technique; twisting, turning and sidestepping faster than Oswin had anticipated. Hravn had beamed when he received a justified warm embrace and pat on the back from Oswin at the end of their session.

It was now Ealdgith's turn. Speed, agility and technique were her strengths too. Oswin had pushed her for a while, seax on seax. Although she had won she suspected that he had let her, allowing her to save her strength. Ealdgith had done very well in her second bout, quickly breaking through Oswin's sword-circle to thrust her wooden short-seax against the base of his rib cage. Oswin had immediately and gracefully conceded defeat.

Now, however, Ealdgith felt vulnerable. She was unarmed and, as Oswin circled her, holding her at sword point, she no longer saw him as their friend and tutor, but as a threatening male stranger. As Oswin moved he cursed her, taunted her, called her names she had never thought to hear. She knew, inwardly, why he was doing it, that it was role-play, but she found herself slipping all too quickly into the role of threatened victim. Ealdgith made herself slow her breathing, concentrate on the tip of Oswin's sword, his stance, the pattern of his movement. She didn't look at his face, avoiding eye contact and any opportunity for him to intimidate her further. Her movement, when it came, was sudden. A swift jerk to her left caused Oswin to swing his sword wide to his right to block her move to escape. As he moved, Ealdgith dived forward, under the level of his arm, thrusting her fist into Oswin's groin and then hooked her right leg in front of Oswin's right leg. As Oswin doubled forward in unfeigned pain she turned and pushed him forward, using his momentum to floor him. As he fell, he released his hold on his sword and Ealdgith lunged to seize it, rolling forward to stand up facing Oswin, holding the sword point towards him.

Ealdgith's triumphant smile froze then crumbled. Oswin lay on the ground in obvious pain, gasping for breath. "Oh Oswin, I'm so sorry, I didn't mean to hurt you, really I didn't, I couldn't ever..." She knelt by him, sudden tears falling onto his face.

"Sister, do not fret, you did well. Violence is always hurtful. I played a role, as did you, and you did very well indeed for I did not foresee that outcome. It proves to me that you can go forth with confidence and it reassures me that I have taught you well. Never fear, my breath will come back soon enough." Oswin smiled back at her and breathed deeply before shutting his eyes, "but my old bones do need a rest now."

~~~

Their final bout of sparring over with Ealdgith and Hravn having beaten Oswin roundly in their two upon one bout, he stood bracing his shoulders as he regained his breath before declaring, with a twinkle in his eye and with a chuckle, "I think it's time to bathe."

Ealdgith peered at Oswin as if he'd taken leave of his senses, which prompted him to add quickly: "I know it's not popular in these northern climes, but it is a habit I got into in the East and one I've held to ever since as best I can."

"Go on…." Hravn encouraged him questioningly, half guessing where this was leading.

"It is Lencten, the sun is warming the air and the turf, and it is time to wash away the grime of winter; particularly if you are set on another long journey. I'll spare Sister Edie's blushes, but you and I Hravn are going to take a shower under the spout. Its cleansing and bracing, believe you me, and you will feel much stimulated afterwards as you lie out on the turf to dry."

"I will?" blurted Hravn.

Ealdgith giggled "I'm sure you will, Hravn, I'm sure".

Oswin caught the tone of her jest. "As I said, Sister, we'll spare your blushes, but that doesn't mean that you can escape a bath. We will go first then I will ensure that you have privacy whilst you follow our lead."

Ealdgith stared at them both and her eyebrows rose. "We'll see…"

Ealdgith did see. She watched from the cave entrance as Oswin and Hravn shed their clothes by the edge of the tarn. Oswin ran at the water with a whoop that sounded like a war cry. Hravn shook his head, smiled nervously and followed suit, by which time Oswin was already at the edge of the spout, scooping water in his hands and rubbing himself briskly. Hravn followed, cursing Hodhr repeatedly in loud, short, exclamations. They were only there a few moments. After immersing himself fully under the force of the spout, Oswin raced across the shallow tarn and threw himself down on the sun warmed turf beyond the far bank. Hravn followed immediately, shouting: "Oswin, I don't know how you managed that, but it does feel good now I'm out."

Ealdgith couldn't stop watching. She felt envious of their freedom and their unashamed nakedness. She was impressed too by the physique of both their bodies, realising just how much of a man Hravn now was and feeling surprised at the emotions it instilled in her. Smiling wryly, she shook her head and walked slowly down to the edge of the tarn. She wondered about testing the temperature of the water but decided against it, knowing that if she did she would go no further. She couldn't lose face now. If she was to play her part in a man's world she would prove it to herself and to Hravn now. She glanced around to see where she could lie out in the sun in seclusion once her mad dash into the cold water was over and then quickly shed her clothes, rushing so as not to lose courage. Calling to Hati to follow her she took a deep breath and ran at the water.

Ealdgith's scream shattered the quiet. Oswin and Hravn sat up, looked across and laughed as Ealdgith kicked water over Hati. Oswin lay back on the grass as Hravn continued to watch Ealdgith wash her hair quickly under the water fall. Her nubile beauty overwhelmed him. He knew then that he must one day take her in his arms and truly love her.

Oswin glanced across at Hravn "Brother! There is a time and a place for all things, but this is not the time and place for where your thoughts seem to be leading you. Let Edie have the privacy we promised her. I know what you feel and it is but natural. Just cherish her now and you will know when the time is right. Remember though, you must be prepared for her to be with child after."

As Hravn lay back on the grass, Oswin added softly, almost with a wistful sigh; "I was young once too… and was not always a monk."

"Rouse your stumps, Hravn!" Oswin sat up, fired with sudden enthusiasm. "There's another skill you both need to learn before you go…my brain is getting too old; I should have thought of it sooner."

"Eh! What?" Hravn tore his thoughts away from Ealdgith and focused on Oswin.

"You both need to learn how to fight when mounted. Even a pony gives you an advantage over a foot soldier; a horse is better."

"Yes…I think I can see what you mean." Hravn was uncertain. It was not something of which he had heard.

"It's an ancient art, one the Byzantines have mastered. They fight with large bodies of horsemen called cavalry. Some use long spears, others the bow. Their speed and momentum create surprise and shock and I have seen many battles won that way."

Hravn nodded with understanding, he was already captivated. "Yes, it takes a brave man to stand against a charging horse. I saw horsemen at Hudreswelle cut down a couple who were fleeing. You're right, it is another skill we must learn. Talk me through the details and then we can give Edie the good news that we must stay a few days longer."

Oswin explained with quick simplicity the different techniques; either riding whilst holding the spear over arm, stabbing down or outwards, or holding the spear couched under the arm and pointing directly ahead so that the momentum of the charge would carry the tip of the spear point through the body of an enemy in front.

"It takes skill, balance and practice and would be more effective if you had a saddle and stirrups but even bareback, a skilled rider can control his mount with his knees. It's the same for an archer. You can quickly close with your enemy, loosing several arrows at them before they can react, or instead ride across their front firing sideways. That takes real skill and practice to adjust for your own movement across the target."

Hravn grinned. "I think it's the spear for me and the bow for Edie. Somehow I just know that she will excel at that; and you know how she rides like a wolf on the wind."

Hravn was right. After all the weeks of sword training, their minds were sharp and they learnt the new skills quickly. The ponies enjoyed the challenge too. It was as if their mounts were as one with their riders.

~~~

Eight days later they were at last ready to depart. They all knew that they had dallied. Each was reluctant to rush to go and each found an excuse to keep each other's company as long as possible. The stable weather had persisted too.

Hravn shook Oswin's hand saying, "Thank you, Brother, we owe you a great debt, one that I doubt we could ever repay."

"No, Brother" countered Oswin "the debt is mine for you have given me back a purpose and meaning to life that I feared was lost forever. Go safely and remember your oath. Use these skills with care and in good cause." With that he clasped Hravn to him in a tight hug.

"You too, Sister, remember you may be a woman in a man's world now, but you have the inner strength and ability to thrive in your own right. Don't ever be cowed. But I am sure that you and Hravn will always have each other, that is all you will need – look after each other and, stay safe."

"Oh, Oswin, thank you," Ealdgith took his hand in hers. "You are the grandfather I never had. I can never thank you enough for you have shown me more affection and guidance, and patience too, than I have ever known; certainly more than my father ever showed me." She flung herself into his arms. He held her, stroking her head.

"Come my friends, you must not make this harder than it needs to be." Oswin held the ponies' reins as they both mounted. They all knew that it would be easier and quicker for them to ride away. They would walk soon enough but walking now would simply prolong the pain of parting.

Oswin wiped his own tears away as Ealdgith and Hravn rode past their old training ground, the hounds running ahead. Neither trusted themselves to look back.

Chapter 10

"Edie, remember the route we discussed with Oswin the other day? I think we should take that, don't you?" Ealdgith nodded as she rode, not really wanting to speak for the moment.

Hravn continued "We'll stay in the forest keeping to the right of the Jor, but away from any tracks. We are too far from the land of Pendragon to need worry at the moment, 'til tomorrow at any rate, but it's best to stay in the habit of taking care. We didn't see anyone all the time we were with Oswin, but we've no idea what the forest is really like."

Edie spoke at last "I know; I know; I know I'll miss him too. I meant what I said when we parted. He was more like a father than I've ever known – save for The Bear of course." She smiled across at Hravn. He nodded, understanding her meaning.

"Oswin said he thinks that the Jor slowly peters out in the high ground. There is another biggish beck that will come down from our right and then the Jor should swing to the north and we'll follow it up onto the tops where it starts."

Ealdgith picked up recounting the route that Oswin had advised. "Yes, and after that we should keep on the high ground with the new river on our left. Oswin thought that the east side of Mallerstang valley is said to be a line of cliffs. If that is so, they might help shield us from Pendragon's lands below."

They had both memorised the plan and talking about it helped take their minds off their parting and other challenges ahead.

"We'll need to plan on finding places to camp too, just like old times, eh!" Hravn teased her.

The days were noticeably longer now, giving more time to walk. It was warmer too and in the forest, the dank browns and greys of winter were flushed through with hints of green and buds just beginning to open on some of the trees.

They had crossed the beck that flowed down from the north and shortly after had started climbing towards the north themselves. The forest persisted, but was becoming thin and scrubby the higher they went. By the time the sun sank towards the western fells they had reached a low col just above the edge of the forest.

"It's a bit too boggy to stop here, Edie, let's push up to the right a bit where it's higher, and shelter in the last of the trees. I reckon we're onto the watershed and once we go over the col we'll pick up the head of the Eden. It flows all the way to the sea at Carleol and, as Oswin said, it's also the start of the Mallerstang valley and Pendragon's lands."

~~~

They passed an uncomfortable night. They were so high that there was too little fuel for a fire. They simply huddled together between a couple of boulders, sheltered by a few scrubby trees, and tucked in close with Sköll and Hati. Neither wanted to voice what they felt; that they had grown used to the reassuring embrace of the forest and felt suddenly vulnerable, exposed on the high fell tops. Their only reassurance was from each other's closeness and the warmth of the dogs.

"Hravn, I really don't like the look of that." Ealdgith shook Hravn awake. It was first light. The sun was still below the eastern horizon but its rays were reflecting off the bottom of towering red clouds looming in from the north west and now almost over head. "The wind is getting up too and the temperature's dropped," Ealdgith added.

Hravn stirred, peering at Ealdgith and then at the angry sky that silhouetted her head. "By Thor!" He exclaimed. "Damn! That's not good. We're going to be caught out whatever we do. We can't stay here, that's for sure."

Pushing himself upright he stared at the towering clouds and then turned to Ealdgith, glumly shaking his head. "We really need to follow the tops around the edge of Mallerstang, but if we do, we could be blown off them if that develops into a real storm, and if we go into the valley we go straight through Pendragon's land. We are damned either way!"

"There's only one way now, Hravn, look!" Ealdgith pointed over Hravn's shoulder. Hravn turned. "Oh no! That's snow! Quick, let's get moving. We'll keep to the east side of the valley and try to hug the edge of the forest away from any tracks. We can't be caught up here in that!"

A dark yellow-grey wall was forming, hanging below the reddened clouds blocking out more and more of the view to the north west. "I give it an hour at the most before it hits us. See how the wind's picking up too. Oswin said that this high up it can snow at Eōstre, I just hoped that it wouldn't."

The first flakes fell as they crossed the beck that tumbled in cascades from the fells above. The river Eden was on their left now as they re-entered the forest, making their way cautiously along the bottom of the valley wall. All was quiet, eerily so. It was as if the forest was expectant, waiting. The ponies' ears twitched, alert; the hounds kept close, their heads down and their hackles up. "Do you think they sense our caution or is it the forest itself?" Ealdgith whispered to Hravn, "I certainly don't like the feeling here. It's as if the trees themselves are watching us and crowding in."

The gloom of the breaking snow storm was intimidating. The rising wind whipped the tree tops, wailing through the branches that swayed and creaked above them. "Hodhr, it's cold all of a sudden! It's not been like this since we met Oswin," Hravn cursed their luck.

"Just stay alert and listen as well as look," he urged "At least no one else will be out in this, which is better for us. We'll keep going and try and use the storm and the snow to keep us hidden; and the snow will quickly cover our tracks whilst it keeps falling."

The cousins kept going until they saw the line of cliffs that formed the valley wall and realised immediately why Oswin had thought that they might form a good barrier between a fell-top route and Pendragon's lands below. They also realised just how vulnerable they were now that they were on the wrong side of the cliffs. There was no way up the face and they would be penned in the valley bottom until they could reach the northern exit further down the valley – but just how far?

"Look, Hravn, we can't go much further today. I'm frozen; you must be too and just look at the balls of snow hanging from Sköll and Hati. We all need to get shelter and some warmth, even the ponies."

Hravn was desperate to push through the valley as quickly as possible, but he knew that Ealdgith spoke sense. The risk from almost certain hypothermia was greater than the possible risk of capture. "I know, I know, you win," he said rather grudgingly. "Look, I think our best choice might be to see if there is a cave or a rock shelter in the base of the crags. We've hours of daylight left yet, but you're right, we do need to get some shelter and warmth soon."

What little luck they had was holding. Within twenty minutes, Hravn noticed a dark, narrow, gap in the wall of rocks. It stood out because the earth in the gap's entrance was still green with moss, not covered by the gathering snow. "That's strange, look there. For some reason the snow isn't settling under those rocks, let's take a look." He ran forward trailing the pony behind him.

"Hey! Feel that." He held his bare hand into the gap, sensing a faint draught of warmer air that was drifting out. Its warmth was just sufficient to melt the snowflakes falling into the gap. "I think we've found a cave," he called to Ealdgith, as she trudged up behind. "There is a draught of warm air here. I think it must be from a cave behind the rock. It must be like Oswin's cave, always warmer inside in winter, and with all this cold air outside, the warm air will be flowing out more quickly."

Hravn peered into the gap, it was set slightly back into the rock, maybe four feet high and three wide. He ducked inside, let his eyes accustom to the gloom and then felt his way further in. The cave opened out to the left and up to a higher ceiling. The blackness in front of him was daunting and he hadn't the confidence to feel his way forward; feeling air on his face he sensed that there was space in front of him.

Ducking back outside he called to Ealdgith. "Edie, this looks promising. It's warm inside, but I don't know how big it is. Can you wait while I get a little fire going and some light?"

"Of course, but don't dally! It's freezing me to the bone standing here."

"Don't stand around then. Why don't you see if you can find some decent dead wood, it won't all be wet from the snow yet."

Hravn quickly sorted out a little tinder and kindling and returned to the cave to generate a small fire from his flint and steel. Ealdgith came back a few minutes later with an arm full of dead wood. Ducking into the cave she gasped "Oh! This is good, there's room for the ponies too if they will come in. It's bigger than Oswin's. I wonder where that leads?" She peered up to a gap where the floor rose to meet the ceiling. "That must be where the draught of air comes from."

"I won't bother exploring," Hravn cautioned, "we just need to get everything inside. If we have the fire in here it will be concealed and the smoke will flow outside. I just hope the wind disperses it quickly and that no one sees or smells it."

The shelter from the biting wind and snow was a life-line for them all. The ponies needed little coaxing inside, probably sensing that the cave was not unlike a stall in the stable they had once shared.

Once inside, their combined body warmth quickly warmed up the little rocky chamber, the small fire being needed for light rather than warmth. The air soon became fuggy, the smell of damp pony was very strong; but it was more bearable than the cold outside.

"I really wanted us to keep going," Hravn said "I really don't want us getting caught in the valley, but we can't go on when it's like this."

Ealdgith agreed with his sentiment, but was more cautious. "We could, once it stops snowing and the wind drops, but we'd still need to shelter overnight, unless the clouds clear and there is enough of a moon to see by. We can't risk breaking an ankle in our rush to get by."

Hravn nodded. "I'll keep checking outside, we'll just have to see." Then, changing the subject, added, "Remember, if we are stopped you are Edmund. Let's say you're twelve, which will explain why your voice hasn't broken. Everything else can be for real. You might struggle to understand their dialect though."

Ealdgith smiled at that. "No bad thing, the less chat I get dragged into the better for me. Why don't we speak in broad Saxon English and you translate for me when you need to? That will stop too many difficult questions. Anyway, I hope it doesn't come to that."

The snow hadn't abated by nightfall so they huddled down with the intention of a very early start, weather permitting.

Hravn couldn't sleep and kept checking outside. He eventually shook Ealdgith awake as the pre-dawn light slowly revealed the snow-scape outside. "Come on, Edie, it's stopped snowing and there is a low mist. It's just like when we were in the forest by the Jor. Let's get going."

It was still barely dawn as they led the ponies out from the rocky entrance and started their trudge northward along the bottom of the cliffs. The snow was at least the depth of Ealdgith's middle finger and it made their going very slow as they kept stumbling over hidden boulders "This really is the valley of the cursed," Hravn said, almost to himself.

"Whisst!" Ealdgith's caution stopped Hravn in his tracks.

Two men, both mounted on fell ponies, stepped from the shelter of the forest and blocked their way between the trees and the crags.

Hravn and Ealdgith felt suddenly nauseous and their legs became leaden. Hravn spoke first. "Edie, we've got to bluff this out. Don't show that you're afraid, and hold their gaze. Remember all that Oswin taught you. You will be fine. Come, just keep walking."

They called Sköll and Hati to heel and formed a tight group as they approached the men.

"Hravn, two more to the left!" Ealdgith warned through the side of her mouth as they got closer.

"Good morning! It's a better day than yesterday. I thought winter had returned." Hravn called with a bravado that he certainly didn't feel, but talking did at least restore some confidence.

The four men sat, expressionless, holding their mounts steady. Hravn and Ealdgith kept walking until one, presumably in charge, raised his hand. "Hold there, young sirs!" Hravn's confident greeting in Norse, their seax, spears and the hunting horn over Hravn's shoulder all indicated a degree of status, raising questions that might need an answer.

"Whither are you going? Why have you not paid your respects to Lord Pendragon?" The leader questioned Hravn in Norse, before making a quick aside to his men in a heavy Cumbric dialect that Hravn failed to understand.

"We are from Ghellinges-scir. Our lands were ravaged by the Normans and we are going to my family in Carleol." Hravn continued to speak in Norse, choosing Carleol as the most likely location for Gospatrick's seat of power.

"That may be so, but you have dues to pay on the way. Lord Pendragon expects and requires that." The leader continued, leaving little room for negotiation.

"Huh! Just rob them now! They look rich, but I doubt they fight." One of the horsemen sitting to their flank called across. He spoke in clear Cumbric.

Hravn wheeled around towards him, speaking in Cumbric "You know not to whom you speak. Chance your arm if you like but beware you may lose it!" He half drew his seax from its scabbard. "Our uncle, Lord Gospatrick, holds these lands, not Pendragon, or so I understand."

"Owain, that's enough! There could be more at stake here than we know. We'll take them to my father. Now!"

"Thank you, that is sensible; and what is your name?" Hravn looked the leader directly in the eye

"I'm Urien, son of Lord Pendragon. Now mount and follow; and keep those hounds close else they'll be dead." With that, he wheeled his pony, leaving Hravn and Ealdgith to mount and follow. Hravn told Ealdgith quickly what had been said. She listened, grim faced having understood the gist of the exchange as it happened.

Chapter 11

Hravn again cursed their luck. Lord Pendragon's manor was barely four furlongs away through the forest; they had actually passed parallel to it and now back-tracked up the valley.

He tried to engage some of the men in conversation. Owain ignored them. They could see that he was only a couple of years older than Hravn and they suspected that he might be Urien's son; each had shoulder length black hair, piercing blue eyes and a hooked nose. The other two men were older and more open. It seemed that the group had been returning from Kircabi Stephan the previous afternoon and had also been caught out by the snow, sheltering in a barn further down the valley. It was pure fate that caused their paths to cross. Wyrd could be cruel.

The forest gave way to strips of fields as they came closer to the river. The mist was lifting and they were quickly able to take stock of their surroundings, which didn't inspire them. Mallerstang was a long narrow valley bound by craggy slopes on both sides. The fell tops that towered above them seemed much higher than those they had grown used to. The valley was a prison. As they rode behind Urien they could see a large encampment ahead, unlike any manor they had seen before. A wooden wall appeared to enclose some small wooden buildings with a larger building in the middle. The wooden wall was at least as high as two men, large doors opened inwards as they approached. The sight of the large building inside took their breath away. It was long and high, with low wooden walls on stone foundations and a steeply pitched turfed roof. "This is more like a burgh than a manor" whispered Hravn. "Whoever Pendragon is, he has some clout, there's no doubt about that."

Dismounting at the steps of the longhouse, Urien said gruffly. "Leave your weapons here but bring your hounds, it looks to be better for all if they are under your control rather than left outside." It was obvious that, like all his men, he was nervous of them. Sköll and Hati stayed close, their hackles raised, eyes alert.

Urien led the way up the few steps into the hall. It was gloomy inside. A fire burned in a central hearth and as smoke rose to a hole in the ceiling, it billowed out amongst the beams and rafters; the air was fuggy. The large hall was partitioned along its sides by roughly hung skins. A table was at the far side of the hearth, alongside which a tall, elderly man stood. Bald, with long grey hair and a roughly trimmed beard, he wore a wolf's skin over his shoulders for warmth. He had the same piercing blue eyes as Urien and Owain.

"My Lord Pendragon," Urien addressed the elderly man formally, before adding, "father, we found these two passing through. They claim to be related to Gospatrick and say they are refugees from yon side of the fells. Certainly, the younger one seems to speak only the Saxon tongue."

Pendragon turned, squared his shoulders and stared at Hravn and Ealdgith. Both held his gaze.

"Mmm, why would two youths from yonder be skulking here? Speak up now!" he demanded.

Hravn continued to hold Pendragon's gaze then replied slowly and deliberately in Norse. "My Lord, I am Hravn, son of Ask. This is my younger cousin, Eadmund, son of Thor, and we mean you no offence. Indeed, we did not know that your manor was here. We are refugees from the Norman devastation of our families' lands in Ghellinges-scir. You may have heard of it?"

"Indeed. Continue." Pendragon's response was curt.

"We were out hunting in early Aefter Yule when the Bastard's men struck. We witnessed their evil work first hand and we were prevented from returning home to find what had become of our families, instead being forced to flee along the dale of the Jor, eventually reaching the forest. Snow blocked our route over the fells and we wintered in a cave until the first Lencten flowers encouraged us to take the path over the tops. Winter held a sting in its tail and snow forced us into this valley yesterday. We are heading to find others of our family.   Our uncle is Lord Gospatrick."

"So you say.   'Tis an easy claim to make, is it not?"

"My Lord, Eadmund and I are from two families, one Saxon, one Norse.   Our fathers hold adjoining estates near Ghellinges.   Our great grandfather was Earl Uhtred the Bold of Northumberland.   Earl Uhtred was Lord Gospatrick's grandfather, was he not?"   Hravn deliberately simplified a complicated family tree and challenged Pendragon to contradict him.

"I see," Pendragon studied them both through narrowed eyes.   "Not quite an uncle, but blood-kin certainly, perhaps a cousin at some remove?"

He continued, "I hear you speak Cumbric, how is that?"

"My father is Norse, my mother Saxon. My grandmother is Cumbric though, and I grew up speaking all three tongues.   Eadmund though speaks only Saxon.   His parents are both Saxon, my mother is his aunt, his father's sister."   Hravn spoke quickly, wanting to explain why Ealdgith wasn't involved in the conversation.

"Yours is a tangled web, lad, but you're bright, I'll give you that.   How old are you?"

"Seventeen come Sumor, Lord," Hravn lied, hoping that claiming an extra year or two might give him more credibility, "Eadmund is but twelve."

"I see. Does Gospatrick expect you?"

"No, Lord. As I said, we fled urgently and have been delayed by the winter snow. I know not where my uncle is, but expect to hear of him at Carleol. That is where we are heading."

"Do you, now? Do you?" Pendragon gave a wry smile "What makes you think I will let you journey to Carleol? These are my lands, after all, and you do not have my permission to cross through them, do you!" It was a statement of fact, not a question.

"No, Lord, but surely in these times we have common cause against a common foe? Surely though, you must be sworn to my uncle? Cumbraland is his, is it not?" Hravn tried to plead their case.

"You mistake me, lad." Pendragon drummed his fingers on the table in obvious irritation. "Do not assume! Cumbraland may be Gospatrick's, if he lives. I know not what has happened to him since his failed venture against your King; 'The Bastard' as you so eloquently call him. There is dispute too between Gospatrick and his younger brother Maldred as to who claims what. What I do know is the land you are in is Westmoringaland, if you did not know. It falls betwixt Cumbraland and the English lands to the south. The Scots King and the English King have each long claimed it, as do the Cumbric princes, but I hold it and pay homage to none. I do not, as yet, see the English King as my enemy. Indeed, I profit from the Norman presence. Many want to transit these lands and all must pay me homage in kind."

This was a predicament that Hravn had not anticipated. He did not know that his grandmother's lands were claimed by both Kings and held by Pendragon. They stood, literally and metaphorically, on very uncertain ground.

"What would you have us do, my Lord?"

"That is a very good question, lad, for I doubt that there is much that you can pay me, other than those tawdry bits of silverware you carry." Pendragon's tone was taunting rather than scathing.

What say you, Urien, and you too, Owain?" They turned and realised that Owain had been standing behind them.

"Take what little they have and sell them to the Dyflin slavers." Urien's prompt reply stunned Hravn. Ealdgith hadn't understood the exchange in Cumbric.

"Kill them, grandfather. Why waste time with worthless kids?" Owain added in a mocking tone.

Pendragon paused, looking from his son to his grandson. "I would have expected a little more forethought, especially from you, Urien." He was scathing and both scowled sourly at Hravn and Ealdgith.

Pendragon continued speaking in Cumbric; Hravn just about kept pace with the conversation.

"Surely you both have more sense? We may get nothing from them individually, but if Gospatrick is their uncle, and why would they risk claiming otherwise, then we could raise a hefty ransom. If that fails, we can do as either of you suggest. Though, Urien, I agree that in the short term we might fetch more for them from a slaver; but there is no merit in simply killing something that has worth. Owain; you act the dolt! It is time you learnt to think instead of just bullying."

Owain pouted, scowling at Ealdgith. The bully within him was obvious.

"Well, Hravn." Pendragon turned back to him, again speaking in Norse, "Your uncle owes me a debt, a great one. There is an old score that is long outstanding and as yet unsettled. He once did me a grievous harm. There is nothing that you can give me to satisfy the dues you owe, but if Gospatrick will pay your ransom, and it will be a hefty one for sure, then you will be free to travel to him, both of you."

Ealdgith trembled, desperately trying to hide the fact that she understood what Pendragon had said. She was all too aware what it could mean for her if she was held as a prisoner; and what could happen to them both when no ransom was forthcoming.

Hravn was just as shocked. Their situation had to be regained somehow. He held Pendragon's gaze and immediately questioned in a forthright tone.

"Yes, Lord, but it will doubtless take quite some time for you to present your demands to my Lord Gospatrick. If we are to be kept hostage, surely you do not intend to hold us here to fester until then? What would that achieve? Can we not at least work for you?" If they were to be held hostage, he was desperate to buy some privacy and limited freedom for them; that might at least give Ealdgith the leeway and privacy she would need.

Pendragon scrutinised Hravn through narrowed eyes. He was impressed by the youth's confident and forthright manner. He sensed that here, there was an honesty and determination that was very different to the character of his grandson. Perhaps he could use Hravn to inspire Owain?

"What do you propose, lad? Just what is it that you think you could do for me that others cannot?"

"Lord, it is not for me to say what your men can or cannot do. From the very little that I have seen, I do not think that your men are farmers. I rather think that your need is for those with a more martial ability. Would that be so?"

"Indeed it is, though from the look of you, and your cousin, I doubt you have much to offer."

Hravn was thinking quickly, working out a possible way in which they could help Pendragon and help themselves. He was also speaking more slowly hoping that Ealdgith would understand his Norse.

"Lord, it is obvious that our appearance deceives you. That deception is the strength that we bring you. We are both skilled in the use of the seax and the bow, and with our hounds we can hunt and track. You prey on travellers, do you not? Travellers will doubtless run, hide or change their route at the sight of your men. But travellers will not feel cowed by two callow youths on ponies who may happen upon them. We can be your eyes and ears."

Pendragon turned to Ealdgith, surprising them all by addressing her in a heavily accented Saxon.

"What of you, Eadmund? Does your cousin speak for you in this? Are you skilled in the use of the seax and bow as he says? Can you hunt and track?" His tone was sceptical.

Ealdgith was taken aback but replied quickly with a confidence she didn't feel. She knew that Hravn had thrown her a lifeline; she had to seize it.

"He does, Lord. I, we, may be young, but my father's uncle trained us both in martial skills. He was once the King's man and made sure that we too could fight for ourselves when called upon." Ealdgith made an oblique reference to Oswin, before continuing.

"We have survived the winter in the forest. That alone proves that we are capable and strong enough to work for you until my uncle ransoms us, as I know he will."

"I believe that you at least have the wit and ability to survive in the wild. I have no time for your uncle, Gospatrick!" Pendragon spat into the hearth, "but that does not reflect on either of you. I too once served Lord Uhtred, your grandfather. I sense something of his confidence and strength in each of you, so I am minded to do as you suggest. What say you two?" Pendragon flicked his eyes across to Urien and then to Owain, who was standing behind Ealdgith.

"As you say, father," Urien agreed tersely.

Owain sniggered. Pendragon glared at him and Ealdgith turned to see what was happening behind her.

"Huh! This runt couldn't piss against the wind," Owain aimed a hard, low punch at Ealdgith's groin.

Ealdgith moved instinctively, blocking Owain's blow with crossed arms. Then grabbing one of

105

his wrists she turned underneath Owain and thrust her torso against his knees. Owain's weight and momentum carried him forward, flipping him over onto his back at her feet as she stood up hissing in Saxon, "There's a lot you don't know about me!".

Owain lay prostrate, momentarily stunned.

Urien moved as if to hit Ealdgith himself. "Stop!" Pendragon raised his voice, and then laughed. "Owain, you're a fool! You don't listen, do you! That's the comeuppance you deserve. It is you that could not piss in the wind!"

Pendragon turned to Ealdgith, again speaking in his accented Saxon. "Master Eadmund, I am impressed. It is many years since I saw a move like that. Your uncle's teaching, I assume?"

"Indeed it is, Lord. He served our old King, Canute, and then journeyed to Byzantium and the East."

Pendragon's eyes narrowed, he paused, looking intently at Ealdgith. "He was a Dane then? Are you not Saxon?"

"Ealdgith realised her error. She had improvised her story quickly and would now need to acknowledge a degree of ability in the Norse tongue. "Yes Lord, I am Saxon, he was a Dane, my uncle by marriage. Many of our families in Ghellinges-scir have intermarried."

Pendragon spat. "Norse, Dane, Saxon – whatever! So long as you do as I bid, I care not what blood you are. Now listen, all of you...." He glared at Owain.

"Be quite clear.... Hravn and Eadmund are my hostages. They will work for me, and with you, Urien, until their ransom is redeemed. They will do as Hravn has suggested. Our work will benefit from a proper scout, and I believe that these two can do what your men cannot...is that understood, Owain?"

Owain had pulled himself upright and was now leaning against a chair, "Yes Grandfather." He scowled.

"Remember," Pendragon continued, "Gospatrick owes me a debt and these two are the means by which he will repay that debt. I will make good use of them, and no harm is to come to them. Make sure your men know that, Urien."

Turning to Hravn and Ealdgith, Pendragon continued. "Now, you two, you will work for me. You will scout and hunt, using your hounds. Urien will make sure you have what you need. But, don't think that you can have free rein to leave. You are in my service. If you try to leave, your hounds will die.... slowly.... with you watching....my men will roast them....and you will eat them....is that understood by you?" Pendragon paused for effect. He could see that they were emotionally very close to the wolfhounds and he knew that this was their vulnerable point.

"Yes, Lord," they said in unison. Both believed that Pendragon would not hesitate to carry out his threat, but at least they had bought some leeway for themselves.

"Right, it is early Lencten now. I will give Gospatrick 'til the long day of mid-Sumor to ransom you. If he has not done so by then, I will consider whether to do as my son advises and sell you to the Dyflin slavers."

"Lord, where would you have us sleep? Hravn asked innocently. "You know I speak Cumbric and I doubt that you want me listening to your men's conversation. Mayhap we should sleep with our ponies and the hounds in the stable? That would protect your men's conversation and save them any trouble with our hounds." Hravn was desperate to gain some privacy for Ealdgith and hoped that the stable might provide a form of sanctuary. Ealdgith would soon be found out if she had to sleep in the longhouse. "We can also use the space there to continue our martial training. Our skills will fade if we do not practise daily."

"You speak sense, lad. As you've seen, there is a wall around the buildings and yard and it is guarded, so you cannot stray. If you are content with the discomfort of the stable, then so be it."

Chapter 12

The stable was a smaller version of the longhouse; a low dry stone wall topped with a wooden frame, low wattle and daub walls and a turf roof. It held well over a dozen fell ponies and with room to spare for more. Head height wattle partitions formed several smaller pens. Low narrow slits provided limited light and very necessary ventilation. The strong smell of warm ponies, manure and urine would take a lot of getting used to, especially after so long living outside in the clean air of the forest. Thankfully, there was room to clear a pen for Hravn and Ealdgith's use. Their ponies could join the others and Sköll and Hati would sleep by the door, a deterrent to any unwelcome interest.

Hravn stuffed some straw into the slit window that opened onto their pen. "That'll do until I can get some hessian over it as we don't want any prying eyes. I'm sure that there'll be some, plus we need to keep the warmth in."

As he turned around, Ealdgith flung her arms around him in a tight hug. "Thank God, Hravn and thank you too. I thought we were finished. You really talked Pendragon around, but I don't trust those others. That Owain is a lout, I know he will be trouble."

Hravn kissed Ealdgith's head. "I agree. I think we have to try and keep you away from him. Let's start to make this a bit homelier and then we'll think through how we are going to play things." He released her. "I think we need something to sit on. Let's see what we can scrounge. I rather think that as we now seem to have Pendragon's protection we can risk one or two liberties."

It was not yet time for the main midday meal of the day so they took a walk around the yard at the back of the longhouse. They were reluctant to poke around inside, but did find a pile of sawn logs that could be placed on end to support a plank to make a bench. There was assorted ironmongery in the stable and Hravn quickly found a hammer and some nails and fashioned a couple of benches; one to sit on and another upon which to lay out possessions.

The stable held an assortment of tack for the horses. Some was in good condition, well-oiled and clean, whereas other tack had simply been piled in the corner. As they ratched through it to see if any would serve the ponies, the dogs growled as the stable door opened. A young lad, no more than ten years old, stood frozen. "What? Who are..?" Hravn cut him short, turning with a smile and holding out a hand he spoke in Cumbric. "I'm Hravn, we are under our Lord Pendragon's protection and will be living in here. We need to clear some living space and sort out some tack for our ponies...and you are?"

"Bran," he said uncertainly, eyeing Sköll and Hati nervously.

"Boys! Settle down," Hravn cautioned the hounds and turned back to Bran. "We'll be here quite a while by the look of it so we might as well get to know you. This is Edie, but he speaks no Cumbric. He's my cousin. What do you do?"

"Stable hand. Stable everything, I guess, as there's nobody else to help at the moment, but I'm not sure; I'll need to speak to Urien."

Hravn interrupted, trying to calm the lad down. "Don't worry yourself there, he knows all about it and our Lord Pendragon made it quite clear that we are part of his household. We'll give you a hand here too if that helps, there'd be less for you to do then." Bran havered "I'll still need to check, but yes, alright, I guess..." He backed out of the door.

"I really don't want anyone in here. Why?" Ealdgith looked quizzically at Hravn.

"I know you don't, but it will help to have a friend who can tell us something about what is going on here. More importantly, if we can take on some of his tasks it will limit what he has to do in here. I'm sure Urien will find more for him to do elsewhere. I rather think it might be something I can suggest to Pendragon. He seems to listen and he certainly seems to question how Urien does things."

Hravn finished rummaging through the tack. "Look, I reckon these two saddles would fit the ponies. It's a long while since they wore them and we'll need to check they are happy with saddles, but it will make riding easier for us...there are stirrups too." He added after a pause. "Very handy if ever we have to control the pony and fight with a spear."

Ealdgith smiled, looking a bit more enthusiastic. "Yes, and when we get the chance to run from here it will help us to cover ground faster. If we claim these and keep them close, we could hide some essentials in the saddle bags."

"Right, but not too quick. We've got to play the waiting game. We have a couple of months yet before Pendragon realises that there is no ransom forthcoming. For the next couple of weeks at least, we need to be really obedient. Urien, for one, will check on us and I wouldn't put it past that lout Owain to pry in our kit, particularly the saddle bags. Just be patient Edie and then we can make a plan. It's got to be one that will work. We would do better to sound out some of the men and see how the land lies. They might even have heard of my grandmother's family at Ravenstandale."

"I agree, but we can't risk staying too long. The longer I'm here the more chance there is I'll be found out; God knows that mustn't happen..." Ealdgith stared hard at Hravn. He nodded, touching her cheek gently. "I know."

"Look, what we can do," Ealdgith continued, "is to try and find some of their womenfolk. They must be here somewhere. They are more likely to talk to me. I'm sure my Norse can stretch to that. It's the men that I won't risk speaking to."

"This is what we'll do," Hravn said with sudden confidence. "I'll try and get close to Pendragon and influence how we work for him. I'll even try and get close to Urien and get him to let us look after this place, which you can do. That should keep you out of common sight and maybe give you a chance to get to know some of their women folk once we find out where they are. You can be the shy one that stays in the shadows and I'll be the outgoing one. We'll make sure that you prove your worth when we are out scouting for them."

Ealdgith looked more reassured. "I'm hungry, let's see if there is any food in the longhouse. We'll just sit at the table end and watch the others."

They stepped out of the stable and Hravn thrust the heavy wooden door shut, shaking the building and releasing a slab of wet snow from the roof above that cascaded over his head and shoulders. He stamped his feet, raised his face to the sky and shouted "Why?!" Ealdgith couldn't help but collapse giggling. Hravn's expression froze, then relaxed as he laughed "God curse Wyrd! She conspires to trap us in this hellish valley by sending an icy blast, and then once we are caught she sends the thaw. What else has she got planned for us?"

113

Hravn shook off the snow as they trudged across to the longhouse. "We'll keep Hati and Sköll close. It will deter others and show that we're not to be meddled with," Ealdgith said, more as a statement of fact than a suggestion.

Their meal wasn't as quiet as they had hoped it might be. Food at mid-day was the main meal of the day and for many it was the first. The hall of the longhouse was filling quickly, and groups milled around three women tending the large pot on the central hearth. A fourth was turning unleavened loaves on the hearth stones. Ealdgith breathed deeply, savouring the smell of warm food. Her joy was short lived. Sensing eyes upon her she turned her head and caught sight of Owain glaring at her across the hearth whilst he whispered behind his hand to another youth of a similar age. Ealdgith nudged Hravn. "Let's move over to the side, away from the hearth, we're attracting unwelcome looks from that lout over there."

Minutes later the room stilled. Pendragon walked in accompanied by Urien. It was obvious from the way Urien was gesticulating with his hands and talking quickly in hushed tones that he was trying to argue with Pendragon, who was ignoring him. They were followed by four other men, two of whom they recognised from their ambush that morning. As Pendragon neared the head of the table, a chair was pulled out for him. Urien and the four men sat either side of him and as they did so the groups, who had been huddling around the hearth, joined them at the table, sitting on long benches along its length. "Come, we'll take a seat at the end," Hravn urged Ealdgith ahead of him, securing places at the end of a quickly filling bench.

The women tending the cooking pot were ladling a thick stew into smaller pots that they carried across to the table and placed along the centre to join the trays of stale flat bread, jugs of water and weak beer that were already there. Hravn reached across to claim two flatbreads for them to use as trenchers. As he did so he glanced along the length of the table and saw Pendragon's blue eyes watching him. His heart beat faster.

Pendragon stood, thumping the table loudly with the hilt of his knife. "All...I want you to take note of the two faces at the end of the table...the two youths with the hounds at their feet. Their names are Hravn and Eadmund. They are here at my behest and are hostage. Both are kin to Earl Gospatrick and their ransom will redeem Gospatrick's debt to me. They are to work for me and are free to move about my land on my business…but they are not free to leave my service. They are to come to no harm…. but they are not to be taken into your confidence. Is that clear to all?" Pendragon held the gaze of those around the table. Some just nodded, others confirmed "Aye Lord" before turning to stare at Hravn and Ealdgith. Hravn nudged Ealdgith's knee. "Hold their gaze, we are not being cowed."

Ealdgith held Owain's eyes, staring him down. She could feel the warmth of Hati's flank rubbing against her leg and took strength from the thought that Owain would never have the courage to come near either of the hounds. She refused to blink and felt a secret relief when he dropped his eyes to the table.

The tension broke when Pendragon stabbed at a hunk of mutton that had been ladled onto his trencher.

"Come on Edie, eat up, we can't miss out on free food. We're going to have to get to know these people anyway." Hravn passed one of the flatbreads to Ealdgith and leaned across the table to pull the bowl of stew towards them. He ladled the stew of mutton, turnip and kale onto the bread trenchers.

"Thanks, at least it's wholesome. I guess it's all that's available at this time of year."

Ealdgith glanced around the long table, taking stock of the gathering. Some were attacking their food ravenously, others were more interested in gossiping, and a few looked back, studying them.

Ealdgith whispered an aside to Hravn, "Look, there are some very strong family resemblances around the table. That red-haired lad next to Owain must be related to the two red haired men with Pendragon, see?"

Hravn glanced towards the top of the table. "Mmm, you're right. Do you mean the one that looks like a small ox and the tall one with the cold stare?"

"Yes," Ealdgith continued, speaking in Saxon, "and I think both the men are related to Pendragon too. Their colouring is very different, but they have that hooked nose, you can't miss it, it looks like a crow's beak." She giggled.

Hravn glanced back up the table and grinned, "I see what you mean. It's pretty damned ugly, isn't it. I think they might be his nephews or maybe grandsons. Urien is obviously Pendragon's son and seems to have some authority over them."

"Hell!" Ealdgith cursed under her breath. "This is a real nest of vipers; we've got to be careful who we speak to".

"No," Hravn countered, "we need to gain their confidence and understand where their loyalties lie. We can then use that to our advantage. But I do agree that we need to keep you away from them. There are quite a few women too. I can't say whether they are wives or servants, but they might be more open to talking."

"There's young Bran too," Ealdgith said at last. "I could perhaps befriend him as you suggested. See how he's ignored by the others."

"The red-haired lad with Owain looks pretty relaxed and affable." Hravn observed. "Not at all like his friend."

As the meal was drawing to a close Urien banged the table and gestured with his head towards the other end of the hall. "Hravn, a word!"

Chapter 13

"Right you two." Urien spoke to Hravn and Ealdgith abruptly has he led them towards the other end of the hall. "It seems my father wants you to work for him...for me. Take a seat there, and listen."

The cousins glanced at each other and sat on a bench whilst Urien pulled up a chair and leant forward towards them. "I can't say that I'm happy with what my father wants 'though I can see the sense of it and I'll make it work...as will you," he said, looking each of them in the eye. "Be warned, he will make money out of you, so you'd both best pray that Gospatrick pays up." They held his gaze, nodding.

"My father controls all the land within a day's ride or more of here and, as you found out this morning, this is one of the main routes from the English lands in the south to the Cumbric and Scot lands to the north, as well the routes over from the east. We farm enough to provide for our needs, but the rest of what we need, we take as tribute from those passing through, and from those rich manors north and south of us."

They continued to nod, silently.

"Once you work for my father there is nowhere to run to; like as not, you'll be seen as one of us and hanged for it, for make no mistake, that is the penalty you will pay if caught. Once your ransom is paid, well, that's a different matter."

Hravn sat back and looked squarely at Urien. He understood the very obvious threat behind Urien's message, but he could also see that they would be given a degree of leeway, more if they could gain Urien's trust. He could also see that they would be at great physical risk.

"So, what exactly would you have us do? This morning we offered to be Lord Pendragon's eyes and ears, to scout for travellers. But I must tell you that I, we, will not kill for you. We both took an oath to our uncle not to use the skills he taught us other than to defend ourselves and those we have a duty to protect...you may not care for that, but we do." Hravn's statement sounded a great deal more forthright and confident than he felt.

Urien sat back, smiled tightly and paused before answering. "I would not expect you to kill, not unless you have to. Not because I share your morals, that's just foolish idealism. I'm a realist. I will kill if I need to and demand that my men do too. But we don't wantonly kill those from whom we take. Fear and intimidation work just as well and with less risk of retribution...we've learnt that the hard way." He paused. "My men will take care of any violence. As you say, you will be my eyes and ears. Anyway, your hounds will be intimidating enough for most. Agreed?"

"Yes" both replied.

"We have little choice," Ealdgith added.

Urien drew a deep breath, then continued. "This is how we work".

"I have three teams of four, leading one myself, with my nephews Math and Nudd heading the others. You'll have seen them just now."

"So where does Owain fit in?" Ealdgith had no hesitation in asking.

"He works for me. He was a fool this morning and you dealt well with him. Don't goad him though, else you will answer to me too. The other two lads you no doubt saw just now are Beli, Nudd's son, and Uther, another nephew. He works with Math. The rest of the men in the teams work on the land and we call on them when we need them."

"I can see where we will fit in," Hravn was quick to appear a lot more enthusiastic than he really felt. "We could either be a fourth team or work with a team to cover one of the main routes and then report back to the leader as soon as we spot a likely traveller. That would give you time to summon your men and get into an ambush position."

Urien raised an eyebrow "There're no flies on you, are there?"

Hravn kept the initiative, adding, "And if it comes to raiding a manor we could perhaps check the lie of the land first. As I said to your father, we won't stand out and attract interest."

Urien smiled, paused, "Don't get ahead of yourself, but, yes, it makes sense."

Ealdgith could see where Hravn was trying to lead Urien's thinking, by playing to his needs. She spoke slowly in Norse, reluctant to show that she knew the language better than she was prepared to let on.

"Day to day, could we not take over running the stable? After all we are going to be living in it and when we met Bran this morning, he seemed to be a bit overwhelmed by what he has to do."

"Yes, Edie," Hravn jumped in. "If Bran helps you, I could help Urien, if that's alright with you, Urien? I could do with getting to know the lie of the land and Edie would be kept busy looking after the ponies, grooming, mucking out and exercising them...there's a lot to do in there."

Urien sat back looking quizzically at them both "I hear what you say, but I am surprised at your enthusiasm for lads with an uncertain future, and who are being held hostage."

"That should be no real surprise to you." Hravn was quick to try to allay Urien's suspicion. "We've lost our family, we've lived wild in the forest throughout the winter and we need somewhere to call home, for a while at least. I am sure my uncle will come good, but until then we can't keep running, can we?"

Urien stood up. "Your shrewd lads, I'll give you that. I agree for now and will see how you get on. I'll speak to Bran and tell him to help you, Eadmund. He has no real family and needs a friend. Hravn, Nudd will show you the land tomorrow. He's easy to work with and I fear Owain will be reluctant to befriend you."

~~~

Hravn and Ealdgith woke early the next morning. Daylight and fresh air came in through the unblocked window slits. Hravn looked out and could see that most of the snow had thawed. "Lencturn's returned," he called, feeling naturally enthusiastic. "Let's freshen up before Nudd arrives, and Bran too, I expect." He splashed water from a pitcher onto his face and then flicked drops down onto Ealdgith who was still lying on a bed of straw. Hati took it as a sign for a game and pounced on his mistress, licking her face until she pushed him off and sat up.

"We've half a loaf and a jug of watered ale I saved from the meal last night, that should do for now," Ealdgith said, adding as she pulled herself up "You're right though, I need to relieve myself before we have company". She disappeared behind a stall at the end of the stable, "I'm sorry, but it is more discreet than using the latrine outside and there is so much manure here that we will never notice."

"You're right there," Hravn chuckled as he turned away "I hate to think what we'll end up smelling like. We'll need another of Oswin's swims sooner than you care to think."

They shared the loaf, then Ealdgith set to grooming the ponies, getting to know them individually as she did so. She was always impressed by the alert brightness of their eyes and their placid, intelligent nature. The fell ponies in her father's stables had been the same; so much easier to look after than the horses that he had also kept. She paused, touched by a sudden worry as to what had happened to them and to her family. The pony sensed her mood and twitched its head to nuzzle her hand.

Minutes later, the hounds growled as the stable door was pulled open.

"Whoa boys, stay calm there! I'm Nudd, you must be Hravn and Edie?" Nudd's short, stocky frame filled the door. The hounds stopped growling but held their ground, heads down, watching.

"Yes." Hravn hurried along the length of the stables holding out his hand "Edie's down here too, getting to know the ponies."

Nudd was impatient. "Well, come on then, let's get going. We won't bother saddling up, I'll put a back pad on Woden here and we'll be off."

Despite his stocky stature, Nudd leapt easily onto his pony's back and was out of the stable before Hravn had his pony out of the stall. He too leapt on bare-back and galloped out followed by Sköll.

"So much for 'good bye,'" Ealdgith muttered; but almost in the same moment she realised that it was probably for the best. They had become so used to showing each little signs of affection; her touch on Hravn's arm, his caress of her shoulder and cheek, that they risked catching themselves out in public if she was pretending to be a boy.

Hravn caught up with Nudd and rode alongside him as they took a southerly track towards the head of the river. The forest edge was a couple of furlongs to their left.

"We'll start with a visit to Outhgill. It's the main village in the dale and home to most of Lord Pendragon's people."

"That must be where yon smoke is from then?" Hravn asked before adding as an aside, "by the way, why is your pony called Woden when you are all Cumbric?"

Nudd grinned, with a deep chuckle. "Ha! You've answered your own question. It's because we are Cumbric that all our ponies have Norse names. That way they know who's in charge." "Hah! interesting!" Hravn laughed back "I'm part Cumbric too, you know."

Outhgill was a large village, home to over twenty families and surrounded by long strips of field that ran parallel to the river. In the early sun of the Lencten day, several men were working a team of oxen to plough ready for early planting. Their ready wave towards Nudd reassured Hravn that he, at least, was popular with his men.

"That's my hall over yonder." Nudd jerked his head towards a thatched building that stood to one side of the cluster of houses. "I live here and Math lives up at the head of the dale by Aisgill. My uncle Urien lives with my grandfather at the longhouse."

"Why so spread out?" Hravn realised that, if Pendragon's henchmen were routinely scattered around the dale, it could limit their choice of routes when the time came to flee.

Nudd carried on talking quite openly. "It's for our own security. My uncle, Uther, once had a hall at Lammerside, down the river towards Kircabi Stephan. It was the size of the longhouse and that way we could secure the whole dale of Mallerstang. That is until he was slain by Gospatrick and the hall and houses razed. Grandfather never rebuilt there and it is still a point of weakness. We can control the head of the dale better than the foot......hmm" he faltered, realising that he had perhaps said too much "...that's enough for now, save to say, there is no love for Gospatrick around here; you'd best remember that."

Hravn kept the conversation going. "Is there a seamstress hereby? Our clothes are threadbare and we're growing out of them. I certainly need some trousers and an under tunic made."

Nudd glanced across with an amused smile. "You could ask for old Rhiannon; she was once my grandmother's maid. She takes in work. Come back in your own time and ask for her."

"Thanks, I'll do that." Hravn was relieved and surprised at the unexpected permission and freedom to visit the village by themselves.

Nudd took charge. "Right! We'll head up to Aisgill so that you can see our land from the dale head. Then we'll head over the shoulder of Boar Fell. It'll give you a feel for the land beyond, North to Kircabi Stephan and Penrith, over towards the sea and Sedberge and back whence you came towards the vale of the Jor. You'll see why Mallerstang is so important and why we now raid so much further afield. The dale is fast in the middle of the fells and the more we raid outside that fastness, the more secure we are within."

Nudd dug his heels into Woden's flanks and urged him to a brisk trot along the river bank. Hravn caught up, with Sköll running behind, and called across to Nudd. "I see that you only have ponies, why no horses?"

Nudd grinned "Just take a look about you. How would horses cope with this land? They'd stumble and break a fetlock within a day."

"Good point," Hravn acknowledged, mentally noting that, because there were no horses, they would be unlikely to be out-paced if they fled.

Nudd added, "Anyway, our ponies are bred to these fells, just like our sheep. They are hefted from birth and know instinctively the lie of the land. We can always rely on them to get us home, even in the thickest mist or deepest snow. What horse could do that?"

Hravn dropped back a pony's length or two behind Nudd, as they wound their way past Aisgill and then around to their right onto the shoulder of the fell. The ponies picked a route around the craggy outcrops, quickly gaining height above the dale that now fell away to their right. They paused on the top. The surrounding fells held the last of the thawing snow and, in the clear light, looked as if they were close enough to reach out and touch.

"Look yonder," Nudd pointed to the north, "that is the length of the Eden, all the way across your Gospatrick's lands to Carleol; and there...," he swung around pointing to the south west, "that is toward Sedberge and beyond is Lauenesdale and the soft sands of the great bay. That is Norman land and is where we take advantage of the richer manors."

Hravn gazed around, impressed by the beauty and clarity of the view. The land was different to that of the dales; the fells were higher and more rounded, particularly to the west, and the valleys were lined with dense patches of wood that would provide good cover for any scouting parties. He strove to quickly imprint the scene on his memory, linking the summits and ridge lines and imagining a bird's eye view. He looked across to the south east, squinting towards where the sun was still rising higher in the sky, feeling a tug in his stomach as his eyes traced the line of the great forest and he made out the pass over towards the vale of the Jor. He then followed the northward line of the high Mallerstang crags and again cursed Wyrd for sending the storm that had forced them down into the valley and capture. He could see that towards the far end of the crags, there was a northward descent to the Vale of the Eden and the way through to Carleol. He knew that there must also be an eastward route down into Swaledale; a route home, if home was still there.

"Nudd, where is Ravenstandale?" Hravn asked, sounding innocently curious. "I only ask because I heard that my grandfather's family once had land near there. It's where my Cumbric blood comes from."

"Indeed?" Nudd's eyes narrowed as he peered across at Hravn, "That must be many years ago; before my time, I am sure, for the land is my grandfather's now. It is just at the foot of the fell, down to the north west. It is the land at the head of the Lauen, along the top of the high scar at the head of the Vale of Eden."

Hravn nodded slowly, narrowing his eyes to discern the distant grey strip of valley and white limestone crags beyond, fixing it in his mind's eye. It was strange to see his grandmother's homeland.

Nudd interrupted Hravn's thoughts, jerking him back to the present and reality "So there you see it, our family's lands and how they fall betwixt the land of the Scots' King and Gospatrick's to the north and the Norman King's to the south. You can see, now, why many of those who travel between them must perforce travel through Mallerstang and why we require them to pay us homage."

Hravn nodded. As far as he could tell, the Mallerstang valley was the only natural route through the high fells that formed the border of the kingdoms. He looked again at Ravenstandale. "Surely, Nudd, if the Lauen starts in the high ground down there and then flows to the west, where does it flow thereafter? Is it not another natural route around these fells?"

"Hah! You're a shrewd lad, Hravn, I'll give you that." Nudd couldn't help chuckling. "No wonder grandfather said he wanted you to work for him whilst he holds you hostage. Yes, you're right, in a way. The Lauen does indeed skirt our lands and then it turns and flows south at yon side of the Haugr-gils. That's the name of those fells to our west. There is a way north from there, over high and boggy ground, to the head of the Lauder that drops down to Penrith. It is a route over the watershed, but not as easy going as it is through Mallerstang." Nudd hesitated a moment before adding, "There is also the old military road beyond that. It is broken in places but is passable."

"Aye, Nudd, but does the Lauen itself give another way around to the south? If so, Ravenstandale would surely be key ground?"

"Indeed it is, particularly for those heading east to Northumbrian lands." Nudd agreed, nodding slowly. Hravn turned away, sure that he now knew why Pendragon had taken the land from his grandmother's family. He was sure too that his heritage was a secret that he must guard from Pendragon and his family.

"Remember," Nunn added pointedly. "The Cumbric border with the English, I should say the Normans now," he added with a shrug, "lies along the old Roman road over Stanmoir and then follows the line of the Eamont to Ulueswater. You can make it out in the middle distance, look!" He pointed out a line from right to left. "Gospatrick may think he holds Westmoringaland; he doesn't. Grandfather will bide his time to get his lands back, but there is more than one way in which your ransom may be paid..." He dropped the conversation and wheeled his pony around, heading back down the fell.

Hravn followed, lost in his own thoughts.

~~~

They arrived back at the longhouse well after the midday meal. Nudd was not to be gainsaid and quickly persuaded the cook to provide them with large helpings of stew and fresh, unleavened bread. Although he was ravenous Hravn didn't want to be kept longer than needs be; he was desperate not to be away from Ealdgith longer than necessary. He was confident that Urien would not be a threat to her, but Owain was a worry.

On the other hand, he didn't want to give Nudd the impression that he was unhappy in his company. It was a long time since Hravn had chatted freely with a man, other than Oswin, and he found Nudd relaxed and with a common sense of humour. Nudd obviously didn't have any concerns;. As he scraped the last of the gravy from his trencher, before throwing the remains to Sköll, he smiled across to Hravn saying, "We've done well today and covered a lot of ground. Would you be confident to scout through the area by yourselves?"

Hravn nodded in confirmation, and then Nudd added, "Good, Urien is keen to make the most of these longer days and the good weather. He thinks that there will be more folk fleeing the Normans, particularly through Lauenesdale where there has been less harrying. I want you to ride with Urien and me, covering the lands south of where we were earlier, scouting the dales of the Rawthey and Clough for travellers coming from the direction of Sedberge and Lauenesdale. Work with Edie to get the ponies ready tomorrow, then we'll leave the day after. We may stay out overnight so see Freya, she's the one that stirs the pot, and get something to tide you through."

Hravn pushed his stool back and stood up. "Thanks, that sounds good, we'll be ready. I'd best get back and make sure Edie knows...but thanks, Nudd, I appreciate your openness." He clicked his tongue as a sign for Sköll to follow and hurried out of the longhouse. Hravn was lost in his own thoughts as he walked back to the stable. He had found Nudd good natured and with a ready smile; he had also noticed that the smile never reached Nudd's eyes. He was sure that, despite Nudd's apparent good humour, there was a hard, cold edge to his nature.

Sköll ran ahead and was pushing the stable door open with his nose before Hravn got there. Ealdgith opened it and pulled Hravn inside to throw her arms around him. She pulled back and turned around swinging her arms in a wide gesture. "See! What do you think?"

The change in the stable was obvious. The floors had been swept and fresh straw laid, decaying manure had been cleared, tack had been polished, oiled and laid out in sets. The ponies looked healthier too, although Hravn was sure that it was just the result of a good grooming.

He gasped in genuine amazement. "You and whose army? This is fantastic. How did you do it?"

"It was just Bran and me. He turned up just as you left. He's a good lad and seems almost scared not to work once he knows what to do. I think he just wants to be wanted."

Hravn was relieved that Ealdgith seemed to have the young lad's confidence so quickly. "How do you manage to chat to him?"

"Well, it certainly wasn't my Cumbric was it" Ealdgith teased him. "In Norse of course. He's speaks both tongues and I'm better than I let on, not that I let him realise it. He chatters on when he's relaxed. It seems that some of the others bully him, not least Owain, so he sees me as a friend now." Ealdgith paused for a moment then added with a deliberate glance at Hravn, "He let it slip that his parents and grandfather were killed by Earl Gospatrick when he was a baby..."

The significance of this wasn't lost on Hravn "Really! Nudd said that his uncle Uther, that's Urien's brother, had been killed by Gospatrick and his manor just north of here was burnt by Gospatrick some years ago. There's a feud for certain...and we're in the middle of it. We need to find out more. What's more," he added "we are going to have our first test the day after tomorrow. I'll explain..."

~~~

Hravn had placed a bar across the inside of the stable door to prevent sudden unwanted visitors and they had then snuggled down on the straw bed to swap accounts of the day and make some more sense of their situation, who must be avoided and who might be befriended, but not trusted. Thanks to Ealdgith and Bran's hard work, the ponies and tack were as ready as they needed to be for their patrol of the southern valleys, so Hravn suggested that their first task in the morning should be to visit Pendragon's wife's old maid, Rhiannon, in Outhgill and arrange for some more clothes to be made. He was now in desperate need of clothes that fitted and both of them were daily looking more ragged and threadbare. If they were to flee in a month or two, they would need to be far more respectable if they were to claim right of access to Earl Gospatrick.

The light outside faded away and they were left in the pale glow of a guttering candle. It was only a stub and would burn out soon enough. Hravn sat up to pull the blanket higher over them and, as he lay back, Ealdgith turned towards him, her hand brushed his cheek and turned his face towards hers as her lips gently sought his.

Chapter 14

The following morning was again bright and warm. They broke fast early with a bowl of porridge from the big pot in the longhouse and then rode out to visit Outhgill. As they left the stockade wall behind, Ealdgith felt as if a weight had lifted from her. She felt free again and she smiled as she breathed in the Lencten air, scented by the earthy smell of dew-damp grass. She smiled too at the fresh memory of her first true kiss from Hravn.

The land immediately around Rhiannon's small A-frame cottage was fenced by interwoven branches. It was just enough to prevent the pigs that rummaged around all the cottages from raiding the few vegetables that she managed to grow in the thin soil.

They hobbled the ponies outside the rough split-rail fence and then went through the low gate. Ealdgith hung back with Sköll and Hati as Hravn knocked gently on the cottage door. It was ajar but he didn't want to intrude and shock Rhiannon. Nudd had said she was old, but was she frail too?

Hravn stepped back as the door opened. He gasped, his greeting catching in his throat. Rhiannon's dark brown eyes and oval face, framed by thick, wavy greying brown hair were the perfect reflection of his grandmother, Bron. Hravn's surprise turned quickly to shock as Rhiannon gasped, her petite frame frozen. "No! Father?"

Hravn was immediately drawn to her. He stepped into the dark interior and gently held her arms in his hands, supporting her. He spoke in Cumbric "I am Hravn, son of Ask, from Raveneswet in Ghellinges-scir, but…I sense there is more to our meeting. My cousin, Edie, is with me. Can we come in for a moment?" Rhiannon nodded, still speechless. Hravn gently lowered her to a stool by the central hearth and ducked outside; his mind racing at the possible implications. "Edie! Quick! This isn't quite as we thought." Ordering Sköll and Hati to lie by the door, he quickly re-entered the cottage. Ealdgith followed and they knelt beside Rhiannon.

"I'm sorry to have shocked you," Hravn apologised gently, "but you seem to recognise me and I know someone very dear to me who is the image of you…I think I may know why; but first, I must tell you a little of our story. May I?"

Rhiannon smiled, nodding slowly. "Please".

Hravn took another stool and sat looking into Rhiannon's eyes as he gently held her hand and quickly explained who they were, how they had come to be in Mallerstang and what they must do for Pendragon. He still called Edie 'Eadmund,' but held nothing else back for he was sure that Rhiannon must be his distant kin.

137

"My father's father was called Dag. He was Norse, but his wife, my grandmother, was Cumbric. She is Bron; she is still living...I hope. She came from Ravenstandale. Her family lived there until it was taken by Pendragon...but I think you know that."

Hravn watched tears run slowly down Rhiannon's cheeks. He knew before Rhiannon said, "Bron is my sister. I knew we must be kin for you are the very image of my father." Hravn leant forward and gently held Rhiannon as her years of loneliness were released in waves of tears.

He looked across to Ealdgith who, not understanding Cumbric, was puzzled by the deep emotion. Hravn explained quickly, "She's my grandmother's sister, my great aunt. Pendragon took her when he slew her family and seized their lands."

Ealdgith looked for a cup and poured some water from a flask. She knelt beside Rhiannon and passed it to her. She spoke slowly in Norse, hoping Rhiannon would understand. "I have more to tell you. My name is Ealdgith. Hravn protected me by calling me Eadmund. We are cousins by marriage and we are sworn to each other. This secret is ours alone for no one else must know...I cannot be found out and we cannot stay here for long. We must leave as soon as we can be sure of our escape."

Rhiannon took the cup in one hand and grasped Ealdgith's arm with her other. She replied in

Norse, "I understand, and you are right to plan to flee. You must." She looked the two cousins in the eye and continued speaking in Norse.

"Hravn, the lands of Ravenstandale are your birthright for there is no one else left in our family to claim them. I was only a girl of ten or eleven when Pendragon seized them. You know what his business is now; it was worse then, in the days under his father 'The Elder'. The day Bron went to market at Kircabi Stephan, he raided our manor. He slew our parents, Bedwyr and Agrona, and our reeve. All who resisted were taken and sold into slavery; those who acquiesced were left to manage the land for him. My brother and sister were sold into slavery too. I only survived that fate because I was the youngest and his wife, Eigyr, wanted a personal maid. I was their slave until she died. I was an old maid by then, but I was a good seamstress and I got by…I never knew what happened to Bron. I'm so glad she found a new life and happiness."

Hravn and Ealdgith were silent. The brutality of Rhiannon's youth and the sadness of her life took a while to sink in, as did the reality of Hravn's status, his right to the manor of Ravenstandale and the even greater threat that Pendragon would pose if he found out.

"What can you tell us of Pendragon and his family?" Hravn asked. "We need to know those who pose the greatest threats."

"Well, Pendragon of course cannot be trusted. He was once known as 'The Dark Lord' due to his cruel nature and his dark looks. Age has mellowed him, but if you cross him, his wrath can be brutal."

Ealdgith gasped, "That is as I feared, and he threatened to make us eat our hounds, Sköll and Hati, if we ever tried to escape"

"You can be sure he would. Do not trust Urien or his son either; neither are bright and Owain is lazy and a bully. Nudd has the brains and is more relaxed; he is not cruel. You can trust him so long as you do not cross him. Beli is his son and a close friend of Owain; he's not a bully like Owain but he is led on by him. Uther the Younger has his grandfather's cruelty too and he carries his own grudge; his parents and his elder brother, Mordred, were slain by Gospatrick when he was a lad."

"I wondered about that," interrupted Hravn. "Why?"

"Gospatrick had just cause, not that Pendragon has ever seen that," Rhiannon was quite scathing in her tone. "Pendragon was raiding more and more into the lands along the Eden. Gospatrick had to stop him. He burnt the manor at Lammerside and deliberately slew those of Pendragon's family who were there as a warning and as retribution. Have you met Bran? He's Mordred's son, but Mordred wasn't married to the babe's mother."

"Wow! I befriended Bran yesterday. I can see now why he's had a sorry life." Ealdgith was genuinely sorry for the boy.

"Rhiannon, if, or rather when we flee from here, which direction would you suggest?"

Ealdgith's question surprised Rhiannon. It was a question she expected Hravn to ask. She thought awhile before replying, "North, into the lands of the Eden, but stay on the west bank if you can. That way, you will have more room to flee and will be quickly into Gospatrick's lands. The lands east and west from here are too rugged and the men here have a hold over them. I don't know the lands to the south, but they are Norman now, so I hear."

Hravn nodded and smiled. "It is much as I thought. I saw the land yesterday when Nudd took me up the peak over yonder." He gestured through the wall of the cottage in the direction of Boar Fell. "I could see down to Ravenstandale too and I can see why the lands there matter so much to Pendragon."

"Now, if you two don't mind me saying, you could both do with some new clothes. I could help you there." Rhiannon stood up, rubbed her hands on her sides as if to help pull her thoughts together, and smiled at them both.

Hravn bent to hug her. "Aunty, that is why we came."

"You, Hravn, are growing out of yours. You need something to grow with you and that will help add to your age. Edie, I will see what I can do to help hide your natural curves. I am sure you will want to dress as the lady you are, but for now, I will make sure you look a youthful lad."

Ealdgith kissed her. "Thank you, but could you perhaps also make me something that a lady can wear? I will need to dress as a lady again one day"

"Of course, my dear. I will keep them here until you are ready to leave, and find you a pack to keep them in. That will avoid any risk of their discovery."

Hravn added, "Look, we have funds that we have hidden. I will leave something with you, now. It will pay for all you need to buy for us and maybe one day, you will have the opportunity to be free of this family and it will help you pay your way; even if I can't be here I can try and help you."

"I rather think that I will see my days out here, but the money will help. I will go to market in Kircabi Stephan tomorrow and buy what I need for you. I can also buy something to barter with in the village here, which will help me a lot."

"Rhiannon, could you also perhaps get us some soap and a new comb? This tangle of knots is becoming unmanageable living as we have been." Ealdgith's look was almost pleading.

"Oh, and a honing stone too, if you can? Hravn really needs to sharpen his seax and could do with starting to shave that boyish fluff. It would actually make him look older if he shaved and it might help some real whiskers to grow."

Rhiannon couldn't help but giggle at Ealdgith's tease, although she tried to suppress it with a smile. Hravn pretended a sulky scowl before squeezing Ealdgith's midriff sharply, causing her to squeal.

"Aunty, we must leave you now, but we will be back soon. For all we know, we are each all the family we have now," Hravn said, hugging her tightly. As they left the small, dark cottage they looked back to see Rhiannon smiling after them from inside the entrance, tears upon her cheeks.

Chapter 15

Hravn wriggled his body and flexed his toes to try and stop his legs stiffening. It was the start of their second day watching for travellers heading north from Lauenesdale. He was on one side of a spur, observing the track down a valley to the north. Ealdgith was doing likewise, observing the valley on the other side of the spur. It was pleasantly warm in the Lencten sun, but tedious; nothing stirred and he anticipated another long and lonely day. He kept his mind busy by studying the lie of the land and testing in his mind's eye the different scenarios by which he might move through the natural cover without being observed.

A curlew called, the first that he'd heard. No; the call was too high pitched. It was a good imitation, but not quite good enough. Sköll noticed it too, his ears pricked and his head turned; he knew. Hravn rose, turned and took a route through dead ground across to the other side of the spur. Ealdgith had called him.

He crawled across the heather, settling beside her with a kiss to her cheek. Sköll nuzzled Hati, pleased to be back with his brother. The cousins blended perfectly with their surroundings, their cloaks and breeches providing the perfect camouflage. Ealdgith pointed, "Look, do you see? Just coming around the side of the spur across the valley." Hravn nodded. Two furlongs away, a small party, maybe half a dozen or so, and at least one horse, were very slowly following the far track along the valley.

They were startled by a shout from behind. "Ha! I knew it. You're just up here sleeping. Why aren't you watching both valleys? Wait 'til my father hears."

Hravn turned. Owain was standing on the sky line, his hands on his hips and his black cloak billowing. He looked like The Reaper himself.

"You fool! Get off the skyline now! I swear, Owain, if you had even half a brain you'd be brighter than you are now. Look!"

Owain scowled, but crouched down reluctantly and crept forward. "What? Where?"

"There!" Hravn's frustration was obvious. "Just coming along yon track. Do you see where it winds around the spur across the valley?" Owain nodded.

Hravn didn't hesitate. "Right! Get back to your father now and tell him that, at this rate, a group of six, with a horse, will be with him before noon. We'll watch them and, if anything changes, I'll report to him whilst Eadmund keeps watching them. Now go!"

"Bloody idiot". Hravn's spat, cursing in Norse as Owain left. "At least he kept below the skyline this time."

Ealdgith hadn't understood the exchange in Cumbric, but she had the gist of it. "He was trying to catch us out you know. Maybe he won't be so hasty in future."

"Hmm, maybe," Hravn muttered sceptically.

They kept watch as the party came closer. They could now see that an elderly woman was on the horse, led by a well-dressed man. It looked as if there was another woman, a maid perhaps, and three other men, probably their retainers. Hravn and Ealdgith moved slowly along the ridge line keeping pace with the party. The track slowly dropped down into the wooded valley bottom, crossed the beck at a small ford, and then continued to follow the beck. It was difficult to see just where the track was and the cousins dropped cautiously into the woods below. They were closer and had a clearer view, but were also concealed better by the trees that were busting into leaf.

Suddenly, the horse stumbled and whinnied, nearly throwing the old lady off its back. The party stopped and gathered around the horse as two of the men helped the lady down to sit on a boulder with her maid. One of the horse's back legs seemed to be lame.

"I think it's thrown a shoe," Ealdgith suggested. "They could be there a while. That is really going to slow them down."

Hravn nodded in agreement. "I think I need to tell Urien. He might want to come here instead of waiting to ambush them. Can you keep watch whilst I go back? Come yourself if they move on or turn around."

"No problem, I'm fine here." Hravn blew her a kiss and was gone, Sköll trotting behind him.

It was a good three furlongs to the point where Urien had set the ambush. Hravn saw the ponies before he saw the men in the valley bottom. He moved skilfully, quickly and with little noise and was close behind Urien before the man turned in surprise. Hravn had done it deliberately, intending to make a point. He couldn't imagine that Owain's field craft was up too much.

"Well?" Urien's tone was as much censorious as it was questioning.

Hravn explained the situation and suggested that Urien might want to surprise the party whilst they were stranded. He agreed. He also agreed that Hravn and Ealdgith should get into a position from which they could block the group's retreat down the track. The two hounds would be enough of a deterrent. Before he left, Hravn said, "Once you've sprung the trap, we'll make our way over the ridge to Nudd, reclaim our ponies and then lead him to join up with you back at the meeting place."

"Good, you've done well. Thanks." Urien's praise was gruff, but genuine.

Hravn returned the way he had come. He moved quickly and was breathless when he slipped quietly behind the bush from behind which Ealdgith was still watching the group on the path below. "Nothing's changed," she said under her breath. "I think they may make camp and see what they can do about the horse."

"Good, Urien's making his way here now. He wants us to set up a blocking position just out of sight back down the track. We can back-track on our route and then cut down the line of that little stream we crossed. That'll give us the cover we need."

"I can't say I'm looking forward to this." There was an obvious reluctance in Ealdgith's voice. "I enjoy the chase, but it's not like taking a hind. We are going to cause real hurt to people, even if we don't make any threats or cause injury ourselves, we are still an instrument in its doing."

"I know. I don't disagree, but we have no option. The more we make a name for ourselves, no matter how unpleasant the doing, the more we'll win their trust and gain the freedom to create the chance to escape. Come on, there's no room for compassion and second thoughts." Hravn ran, leaning forward, hugging the contour line and keeping low as he moved out of cover and retraced their steps.

They took up a position on a small spur that overlooked the track itself. From there, they could see the group who were less than half a furlong away. They were close enough to show a very visible presence if needs be, but far enough away not to be drawn in to the group's ambush and demise.

They'd been there barely twenty minutes when Ealdgith nudged Hravn. "Look! That's Urien, dropping down through the woods. He's just about in line with the group. Owain's above and behind him."

The excellence of Urien's field craft impressed Hravn and he regretted his earlier assumption. Urien's skill was in marked contrast to Owain's. "In Thor's name! Why doesn't his father grip him? He's going to be spotted…it's just a question of when."

Ealdgith wasn't so sure, "I don't think so. They're so engrossed in the horse and their own misery that they aren't aware of the dangers around them. Just you watch; Urien will be within a stone's throw before they look up, and then it will be too late."

Ealdgith proved right. Urien's stealthy use of the cover of crag and scrub allowed him to get twenty paces above the group before he stopped, sheltered by a low outcrop. Owain proved more adept too, dropping into the cover of a shallow re-entrant valley to take up a position on the track between the cousins and the group. He too was very close to the group; both waited, watching for sight of Urien's two other men.

The trap snapped shut. Neither Hravn nor Ealdgith had seen Urien's men before they pounced. Urien leapt from behind his cover on to the top of the small crag above the group just as another of his men stepped on to the track in front of the group. A third appeared on the river bank, blocking any attempt to flee across the valley. To Hravn's surprise, Owain didn't move.

"Come, Eddie, we need to block the track!" Hravn stood up quickly, showing a very visible presence on top of the crag by the bend in the track. He was still puzzled as to why Owain stayed concealed just behind the group.

The group's distress was obvious. Although they outnumbered their attackers, they knew that they were in no position to resist. The elderly lady stayed sitting on the boulder, slowly swaying; her maid stood in front of her, staring fearfully from one attacker's face to the next. The well-dressed man turned to look up towards Urien. Ealdgith could see that he too was elderly, presumably the lady's husband. She remembered the shock of her own ambush by One Eye and Scar Face and felt sick at the thought of the anguish the couple must be going through. She felt guilty too.

Hravn read her mind and took her hand; he too was far from happy with the situation.

Urien called down to the group. Hravn couldn't hear at that distance but it was very evident to him that the group didn't understand.

Presumably, they were English, fleeing the Normans and came from lands beyond the reach of the Cumbric and Norse tongues.

Their lack of comprehension caused Urien to become more aggressive in his manner. The elderly man looked about, obviously confused. He took a step back and as he did so one of his retainers stepped forward and drew a seax from under his cloak.

Hravn tensed, his hand gripping Ealdgith's. "This isn't good, I fear…" His words died in his throat as Owain stepped sideways from his cover and hurled a small seax at the back of the retainer. The blade pierced the middle of the man's back. The force of the throw was sufficient for it to penetrate to the hilt. The man staggered, his hand slipping from the hilt of his seax as he dropped slowly to his knees, then pitched forward with a jerk to fall on his face, his arms outstretched and still; only his fingers twitched.

Owain followed through on the momentum of his throw, jumping forward to kick the man's body onto its back and bending swiftly to draw the seax from the man's belt. The elderly man turned on Owain, grabbing his hair, pulling his head down swiftly in a gesture as much of hate as defence. Within a matter of seconds, the situation had deteriorated from one of tense control to potential chaos.

"Enough!" Urien bellowed. He leapt from the crag and as he landed on the track, he pulled the elderly man off Owain, then spun around and cuffed Owain across the face with the back of his hand. The youth froze, a sullen scowl on his face. As he did so, the horse reared in fright, then squealed in pain as a back leg gave way and it stumbled to its knees. The two remaining retainers jumped to it, holding its flanks and trying to calm it down.

The elderly lady pitched forward off the boulder clasping her hands to her chest as she gasped for air. Urien's two men jumped forward, seaxes drawn, unsure what to do.

Placing two fingers in his mouth, Urien whistled sharply then, pointing to Hravn at the end of the track, he swung his right arm in an arc and pointed down towards his own head. Hravn immediately understood the basic field signal – 'to me, now!'

"Come on, Edie, Owain's botched it up and like it or not, we're in the thick of this mess." They ran down the track with Sköll and Hati following closely, heads down, hackles up.

They paused at the edge of the group. Hravn called the hounds to heel and then to sit. The hounds' focused stare was enough to calm the situation.

Urien shouted to Hravn, "The fools don't understand. Tell them I don't want their lives, I want their silver and jewels, now! They must then return whence they came."

Hravn called to Ealdgith loudly and in English so that the group would understand. "Edie, get the old lady some water." He then turned to the elderly man and quickly translated Urien's order.

Ealdgith's sudden cry of annoyance caused Hravn to look across to where she was pulling a pewter chalice from the hands of one of Urien's men who was quickly emptying the group's saddle bags and sacks.

Choking back his rising anger, he turned to Urien again, "For God's sake leave them the means to carry water and feed themselves in the wild. Surely their coin and jewels are enough for you!" He paused. "Would you give them their lives then let them starve?" Urien looked back, coldly, hesitating before replying. "No, they can keep their metal ware." He turned back to his men. "Take their jewels and silver. Leave them some coin and what else they have. Be quick about it, I want them away from here; and throw that body into the scrub. I don't want any obvious evidence. You, Hravn, take them back across the ford, see them gone, and then fetch my brother's group back to the meeting place."

Hravn nodded, then ran to help Ealdgith with the elderly couple, explaining in English what Urien had said.

He looked up at the sound of raised voices. Urien was jabbing Owain in the chest. His anger was evident. "A bit bloody late," Ealdgith muttered angrily.

The old lady recovered as Ealdgith slowly gave her sips of water from the chalice. Her maid stood by her, holding her shoulders but still shaking herself. Hravn called the old man and his two retainers to him and explained in English that he and Edie were hostages, but forced to work for Urien. He stressed that they needed to leave quickly. He couldn't guarantee their continued safety but he would take them back down the track, away from Urien and his men, and across the river. They would be on their own then.

The old man nodded resignedly "Thank you, my boy, I know you have done what you can. I can't ask you for more, but I fear we have little to hope for". He turned to his wife and gently took her trembling hand. "Come, my dear, you must walk from here. We will go slowly, but go we must." He led her slowly down the track, leaving the retainers to urge the horse to follow. Hravn nodded to Urien, called the hounds to heel, and caught up quickly with the old man, falling in step alongside him.

"Sir, I don't know where you are from, but we have been forced to flee the Norman destruction of our own land and family in Ghellinges-scir. That is how we came here and have been held hostage pending our ransom. I have been looking at your horse and I think I know why she is lame. Wait until we are out of sight at the ford and I will examine her hoof."

The old man turned, his hand grasping Hravn's wrist in gratitude. "Thank you. We too fled the Norman scourge. My land was south of Lauenesdale. The Normans have dispossessed us all. I was given a choice. I could stay and work my land, the land my family has held for generations, serving a Norman lord!" He spat angrily. "Or we could flee north. I chose to flee, but as you have seen, these Cumbric bastards are no better."

"These men aren't true Cumbrians, my Lord, at least I hope not. My uncle is the Earl Gospatrick and it is for him to ransom us. Rather, they are bandits. They hold most of the passes from Lauenesdale through Westmoringaland to Cumbraland and they rob and pillage across the border land, playing one side against the other. I know my lord Gospatrick has punished them once already but the Normans have yet to get a grip of them."

"I understand, and I see you for the prince that you obviously are, but what do you suggest? How are we to escape if they hold the border lands?"

They had reached the ford. Hravn stopped and turned to the old man and his wife. "I'm not sure, for this is not my own country, but I can tell you that Lord Pendragon's stronghold is in the Mallerstang valley which is to the north east of here. His power is less the further west you go. I understand that there is a route to the west of here, through the Shap fells. It will be high and slow going. Keep the rounded fells of the Haugr-gils on your right as you make your way back down this valley and then slowly go west and then north, always keeping the Haugr-gils on your right."

The old man nodded, his eyes holding Hravn's as he strove to memorise the directions. Hravn continued, "I haven't seen it myself, but I hear that you will finally see the vale of the Eden in front of you. You should then make your way down to Penrith which lies just to the west of the river itself. When you cross the river Eamont that runs eastward from the high fells into the Eden, you will be across the border into Cumbraland ...now, my Lord, let us see to your horse's hoof."

Hravn bent down and gently raised the horse's fetlock whilst Ealdgith looked under the hoof. "Ah, I was wrong and you were right." She smiled across to Hravn. "There is a large thorn embedded in the soft tissue." She looked up at the old man and his retainers. "Hold her, and keep her calm, please and I can pull it out...ready?" They nodded and she paused until the horse settled, then she deftly pulled the thorn clear in one swift movement. The horse whinnied then settled, tentatively placing its hoof back on the ground.

"Lead her to the river and bathe the hoof. The cold water will help too." Ealdgith spoke with a confidence that encouraged compliance.

Hravn turned to the old man and offered a handshake. "Sir, we must go now, but

Godspeed, and warn all you may meet about Pendragon of Mallerstang." With that he turned and, calling the hounds to heel, he walked briskly, climbing up the fell slope to make his way over the spur to find Nudd. Ealdgith smiled quickly at the elderly couple and ran after Hravn.

~~~

Hravn and Ealdgith scrambled down through the heather into the scrubby wood, still some distance from where Nudd's group was waiting. Ealdgith stopped in her tracks and jerked Hravn's arm. He stopped, turned; he had been lost in his own thoughts about the day. "Quiet! There's movement, there, look!"

Ealdgith was hushed, insistent. Her eye sight was sharper than Hravn's and it took him a moment to see the movement in the dappled forest light. "It's a deer; a young roebuck, I think. We're down wind of it." He paused, thinking. "Why don't we try and take it? Fresh meat is always welcome and the boys need more practice; what's more, I want to keep on the right side of the Pendragons." They'd both taken to referring to the whole family collectively.

"What about Nudd? He'll be getting impatient by now." Ealdgith was unsure.

"He can wait. Anyway, if we are quick, this won't take long. I'll take the boys down the shallow valley on the left; that'll give us the cover to within maybe fifteen paces of him. We'll still be down wind and its quiet moving on the turf. Watch until we're in position then go to the right. Still keep down wind and then give an owl call. It should spook him to run. There's a crag the far side of him so he is almost certain to run onto us. Let's give it a go."

Ealdgith was cheered by his confidence "Why not? We've nothing to lose; off you go. Good luck."

Hravn calmed the hounds with a hand on each of their collars and then led them quietly and quickly away, dropping into the shallow valley that would take them around to their flank.

The chase was over almost before it started. Hravn had been in position for only a couple of minutes when Ealdgith's owl call startled the roebuck. It looked up from grazing and, sensing the high craggy ground to its right, bolted for the cover of the shallow valley. The two wolf hounds took it in mid-flight, bowling it to the ground in a frantic flurry of leaves and broken undergrowth. The roebuck lay twitching in the last of its death throes as Hravn called the hounds to heel and Ealdgith ran in to join them.

"We'll mark the place and then bring the ponies back to collect it as soon as we've caught up with Nudd." Hravn's mood was noticeably brighter as they patted the hounds, praising them for their swift and efficient hunt.

~~~

Nudd's boredom and irritation were very evident. "So, you're back at last! The sun's already dropping. What's up? Did you fall asleep up there?"

Hravn gave him a disdainful look and then quickly explained about the ambush and how Urien had nearly lost control due to Owain's hot-headed and needless violence.

Nudd's pent up frustration exploded. "The bloody dolt! Grandfather and my uncle need to take him in hand. They've indulged his reckless vanity too long and this is the result. He'll cause us all pain if he doesn't change his ways...but I'm not happy that Urien let the old couple and their retainers go. There's now the likelihood that they will spread the word and it risks a backlash. Urien should have made sure that there were no witnesses."

Hravn and Ealdgith were speechless. This wasn't the reaction that Hravn had expected from Nudd and he feared that Nudd might even go after the elderly couple and their retainers to make sure that they didn't escape. He spoke quickly "Nudd, I don't think there is a problem. The couple were old and the old woman suffered from a bad heart, she nearly died with the shock. I can't see them surviving in the wild, not with a lame horse. The old lady will collapse again within the hour and her husband lacks the will to go on. Their men were but serfs; they will be lost and starving within a day or two." He hoped he'd calmed Nudd's concern and prevented further action; the more that word of Pendragon's banditry spread the happier he would be.

"Anyway, there's better news." Ealdgith was quick to move the conversation on. "The hounds took a roebuck on our way down here. At least we have fresh meat to take back with us."

"Did they indeed; you never cease to surprise me." Hravn couldn't tell whether Nudd was being complimentary or scathing.

"If it's fine by you, Nudd, we'll take the spare pony to carry the carcass and then catch up with you on the way back to meet Urien." Nudd nodded.

Hravn and Ealdgith reclaimed their ponies from where they had been left with Nudd's group and, leading the spare one, they trotted back through the fellside woods to collect the roebuck carcass.

Nudd made quick time across the spur and down to the meeting place; Hravn and Ealdgith only just managed to catch up. Urien was waiting and Nudd rode up to him scowling. The two exchanged terse words then turned to lead the men home towards Mallerstang. Owain held back, allowing others to separate him from the two section commanders, obviously wanting to avoid their attention. He scowled at the cousins. Beli hung back too, waiting for Owain to catch up; he laughed at something Owain said, with a quick furtive glance over his shoulder towards the cousins.   Hravn and Ealdgith fell even further back; they had no desire to be near Owain.

As they rode, Ealdgith looked across to Hravn. "I was watching the sun as I lay on that fell top this morning. Have you noticed how high it now rises?"

Hravn nodded, he'd noticed it too.   "I know, Edie, Sumor is almost here and that gives us six weeks, eight at best, before mid-Sumor when Pendragon will expect his ransom from Gospatrick." "Yes, and we have to be long gone by then. We both know that there will be no gold coming."

Hravn halted his pony and looked across to Ealdgith. He could see she was scared, although she hid it very well. "We'll be gone by then, Edie, never fear.   We'll make the Pendragons trust us and then we'll break that trust and flee. I just need to plan how."

~~~

The kitchen in the longhouse was open, waiting for their return, and the group's mood picked up considerably when bowls of stew and fresh loaves were spread across the trestle table. Pendragon banged the table with his fist "Eat! You've done well. Your food and ale are well deserved." He scattered the gold and silver coin from a purse across the table in front of him. "This is but one…there are several more."

He looked across at Hravn. "Thank you too for the fresh meat you brought back. That was quick thinking, good work and much appreciated. We will talk tomorrow." Then pausing, he looked across at Owain, his brow furrowed, "As will we".

Ealdgith leant across to Hravn and whispered, "Come, let's eat up and go. I want to be away before ale flows. Something tells me too that we could do with practising the skills Oswin taught us. We need to make some time together to do that."

Hravn nodded, looking under his lowered brow at Owain, then at Urien and Nudd. "I agree; I don't trust any of them. Come on, my Valkyrie, I'll grab a loaf to take with us."

Sumor

Chapter 16

"Well done, lads. You've proven yourselves these last couple of days, both of you. Urien said that your quick thinking helped him. You could have fled, you know, so I'm glad you have shown that you keep to your word."

Pendragon had called them to him in the longhouse when they had gone across to eat in the morning. He was sitting by the hearth, his wolf skin over his shoulders despite the warming weather. They both sensed that he was frailer than he liked to show. He was no longer the Dark Lord of his youth. He was speaking in Cumbric and, although Ealdgith could sense his good humour, she couldn't follow the conversation. She just listened.

He continued, speaking gruffly, "I've told Urien what I want you to do next, and he agrees. I plan to raid some of the manors in Lauenesdale. There's still good pickings there, but the Normans will be taking more of a hold by now. I want to get what I can whilst I can. I want two quick raids, one after the other, first in Kircabi Lauenesdale and then in Sedberge." Pendragon spat into the hearth then held their gaze, looking each in the eye, "Like I said before, you'll be my eyes there. Urien will tell you more; but remember, you hold to your word and I'll hold to mine. Now go."

"Thank you." Hravn spoke with a confident nod and deliberately refrained from calling Pendragon 'My Lord'. He then turned to Ealdgith speaking in English, "Come, Edie, I'll explain. We'd best find Urien and see what is really planned for us."

They caught up with Urien as he was talking to a guard by the gated entrance. He gestured at them, indicating that they were to wait by the longhouse. The guard looked relieved; he had no wish for the hounds to come any closer. Urien joined them a few minutes later, ushering them inside to take a seat. He started speaking in Cumbric. "Right, I know my father's told you what he wants. Now, this is what I want."

Hravn interrupted, "Urien, surely you can tell us in Norse. Edie will understand then and he needs to know exactly what you want as much as I do." Urien's blue eyes flashed angrily at Hravn, but he did change to speaking in Norse.

"You proved the other day that you're both quick witted enough to work by yourselves unlike..." he paused. "Anyway, you're to scout out the land around Kircabi Lauenesdale and Sedberge and find manors there that are suitable for us to raid. I want good pickings from the raids, so find ones that have not yet been impoverished by the Normans. They need to be remote with concealed routes in and out, if possible. I also want a secluded spot an hour's ride away where we can rest before attacking. You'll need to find out how many live there, their routine, the best time to move in and so on. You'll find that English is spoken more than Cumbric there and so you are less likely to stand out than my men. Don't run, you've no escape. I have my own eyes on the routes about here." Urien's implied threat was quite obvious.

Urien got up and moved to the hearth. "Come over here." He smoothed the ashes with his boot. "Look, I'll show you the lie of the land." He sketched a map of the lands to their south, placing kindling on the ashes to show the ridge lines, stones for the market towns of Sedberge and Kircabi Lauenesdale and then etched the lines of the tracks that he knew. Sedberge was close on a day's ride away; Kircabi Lauenesdale was a half day's ride south of Sedberge. Hravn watched closely, relating the model in the ashes to his recollection of the view from Boar Fell.

"Just how long do you expect this to take?" Hravn sounded a bit sceptical.

"A dozen days or so. You've proved you can live off the land so you shouldn't have a problem." Urien was bullish.

Hravn was far from persuaded. "I can't see how that would work, Urien. Surely you want us to spend our time scouting? We need to get in and out again as quickly as possible and report back. The longer we take, the more suspicion we raise. Sure, we can live off the land, but I'm not going to live off someone else's land and risk capture and questioning; just where would that leave you? We need some coin to pay our way with the locals; that's common-sense! Call it a down payment on your investment in the raid if you like."

Ealdgith felt a cold chill as she watched Urien clench his fists. Hravn wasn't fazed. He knew Urien was a bully; the Pendragons all were. He had to stand up to him now and he wasn't going to jeopardise their safety for an ill thought through plan.

Urien glared at him for a moment, then nodded. "Hmm, it makes sense. Get yourselves sorted out. You leave tomorrow. I'll give you coin before you go." He turned and left, walking swiftly away from the hearth.

Ealdgith stood and looked at Hravn. "Well? I thought he was going to explode!"

Hravn smiled at her, and spoke quietly, "He didn't, did he? He knew I was right. I rather like the sound of this job. It will get us away from here and from Owain's taunts. If we do well again, we should be given even more leeway the next time; and then we can think about escape."

"Come on then!" Hravn grabbed her hand enthusiastically. "Let's get our kit ready as best we can. We need it sorted so that we're ready to flee, as well as for this trip. Then maybe we can go over to see how Rhiannon got on at the market." "Yes, and don't forget that we will need as much dry food as we can carry too. Maybe we should try and hoard some now and store it with Rhiannon?"

Chapter 17

It was a beautiful, still Sumor day, with a bright sun and the heady smell of new grass and tree pollen, although white clouds were gathering above the ridge of fells to the east.

They had left early, their saddle bags stuffed with food and as many of their belongings as possible. Yesterday's visit to Rhiannon had been a real treat for all of them. Rhiannon had hugged each of them closely and then proudly shown them the clothes that she had made. Some they wore now, others they had left with Rhiannon, including the clothes that she had made for Ealdgith; a mantle, gown, under dress and a wimple. Ealdgith had gasped at the sight of them, but Rhiannon had reassured her that she might have to dress to pass as a married lady, covering her hair too. Rhiannon had then caught Ealdgith's eye, smiled mischievously and said that, although she and Hravn weren't married in the eyes of God, they were sworn to each other and that was good enough for her. Ealdgith had blushed, speechless.

Thanks to the new honing stone Hravn had been able to sharpen the blade of his small seax to a very fine edge and he had managed his first shave. Ealdgith was right, it did make him look older, despite the odd cut and graze on his neck.

Hravn had been surprised at Urien's generosity. His humour had improved and he'd given Hravn more than he had expected; a large purse of small coins and silver clippings that would be easier to use than anything with a high value. Urien had also told him more about how the land lay; suggesting that, although the track from Sedberge to Kircabi Lauenesdale followed the Lauen, there was a range of fells to the east that might be passable, or the valley behind the fells might offer an even more discrete route. They were to have a look at this as it might give the main group a better escape route from Kircabi Lauenesdale for their follow-on raid on Sedberge.

They made good time as they followed the track through the woods, retracing the route from a few days earlier, moving as quickly as their ponies would allow and not worrying about concealment. After all, as Hravn had assured Ealdgith, they were posing as Saxon refugees who had passed the winter in Cumbraland before trying to return to English lands that had not suffered from the Bastard's harrying. They had nothing from which to hide.

The sun was at its zenith as they came to a break in the forest. The land sloped away below them with a view to a great combe sliced into the side of the mountain across the valley to their west. The midday air hummed with the distant sound of falling water that cascaded down the grey crags at the head of the combe, possibly half a league away. Hravn whistled in surprise, Ealdgith just held her breath in awe.

"That can only be Laga's throne, a place to respect and avoid," Ealdgith said at last, mindful of the Norse goddess of wells and springs.

"I thought Oswin's water fall was a true wonder, but that has a magic all of its own," Hravn agreed. "I wonder what it's like to bathe under?" he whispered as an aside to Ealdgith, before urging his pony to move on. He wasn't quite quick enough to avoid the punch she aimed at him.

Hravn turned to cheekily thumb his nose at Ealdgith, but his smile faded as he saw the clouds towering above the woods and fells behind them. "Edie, look! We'll need to find shelter or get to Sedberge quickly. That's not good!" Just as Hravn spoke, a chill wind swept suddenly down the valley, blowing the dust in whirling twists.

Ealdgith nodded, frowning. "I'm not surprised; I thought it had got too hot too quickly these last few days. There'll be thunder on the way."

"You're right, let's get to Sedberge if we can. If I'm right, it's at the foot of this valley and only a league or so away." They urged the ponies to a brisk trot, thankful for the saddles that eased the hard rise and fall of the ponies' backs.

Hravn was right. Sedberge was close by and they were within clear sight of the jumble of thatched houses when the first large drops of rain fell, hitting the dry dust of the track, releasing an acrid, earthy taint in the air. The track widened, leading to a small, open market place with thatched, open-sided stalls in the middle. To the side of one of the stalls, blue wood smoke curled from an earthen oven.

"Come, Hravn, let's see what they've got." Ealdgith was seized with sudden hunger and excitement. The small crowd in the market place cleared quickly as heavy rain drops continued to fall. Distant thunder echoed across the fells behind them and by the time they reached the market, most of the townspeople had taken shelter. There was room for them and the hounds under the thatched canopy of the pie stall.

"What can I offer you, young sirs?" a stocky, ruddy-faced wife asked as she straightened up from stooping over the oven, studying them as she wiped her hands on the apron tied around her waist and then tucking a strand of greying, black hair behind her ear. Her tone was one of curiosity and respect. The cousins suddenly felt conspicuously out of place.

Ealdgith gabbled. "Those pies look good, what's in them?"

The store holder laughed. "They look good for sure. I should say they're brim full of the best mutton, but we all know I would be lying for there's little enough of that hereabouts now. Let's just say there's meat in them, gravy too and more than a touch of grain."

Hravn smiled, "I'll take four please. Two fresh, hot ones and two cold ones if you have them. The boys here are hungry too," he said, gesturing to Sköll and Hati, much to the woman's amusement. He continued, sensing that an explanation of their presence was very much expected. "Tell me, what's the situation with the Normans? We fled their killing in the east, wintered in the forest and have recovered somewhat serving a Cumbric lord. We're heading south now to family lands near Loncastre." The woman shook her head slowly, lent forward and offered Hravn her hand. "I'm Elfreda, and you are...?"

"Hravn and Edie," they answered together.

"Well, Hravn and Edie, you might regret that plan. The Norman...bastards, have a strong enough grip here and yet more so further south where you are headed. We were spared the killing across in Jorvale, but they take our land and our grain, and push our own lords into servitude too; those that don't buy into their favour, that is. You might want to think again and return to Cumbraland."

Ealdgith pulled a face. She was keen to gain Elfreda's confidence, "I did wonder; can you tell us more?"

"Well..." Elfreda paused, "Do you have anywhere to stay tonight?"

Ealdgith shook her head. "No, we want to avoid the bawdiness of an alehouse and were about to ask around."

Elfreda smiled, perhaps sensing Ealdgith's vulnerability. "I can help if you like as there's an empty stall in the byre below our room. It'll be dry and you can eat with us. There's my husband, Aelfnod and our three lads."

"Please, that's most kind, if that's alright with you, Hravn?" Ealdgith was very quick to accept, so relieved not to have to stay at an alehouse.

The rain continued to hammer down, quickly turning the dusty tracks around the market place into a thin layer of mud. The three stood, talking, sheltered by the thick thatch roof of the stall. The ponies shifted uneasily at the cracks of thunder and pushed their way under the shelter whilst the hounds sniffed around, scavenging for scraps beneath the trestle table. They talked about the weather first, as the English always do.

Elfreda was keen to learn more about Cumbraland and how they fared there. Ealdgith struggled to answer, but Hravn was quick to resort to tales of his past experiences in Kircabi Stephan market. Hravn gradually turned the conversation back to life around Sedberge and Kircabi Lauenesdale. It seemed that a couple of the Saxon lords had managed to keep control of their manors but only by paying a great sum in tax and accepting a Norman overlord. Most, though, had lost their lands by force; some had died defending them, their families dying with them or forced into servitude. Others had fled, much as the couple that Urien had ambushed.

"Are there Normans here now?" Hravn asked, suddenly aware that he hadn't seen any soldiers and had rather slipped into a false sense of security. Elfreda nodded grimly "Of course, look yonder." The cousins' eyes followed her glance towards the low hill that overlooked the small town.

The cousins hadn't noticed the hill; it was a high, earthy mound that had been piled up behind the houses that surrounded the market place. A wooden stockade surrounded the top of the mound and a large wooden tower had been built within the stockade. As he looked, Hravn could also make out the top of another stockade encircling the bottom of the mound. He whistled softly through his teeth. "I've never seen the like before." It reminded him of Pendragon's longhouse and stockade, but the height of the mound and high tower walls were obviously built for defence.

"That's where the soldiers live. The Normans call it a castle. They ride out to take what they want, but keep safe inside." Elfreda's tone was scathing.

"How many are there?" asked Hravn.

"Mayhap twenty, with a good dozen horses... and before you ask how so few of them built the place, they didn't, we did! There's no talking to them, as they don't speak our tongue, save for one or two. We can't fight them either, so we have to obey them. 'The Bastard' is well named!"

~~~

The two cousins cuddled together in the impromptu straw bed in the byre. The hounds snuggled in close, the ponies rested in the neighbouring stall, and dusk faded to dark.

"Whatever we do for the Pendragons, we can't harm people like Elfreda." Ealdgith was emphatic, speaking in low tones, conscious of the floor boards creaking above them.

Hravn idly stroked her hair "I know we can't, we won't".

The cousins had made their excuses, pleading the strain of travelling, and had turned in for the night almost as soon as the family meal was over. This had been filling enough, a communal bowl of stew made from the left-overs of the pie making, but it had been poor, gristly meat that needed sucking and chewing to make the most of it.

Conversation had been slow. Aelfnod and the three boys were withdrawn and reticent to talk, tiredness showing in their drawn faces. Although Aelfnod was a freeman, it was obvious that they were struggling to keep going, working their land for very little reward thanks to the taxes that were imposed on them and the amount of grain that was taken from them without payment. As they bade them goodnight, Hravn had pressed coin into Elfreda's hand in payment for their board. She had looked and then shaken her head, words of protest forming on her lips as Hravn had said quietly, "Our Cumbric lord was generous when he gave us coin for the trip. Take it, your help and kindness means a lot. It is yours...please."

Ealdgith continued, "I feel sorry for Elfreda; you can tell that she welcomes company, that's why she was so warm and welcoming when we met. It can't be easy being the only woman with four men to look after, men who are worn down by endless work and servitude."

Hravn nodded. "They are our people; the people that our fathers are...were... responsible for." He faltered, knowing the meaning of his words and hating the implication. "Without their labour, we have nothing. It's a building block of our way of life and now the Normans are destroying it. They are breaking the foundations of our society and building their new one on very different ground. Believe me, whatever we do, we have to make sure that we harm the bastards and their new way of life, and look after our people, whoever and wherever they are. Remember our vow to Oswin; to only raise a sword in the defence of others."

Hravn continued in the same theme, "Did you pick up on what Aelfnod said about Ulf the miller?"

"Of course, he said very little, but he did say that Ulf was the one real traitor, the one who had sold out to the Normans and was now doing their business for them, taxing every sack of grain and getting fat in the process."

"Well…" Hravn said with a grim smile, "I think he should meet the Pendragons."

"What about Kircabi Lauenesdale?" Ealdgith asked, "From what little they could say about it, the Normans haven't yet built one of their castles there and the town's much smaller." "That might work better for us." Hravn replied, "I got the impression that there are only a handful of manors and all are now held by minor Norman lords. I think we should still make our way there and have a look at the manors that are on this side of the town. We can choose the most remote one and look for a quick way in and out."

~~~

They woke to the sound of heavy feet on the floorboards above their heads. Although it was early, Aelfnod and his sons had already left, starting work on their land at first light to make the most of the lengthening days.

They splashed their faces in water from a pail and left too. The cold wind hit them as they stepped outside. The storm had abated, but heavy black clouds hid the mountain tops and the wind battered their ears making it hard to hear. At least it was dry.

Hravn had gathered from their conversation the night before that Ulf's mill was on the south side of the river to the east of the town. That suited Hravn's plan. The new Norman castle was on the north side of the river and he wanted to try and find a target and routes in and out that kept the river between them and the Normans. The river wasn't much of a barrier, but it all helped. Pausing whilst the ponies drank from the river by the ford, they then crossed and turned to their left, riding slowly, cautiously hugging the cover of the tree line that followed the river.

Hravn wasn't sure where the mill was and he was surprised to find another river joining from their right. From looking at the lie of the land, it was quickly clear that this was the junction of two valleys.

As they turned to their right to follow the new river until they could find a crossing place, Ealdgith noticed a curl of smoke coming from a line of thatched roofs beyond a thin line of trees. "Look, Hravn, that must be Ulf's mill, by the edge of the river beyond the trees…and if you follow the tree line to the left, you can see a small bridge."

"Aye, I've got it." Hravn saw where Ealdgith was looking. "See the wood across the river? Why don't we make our way into there, then lie up for a while and watch who's coming and going? We might be able to work out the use of the buildings and see if there is a routine they follow."

Ealdgith agreed. It would be better to have the river to help separate them from the mill. "Yes, we could then back track, go around the mill to see where the tracks are and be on our way without looking too suspicious."

They dismounted to cross the narrow bridge of hewn planks and made their way cautiously around to the back of a thick wood that covered the far bank of the river. Although the river wasn't wide, it was fast flowing with steep banks and made quite an obstacle to cross. Hravn led the ponies into the wood and tethered them where they could not be seen by anyone working the nearby fields. Ealdgith backed her way carefully through the brushwood that had been disturbed by the ponies and pulled it back in place to conceal signs of their passage. Hravn called in a low voice, "Come, follow me, and we'll find a spot a few feet in from the far edge from where we can watch the mill."

They moved quickly but cautiously. Hravn chose a spot behind a large holly bush from where they could observe the mill on the far bank; the holly's broad leaves would screen them and break up the outline of their faces. He had chosen the site well. The mill was a collection of thatched buildings that faced onto the river bank. They quickly formed an idea about the function of each of the buildings. Hravn pointed out the mill-race that led in from their left to power a large wheel on the edge of the first building. The building was tall, with a second floor above the milling room. Presumably, this was the store. The mill wheel turned slowly and they could hear the grinding screech of the stones above the sound of the river. To the right of the mill and set further back, a larger two storey house with a steep, thatched roof dominated a little paved square. This must be Ulf's manor. Smoke curled from the centre of the roof. To the right, the manor joined onto a terrace of low buildings that were either store houses or stables, fronting onto a wide track leading towards the thin line of trees that screened them from the plank bridge.

Having studied the mill and manor for a few minutes, Ealdgith said quietly, "I might not have your eye for a plan but this looks very simple to me."

"Go on," Hravn encouraged her.

"Well, we need an approach that is covered from view. This wood provides it. Of course, we will need to check that we can cross this river much higher up and work our way down to the wood. If we arrive at dusk the fields will be empty. We should hold the ponies here, behind the wood, whilst Urien takes his men across the bridge, through the line of trees and into the courtyard. That whole route is also covered from view and there's no real risk of them being seen. We'll need to have a look at the other side of the manor, but I got the impression when we first looked that there is a stockade around it. Once Urien and his men have done their work, they can then retrace their steps and we can be away with two rivers between us and the Norman castle."

Hravn pulled a face. "You're good Edie," he paused, "but what about dogs? There's one sleeping, chained to the wall of the first store house by the track."

Ealdgith looked back at the mill and then tweaked a holly branch so that a sharp leaf caught Hravn on the cheek. He smiled. "Seriously, it is a good plan. There will always be dogs somewhere; but they will be Urien's problem to deal with. We'll watch the place a bit longer though, just in case."

Just as Hravn spoke, a cart pulled by an ox rumbled slowly up the track; waking the dog that snapped aggressively at the ox's shanks. Three men, alerted by the barking, came out of the mill and stood waiting. One, the burliest of the three, stood back with his arms folded across a broad chest and portly stomach. "No doubt that's Ulf," Ealdgith muttered scornfully.

"Come on, let's leave whilst they are distracted." Hravn moved slowly back from the cover of the holly bush.

The cousins skirted around the back of the mill, confirming that Ealdgith's plan was their best option, and made their way up river for a league before they found a suitable crossing point at a shallow ford. Hravn noted that there was a large, solitary rowan tree growing just above the ford. It would make a good marker. They then retraced their route and riding at a canter returned to Sedberge to follow the track to Kircabi Lauenesdale.

~~~

The wind still thrummed in their ears making it hard to talk. Hravn was lost in thought as he pondered plans for the raids on Sedberge and Kircabi Lauenesdale. He was trying to memorise a bird's eye view of the land around the mill and, at the same time, develop a picture of their route. Ealdgith was distracted by a flock of sheep and lambs in the distance. They were grazing by the track and she hoped they would not move on; the playfulness of lambs always amused her.

The flocked scattered suddenly. Ealdgith sat up in her saddle with a jolt. "Hravn!" She screamed. "Hide!" Four horsemen had burst out of the wood just beyond the flock and were galloping along the track towards them. Ealdgith followed Hravn as he wheeled his pony and dropped quickly down the slope into the wood by the river. They dismounted and stood screened by the ponies as four armed men wearing chain mail galloped past.

"Thank God you spotted them, Edie." Hravn felt thrilled rather than threatened by the experience. Ealdgith was far less confident and gave him a wry look as he said, "At least we now know that the track isn't a good route. Although there isn't a castle in Kircabi Lauenesdale, it's obvious that the track is patrolled. It's possible that there are soldiers living in Kircabi Lauenesdale that report to the castle in Sedberge."

"I don't think we should stay on the track anymore." Ealdgith was not at all happy about their choice of route.

"I agree," Hravn reassured her. "We'll cut up to the trees above the fields and then follow the line of the track from a distance." He paused, before adding "We need to have a look at the route behind these fells. We'll go back to Sedberge that way after we've been to Kircabi Lauenesdale."

It was a good half dozen or more leagues from Sedberge to Kircabi Lauenesdale and the shadows were lengthening before they reached the town. A few carts had passed along the track below them and late in the day, a party of soldiers had returned from Sedberge galloping towards Kircabi Lauenesdale. "If those are the same men, I hope they have fresh mounts" Ealdgith muttered scornfully, "or perhaps they treat their horses like they do us."

"It's late and we're tired," Hravn called back to her. "Let's rest up in the wood for the night. There's no one working the fields now so I reckon we can risk a fire if we go deep enough into the trees."

They had a cold meal of bread and hard cheese before cuddling by the fire, hugging Sköll and Hati for warmth. Just as they were falling asleep, Hravn wrapped his arm around Ealdgith and gently whispered in her ear, "I love you Edie".

Ealdgith stirred, turned her face to Hravn and delicately kissed him, teasing his lips with her tongue, "And I you". She smiled into his eyes, "and now, sleep."

It was a hard night; the damp from the rain-sodden ground soaked through their bed of ferns and they woke to the early dawn chorus feeling cold and stiff. Hravn challenged Ealdgith to run on the spot to get her circulation going, reminding her that Oswin would have demanded the same from them both. Minutes later, they collapsed breathless and giggling, but warmer and happier too.

"I'm sure that we must be within a league of Kircabi Lauenesdale by now," Hravn said, as they left the wood cautiously, ducking under the branches that hung low on its outer edge.

"Look, you're right," Ealdgith almost cheered. "There's smoke yonder, just around the corner of the valley. Look, you can see it rising up behind those crags. It must be from Kircabi Lauenesdale."

Ealdgith was right. They made their way down to the crags and dismounted; from the top, they looked down onto a large village. Kircabi Lauenesdale was too small to be called a town. It was just an unstructured collection of houses, clustered around the wooden tower of a church.

The crags were a good vantage point and the ground rolled before them as if marked on a map.

The view was stunning. Low hills rolled away from them to the West, blurring into a band of yellow that merged into a smudge of blue. Ealdgith's jaw dropped in surprise "What's that? Look, between the land and the sky?"

Hravn put his arm around her waist and pulled her close "That, my Edie, is the sea. My father showed me once and said that it was from across there that our fore-fathers came in their long ships." They stood together, lost in wonderment until Hravn suddenly pulled his mind back to the present.

"There's the track from Sedberge, coming in from our right and see how it splits in two in the middle of the village." Hravn was delighted. The viewpoint would save them so much work. "Look how each of the tracks that runs out of the village leads to a manor."

Ealdgith nodded, imprinting the view into her memory. Hravn was right. Clusters of thatched roofs showed where the manors lay. "Hravn?" Ealdgith's tone was questioning. "You planned on raiding the manor nearest to Sedberge?

"Mmm, yes?"

"Well, if we aren't going to use the main track and are going to find a route behind the fells, we need to raid the manor closest to that route instead, don't we?"

Hravn poked his tongue at her and winked. "My thoughts exactly." He continued studying the ground below before coming to a decision.

"Right, Edie, see how the river flows around this side of Kircabi Lauenesdale but that the left-hand manor is also this side of the river? I reckon that, if we can find a route around the back of the fells, then Urien could raid that left-hand manor without ever going near the village and always keep the river as a barrier to protect his back. Let's drop below the crag line, follow the fellside around and then approach the manor from the far side."

Ealdgith nodded her head slowly, agreeing, whilst still studying the ground below. "Do you see the large wood at the base of the fell? There's a finger shaped wood that stretches from its far side almost as far as the manor. It splits the fields in half. It's almost as if the wood was cleared to make space for the manor house. I think we could get really close that way." Hravn gave her a tight squeeze, prompting a squeal. "You're not a Valkyrie for nothing!"

Ealdgith smiled at the compliment. She really enjoyed their increasing closeness and the way in which their life together gave them so many special, shared secrets and jokes. "Well, look really closely and you'll see that the families that work the manor's land don't live there. See that group of roofs, across the fields beyond and to the right of the manor, probably two furlongs away?"

"Aye, well spotted." Hravn instinctively picked up her line of thought. "That means Urien could keep the ponies hidden at the foot of the fellside behind the main wood, approach through the finger wood and be in and out without risk of being seen."

~~~

The wood was surrounded by dense thickets of hawthorn but was open inside with mature larch and ash trees towering above a dense blanket of flowering bluebells and white wild garlic. The clash of colours, with dappled sunlight reflecting off fresh green leaves, and the swathes of larch onto the blue and white below, gave it a mystical, magical feel and they trod carefully, leading the ponies behind them. "Ssh, this is Freyja's bower," Hravn whispered to Ealdgith with a cheeky smile.

She cocked a wry, coquettish, glance at Hravn. "Would that be Freyja the goddess of love, or Freyja the goddess of spring and flowers; you Norse have so many gods?"

Hravn shrugged cheekily, "Both, perhaps."

Ealdgith paused, blew him a kiss and turned away with a smile over her shoulder, "I'm a Valkyrie, remember, we have a job to do. Come on now."

Hravn sighed, but he knew that she was right. The surrounding screen of hawthorn rendered them invisible to the outside world and they tethered the ponies in the middle of the wood, confident that they couldn't be seen. Hravn led Ealdgith to the edge of the wood and wriggled under the low branches of a hawthorn bush, taking care not to snag his clothes on the sharp thorns. Ealdgith rolled over to his side, muttering something rude about his choice of view point. The hounds looked at each other and lay down with a deep sigh. They knew better than to crawl under a hawthorn.

The edge of the manor was very close and they kept perfectly still, watching. They were just to the front of the manor's small group of buildings. There was a track twenty paces to their front that joined the main track to Kircabi Lauenesdale, someway off to their left. A shimmering swathe of bluebells floated above the grass both sides of the track. To their right, the track passed through an entrance in a low earth wall that encircled the settlement. The buildings formed a horse-shoe shape with the central manor house facing across a cobbled area towards the entrance in the earth wall. There was a barn to either side of the manor; each had a large central door flanked by the thatch of a low steep roof. Hravn looked across to his left towards the distant workers' houses and realised, with a thrill, that they were out of the line of sight from the courtyard. "Edie I love it when a plan comes together, the courtyard's in dead ground and anything that Urien does there can't be seen from yon village."

The morning wore on as they lay watching for any movement that would give them a clue as to who lived at the manor. As the sun rose, the clouds cleared and the day warmed up. Bees hovered around the hawthorn blossom that was inches above their heads; the constant buzzing proved to be a lullaby and both their heads gradually dropped as the strain and tiredness of the last couple of days took its toll. The ponies, tethered behind them in the forest, suddenly whinnied, startling them both back to reality. "Hravn! Get your head down!" Ealdgith hissed urgently, "Horsemen are coming." They buried their heads in the bluebells to prevent the risk of sunlight reflecting off the white skin of their faces. Squinting under their eyebrows, they could see a troop of four armed horsemen gallop from the track junction towards the manor. They held their breath.

The horsemen were Norman soldiers. Their horses skittered to a halt on the cobbles in the courtyard, where they dismounted and pulled open the door to one of the outbuildings. "Oh no!" Hravn's whispered sigh was full of concern "They are quartered there. Look, the horses are stabled in the building to the left of the courtyard and the soldiers seem to be living in the other one."

"I think they are the ones we saw on the road yesterday." Ealdgith was perceptive. "They have the same coloured cloaks. If the Normans don't have a castle here, I wonder if they are quartered at the manors instead?"

"We'll need to stay a bit longer and see what they do. Stay here whilst I crawl back and check that the ponies are all right. I don't want them feeling spooked by the presence of the horses." Hravn eased himself backwards, taking care not to disturb the blossom on the branches above him.

Ealdgith watched one of the soldiers walk briskly to the door of the manor and knock for admittance. A moment later, a man in drab clothing opened the door and the soldier entered without speaking. Ealdgith smiled to herself; she noted that no dogs had barked and that the servant must be Saxon to be treated with such disdain by the soldier. Hravn nodded in agreement when he returned and she told him what she'd seen; he continued looking at the manor, lost in thought.

"Edie, have you noticed how the manor is built for defence?" He whispered at last. "There are no windows in the outside wall, just a few slits for archers, yet there are plenty of windows overlooking the courtyard. That could work to our advantage, but the soldiers are a worry. Urien can't risk a fight that he can't win."

"I know," Ealdgith agreed, "but what if they could be penned up in the outhouse? Look, there are no windows, just the big doors. Remember how the Normans penned the people of Dune in the barn?"

190

"That's it, Edie, that's the answer!"   Hravn
flashed a grin at her.   "We could use one of the
two carts that are by the side of the out
buildings.   We just need to pray that all the
soldiers are inside.   We can block the doors,
release the horses from the other building and
then force entry to the manor.   If Urien is quick
and quiet, the soldiers might not even be aware
they are captive.   It would take them time to
break through the wattle walls or the thatch and
if needs be, they could be picked off if they do."

As he spoke, the manor door opened and the
soldier held it while an elderly man, well dressed
in a dark green robe, walked slowly outside.
The two stood in the centre of the courtyard,
engrossed in heavy consultation whilst a serving
woman walked briskly from the manor door and
drew water from a well in the corner of the yard.
She appeared timid and it was obvious to
Ealdgith that she was in fear of the older man.

"He's our mark, Edie.   He's Norman, for certain,
a minor lord who has no doubt been granted this
land. I'm pretty sure that he could yield a fair
amount of gold to Urien – money taken from our
people.   Come, we've seen enough, let's leave
and find a safe route back behind the fells."

Chapter 18

It was maybe ten days later when Hravn returned to Kircabi Lauenesdale. He had rather lost track of the passage of time, but was conscious of the lengthening days, and concerned increasingly that the sun was nearing its solstice zenith.

Hravn led Urien forward, moving cautiously around the edge of the finger wood. It was late dusk and the sun had already sunk below the fells to the west, where a dark red smudge lingered on the horizon. The pair halted at the corner of the wood, standing in the shadow of a stubby fir whilst Hravn pointed out the manor, its low earth wall and the two outbuildings. He breathed a quiet sigh of relief; the two carts were still there. Urien nodded in approval as Hravn quietly summarised his plan; stopping to watch closely when the manor door opened. A dull glow from a lamp inside lit the face of a man as he closed the door behind him, before walking across to the soldiers' quarters. He paused, as if breathing the night air, pulled the door open and went inside. They heard the solid clunk of a cross bar dropping into place, locking the door from the inside. Urien smiled tightly "They've done our job for us, penned up for the night already. No dogs either. Well done so far, Hravn."

As they turned to re-join their men, Urien tapped Hravn on the shoulder to attract his attention "I want you and young Edie in the manor with Nudd."

Hravn's heart leapt; it wasn't what he wanted "I thought we were to look after the ponies and bring them forward on your signal?"

"No more; Beli can do that. The Normans won't talk, and if they do, we are unlikely to understand them. On the other hand, the Saxons will talk and you will get more from them. Those hounds of yours will be good to keep control inside the manor too. I'll be in the courtyard containing the soldiers, so Nudd will need all the support he can get."

Hravn shrugged; he understood the logic. At least if they were in the manor, there was less risk of Edie confronting one of the soldiers.

It was fully dark. Urien's group of four moved first. They slipped silently into the courtyard. The cart creaked as it was pushed slowly into position, sideways across the heavy barn door. A loud sonorous snore from within the barn confirmed that the soldiers were blissfully unaware.

Owain took one of the men to guard the barn whilst Urien signalled to Nudd, then quietly opened the stable door. He wanted to lead the horses out without spooking them and set them to stray outside the manor's enclosure. When the soldiers finally escaped, they would find it hard to give chase.

Nudd led his group to the side of the manor, with Hravn and Ealdgith bringing up the rear. Nudd's two men carried a heavy log slung between two ropes. It was an effective battering ram and swiftly took down the manor's door. Nudd burst in followed by his two men. The manor consisted of a large room with sections partitioned off with heavy drapes. A low fire burned in the central hearth, from which its glow threw dark shadows. By the time Hravn and Ealdgith entered with the hounds, the two men had already pinned the Norman lord and his much younger wife against the wall by their bed. The woman, clad in a night shift, shivered in terror. The man was naked. He glared at the men, cursing in a tongue they couldn't understand, his face flushed in rage rather than embarrassment. The sight of the hounds silenced him.

Nudd, who held aloft the torch that he had carried in, noticed a curtained off corner. He clicked his fingers and gestured to Hravn who, with Ealdgith, moved across the room and drew back the curtain to find the two servants cowering. "English?" Hravn asked with calm reassurance. They nodded. "We're not here to hurt you. We're relieving your lord of his gold."

"But the..."

"...soldiers are taken care of." Hravn finished the man's question for him. "The coin, where is it?"

Hravn wanted to get a reply quickly before Nudd had reason to become violent. The man hesitated; sweat was beading his face. He glanced towards his lord and saw that all his lord's attention was focussed on the hounds. His master was frozen in naked terror and was no longer the imposing threat that he had once been.

"It's in a chest under my master's bed. You'll need to pull it out. He keeps the manor's accounts there, and also gold and jewellery that he took when he claimed the manor from my old master."

"Where's your old master now then?" Hravn enquired casually. His tone relaxed the servant.

"He was given the option of fleeing or working his own land. He chose to stay and lives in a hovel across the track."

Nudd's two men pulled the heavy, iron-banded, wooden chest from underneath the bed and dragged it to the centre of the room. A blow with the back of an axe head shattered the lock and they threw open the lid. Nudd gave a low whistle of surprise. Packed into one side of the chest was a stack of leather pouches that doubtless contained coin from the manor's accounts. What really caught his eye was a pile of gold jewellery; arm rings, necklaces, brooches and drinking cups. Hravn could guess where it had come from. Nudd's whistle broke through the Norman's terror. He lunged at Nudd, snarling in fury. Nudd stepped back, distracted, and his two men lunged towards the Norman. Hravn saw a chance and took it. His hand flashed over the top of the open chest, seizing three pouches of coin, which he passed deftly behind him to Ealdgith. As Ealdgith stuffed the pouches into the front of her tunic, Sköll started forward with a low growl and the Norman sprawled across the floor, hands clutching his naked genitals.

Nudd placed his foot onto the man's head, forcing his face into the stone floor, and turned to one of his men. "Tell Urien to get the ponies up here now. We'll need most of the saddle bags for all this."

Hravn spoke to the servant in English "You have a choice. Stay with your master here, or flee. We can bind you both and you can claim that you were overpowered and forced to speak, or you can take one of those pouches and flee. There are probably still horses outside, but you would have to get well clear from here."

The man hesitated, looked at his wife and then spat on the cowering Norman. "We will flee and take our chances, life can be no worse than with him."

Hravn turned to Nudd and explained. Nudd raised an eyebrow in surprise, but did not demur when Hravn passed a pouch of gold coin to the servant.
As he did so, he said quietly in English, "I am Hravn of Ravenstandale but if asked, it was Pendragon of Mallerstang who ordered the raid.

Go with care." The servant's look of surprise and questioning quickly changed into an understanding smile. He nodded his thanks.

With the pack-ponies laden, the Norman and his wife were bound and gagged whilst the servant and his wife were dismissed to find a horse and make their escape. Hravn and Ealdgith followed Nudd out of the manor. Urien was about to lead the laden ponies away and he signalled to Owain to follow. Owain turned to look at the cart barricading the front of the out building, then lowered his arm holding the burning torch. Ealdgith realised that he was about to torch the thatch.

"No!" Her scream was that of a woman, not a boy.

Everyone turned just as Hravn's right fist smashed into Owain's face, sending him backwards into the wheel of the cart. The torch fell to the ground, sputtering. "You murderous bastard! That's how our families died!"

Hravn spat at Owain's sprawling body, then he added in a more measured voice, "and you would bring a Norman army down on us all."

Nudd cursed and placed a restraining arm on Hravn's shoulder. Urien wheeled around, grabbed Owain by his hair and pulled him upright, shouting directly into his face, "Sometimes I wonder that my loins begot you! You fool! Go with the ponies. Now!" He released Owain who staggered forward after the ponies. Hammering and shouting came from within the out building. Ealdgith's scream and the subsequent commotion had woken the soldiers.

"Get that second cart in front of the door too. We've probably got ten minutes until they break out. Scatter the remaining horses and go! We want no trace of the route of our departure."

Urien really pushed the pace of their return. He called Hravn to the front wanting the benefit of two pairs of eyes. He couldn't risk a fall or stumble as they made their way across country at night. Ealdgith came too, her sharper eyes often seeing landmarks before the others. Although there was no moon, the clear sky enabled sufficient star light for them to see. The sumor night was short and it wasn't long before the false dawn slowly illuminated the land around, dark shadows faded to grey and the short horizons slowly lengthened. Their pace quickened.

Urien made no mention of the fight with Owain. The sun had risen well above the ridge of eastern fells by the time they reached the resting-up place that Hravn had previously chosen. It was just below a low ridge that over looked Sedberge. As Urien called a halt, he motioned to Hravn to join him. "Owain was a fool. You were right to stop him, but not to fight with him. Steer clear of him in future...and get a grip of Eadmund. Screaming like a girl doesn't help."

Nudd rode up to join them. Owain stayed at the rear of the line of ponies.

"Urien, Hravn told us about how the Normans support Kircabi Lauenesdale from their castle at Sedberge. Do you not think that they will have been forewarned by now?" Hravn could tell by Nudd's tone that he was seriously concerned about the plan to raid the mill.

Urien nodded and laughed. "Forewarned about what? That naked lord and his hapless men will have to concoct a jolly tale before they admit how they were caught out."

Hravn had to admit that Urien had a point, but he also realised that the theft of the coin raised in taxes from the manor couldn't be concealed for long. He said as much to Urien who scoffed again and said, "We'll raid at last light and then be on our way. Even if they hear about Kircabi Lauenesdale, why would they expect us to raid Sedberge? It would be like poking a wasps' nest. Instruct the men to get some rest; I want one man awake and on guard all the time."

Hravn and Ealdgith settled themselves by a boulder to one side of the group of men. They ate some hard cheese and black bread and were quickly asleep. Sometime later, Hati gave a low menacing growl. Hravn sat up with a jerk, his hand grabbed his seax as he blinked in the bright day light. He could see Owain and Beli walking briskly away. Hravn lay back down and whispered to Ealdgith who was now awake, "Relax; the sly bastard and his mate were approaching us, but Hati saw them off.   We need to make sure we don't split up and we must always keep our seax with us. He'll want his revenge somehow." Hravn did not mention his growing suspicion that Owain, and perhaps Urien, suspected that Edie was a girl.

Urien waited until the shadows were lengthening before he again went forward with Hravn to take a look at the target of the raid. Hravn quickly spotted the lone rowan tree and they crossed the river at the ford before following the bank down to the wood opposite the mill. He suggested that Ealdgith and he should hold the group's ponies by the wood, away from the track and the narrow bridge, just in case anyone else was using the track late at night. Urien agreed. He had already ordered Hravn to control the ponies and Owain to be on the raid. He also wanted Hravn to keep the bridge clear for a quick exit. It was obvious to Hravn that Urien didn't trust his hot-headed son and wanted to keep him as close as possible.

Urien grunted when Hravn pointed out the gate where the dogs were chained; poisoned meat would deal with them. Urien was impatient to start the raid and get on their way home to Mallerstang. He sent Hravn back to call forward Nudd with the raiding party, whilst he stayed to watch the mill and finalise his plan. Hravn suspected that the guard dogs would be dead by the time they returned.

"That's them into the mill house now," Hravn whispered to Ealdgith.   She nodded, having herself seen the shadowy figures force their way in through a wicker screen that covered a high window. Nothing happened for a few minutes. They could see one of Nudd's men by the gate where the guard dogs were conspicuous by their absence. Another figure hovered by the door to the mill itself. Someone else, probably Nudd, was covering the front door to the mill house. At last, they heard voices, low at first, then rising.

Hravn and Ealdgith jumped suddenly, startled by a loud, guttural, stomach churning, male scream that rent the still night. The sharp sound of a smack on flesh followed. Rooks roosting in the branches above them rose into the air in a cacophony of sound. In the background, they could hear the low sobbing of a woman in distress.

"What, in God's name, is going on in there?" Hravn cursed. Ealdgith shook her head slowly; she knew instinctively that, with Urien and Owain in the house, violence was inevitable. A second scream followed; it was louder, more drawn out and even more sickening to hear.

Hravn jumped up, "That's the sound of Valhalla. They'll rouse the castle and cause a patrol to investigate if this goes on."

Ealdgith said slowly and forcefully, "Hravn, we have to leave, now!"

Hravn paused, weighing the implications. "Edie, we can't. We would still have to flee through, or around, Mallerstang and they would run us to ground first. We…"

The choice was taken away from them. "Hravn! Get here with two ponies. Now!" Urien's voice sounded very close.

Hravn turned to Ealdgith and squeezed her shoulder gently, "We've no choice now. Stay here with the other ponies." He led the two pack ponies carefully over the narrow bridge and ran with them towards the buildings where Beli held a torch aloft, lighting the mill courtyard. One of Nudd's men was holding two servants at sword point at the entrance to the mill. All other activity focussed on the entrance to the house.

"Get those ponies here, now!" Nudd was in no mood to tarry.

"What, in Frigg's name, happened?" Hravn wasn't going to be cowed by Nudd's abruptness.

Someone chuckled from the shadow of the doorway; it was Owain. "The fat sod wouldn't cooperate, so I branded him with his own poker. It loosened his tongue, and his coffer. We've got his gold now."

Hravn glanced at Nudd, his eyes spoke the obvious question; Nudd shrugged, "If needs must…"

Hravn realised that there was no point in replying. He clenched his fists, digging his fingernails into his palms to control his anger through his own pain. Urien came out with two of his men and filled the ponies' saddlebags with the miller's gold. Seeing Hravn, he said, "He lives, not that he'll sit for a while. Owain acted well for once."

Owain chuckled from the doorway. "I doubt he'll ever sit again after that."

Hravn turned and led the ponies away. "I'll get them back over the bridge and the others ready to go." He felt sick and couldn't bear to stay close to the Pendragons. Although he had little conscience about raiding the miller, such violence could not be justified.

Chapter 19

Pendragon banged the long table, forcing them all to pause eating and pay attention to him again.

The raiding party had returned to the longhouse in Mallerstang earlier that morning and Pendragon, delighted at the sacks of gold and hoard of jewellery that Urien had presented to him, had ordered a celebratory midday meal. Hravn and Ealdgith had deliberately seated themselves at the foot of the table, away from the bulk of Pendragon's men. Pendragon had started the meal by praising Urien and Nudd and thanking them for the spoils of the raid.

The hounds were lying at the side of the room, watching and catching the occasional scraps of meat that Ealdgith threw them. Hravn was finding it increasingly difficult to engage with any of the Pendragons, even Nudd. The needless torture of the miller had reinforced just how cruel they were and he was increasingly fearful for their own future. It therefore came as a surprise when Pendragon called him by name.

"Hravn! My thanks to you. You've proven yourself a good scout with a sharp mind for a sound plan. Our success is in no small way due to your good work in choosing where to raid.

Well done, and to young Edie too. You gave me your word that you would work for me and you have held to that. I gave you my word that I would decide on your future, should your ransom not be forthcoming by mid sumor. That time has passed."

Hravn swallowed hard, fearful of what Pendragon would say next. His eyes fixed on the piercing blue eyes in the grey-haired, hook-nosed face.

"You've proven your worth and paid for your keep, and more besides. I have my doubts that a ransom will be paid; mayhap your uncle doesn't appreciate your worth. I do though. I shan't sell you on, as others might have advised. You will both stay here and continue to work for me, doing just what you have proved you can do."

Hravn's breath caught in his throat. It was a relief, but also a shock. Pendragon was ahead of them in planning for the future and they were held fast to him now. He stood, breathing deeply to calm his nerves and raised his horn of watered beer in a toast to Pendragon. "Thank you, Lord. Your praise is generous. I speak for my cousin too when I say that we will serve you."

He sat, catching sight of an immediate glare, followed by a smirk, from Owain and a chilling stare from Urien. Pendragon's decision wasn't universally popular. He whispered a quiet aside in English to Ealdgith. "Edie, we have to go, soon…"

Hravn was interrupted as Pendragon banged the table for a third time. "We will continue to raid whilst fortune favours us but I have decided that we will not raid into Lauenesdale for a while. I do not want to draw the eyes of the Normans further north. Our next raid will be into Gospatrick's land in the Vale of Eden. Urien; do you recall the manor at Aplebi that we raided three summers past?" Urien nodded. "I have heard word that it prospers again and that nothing has changed there. Whilst this good weather holds, I want you to lead a raid within the next few days. Let's build upon our good fortune."

Urien smiled. It was a grim, self-serving expression. "Very well, father. It will be done."

Hravn and Ealdgith knew that this was their one chance to escape. Urien and Owain's reaction to Pendragon's announcement that they would continue to work for him gave them good reason to fear that their lives would be in jeopardy if they stayed.

The meal over, they made their way quickly to see Rhiannon to say their farewells. She could sense why they had come. They hugged the old woman in turn and Rhiannon struggled to hold back her tears as she touched each of their faces. None trusted themself to speak.

Hravn broke the silence at last, "Aunty, Pendragon took all you had and has given you nothing in return. We have something of his that is small recompense but it will at least give you some security. Keep it close and spend it carefully, but it will help you if you ever feel the need to flee." He passed her a leather pouch that they had taken from the Norman and her hand dropped as she felt its weight. Rhiannon's tears really flowed as she again hugged them both together.

"We will come back for you one day," Ealdgith promised, "I can't say how or when, but we will."

"And if you do flee from here, try to leave word with the church at Kircabi Stephan, we will ask there," added Hravn.

Upon their return to the longhouse they heard that Urien had ordered that the raiding party would leave late the following afternoon, ride during the fading light of dusk and then make the raid at dawn. They were again to secure the ponies for a quick getaway. As with the Lauenesdale raids, Urien would lead, taking Nudd with him and leaving Math and his men to guard Mallerstang.

Fortunately, most of their belongings were still packed from the last raid. They had little time to prepare because they knew they would also have to get some rest. The raid and their escape would be very challenging. Ealdgith consolidated their coin and packed it into the hounds' collars that she reinforced. She stuffed her dresses into the bottom of the saddlebags where prying eyes were unlikely to see them. They strove to cram as much as possible into the limited space they had but they could not afford to raise suspicions about the amount they were carrying. Hravn hoped the ponies would cope with the burden and he compromised by limiting the amount of food they took. They could live off the land or pay their way in their quest to find Ealdgith's distant cousin.

~~~

Urien led the raiding party down the Mallerstang valley and over the low hills to Ravenstandale. Hravn felt a surge of very mixed emotions as he rode through his family's lands in the company of those who had stolen them by force. He looked at the motley collection of run-down cottages that now remained and he wondered if their future would ever change. He rode up to Nudd and asked about the route ahead.

"The beck we are following flows through a deep wooded gill into Smardale. Once in Smardale, we have a route that takes us well into the Vale of the Eden without taking us near Kircabi Stephan. The vale itself is gently rolling with many shallow, wooded valleys. It's easy for us to move without being seen and many of the little settlements look little further afield than their own land, so offer little threat of our discovery." Hravn encouraged the conversation; he was keen to find out as much as possible about Aplebi and the lie of the land into which they would flee.

The raiding party crested a low ridge south of Ravenstandale and descended into the gill. "Hravn, this is beautiful," Ealdgith said quietly without attracting the attention of the others. The gill was flanked by steep slopes of open woodland. Scattered blossoming hawthorn and birch grew around the outcrops of red sandstone. The sight that took Ealdgith's breath away wasn't the trees; it was the endless sward of late-flowering primroses that seemed to float over the short grass; the delicate yellow blending into the pink and ochre of the rocks. The beauty of the sumor evening belied the menace of their mission and the dangers that lay ahead. Ealdgith sighed, longing to perpetuate the moment for ever.

The sun had sunk behind the western fells by the time Urien called a halt at the edge of an oak wood where a small beck ran off the fields and along the edge of the trees. The dying light tinted the trees' leaves with a tinge of red; long shadows accentuated the inner gloom of the forest. "Move the ponies under the trees and secure them," he ordered. Nudd, Owain, Beli come with me; you too Hravn." Urien led the men through the trees whilst Ealdgith settled their own ponies and kept them apart from the others.

The men moved silently through the wood. It was quite open with little undergrowth and it was still fairly easy to see their way. There was a large clearing in the centre of the wood and then a steep slope down through thicker undergrowth to the edge of the wood. They looked out over the manor whilst Urien outlined his plan. He explained that a track wound its way around the wood to their right and then led into the small cluster of thatched buildings surrounding a small courtyard. Urien would take control of the courtyard whilst Nudd moved around to the back of the manor in order to force an entry though the small door to the manor's latrine. Hravn and Ealdgith were to look after the ponies and guard the track in order to give early warning of unwelcome visitors. Hravn welcomed the task as it would give them the opportunity to gain maybe an hour's lead in their flight.

It was warm and sultry, but they couldn't sleep. Urien ensured that a guard was posted which, of course, prevented Hravn and Ealdgith just stealing away in the night. Dawn seemed to be a long time in coming and they were both groggy from lack of sleep when the guard quietly woke the camp. They busied themselves watering the ponies, keen to give the impression that they were fully absorbed in their duties.

Hravn jumped with a start when Urien tapped him on the shoulder and said that they were off. They watched as the eight men slipped silently through the trees and across the clearing. They saw the groups split to go their separate ways; they noticed too that Owain and Beli were hanging back.

Ealdgith suddenly clutched at her stomach. "Hravn, my stomach's griping. I need to find a bush. I'll be quick, I promise, but I can't flee just yet. Keep Hati here, he'll get in the way." With that, she ran quickly into the wood, finding a large tree to crouch by at the edge of the clearing.

Hati obeyed Hravn's call to heel, but sat staring at the wood, ears pricked. Just minutes later he jumped up and whined. He looked from Hravn to the direction of Ealdgith's sudden flight and whined again. "Go on, boy, go to your mistress." Hravn dismissed Hati without further concern.

Ealdgith dropped her breeches and squatted by the tree, taking a deep breath to try and dampen the sudden cramp that had seized her stomach. A twig cracked behind her; she thought nothing of it as she tried to control the pains. Another twig cracked and she froze, tense; her hands went to pull up her breeches and she started to turn as she stood up. Hands suddenly grabbed her arms, pulling her elbows back and up, jerking her abruptly to her feet. Ealdgith started to scream but, as she opened her mouth, a ball of cloth was forced into it, choking the sound and her breathing. Her heart leapt, adrenalin kicking in, driving the urge to flee or fight. Owain stood in front of her, a lewd grin on his face.

"You're a girl! I thought you were. No one will save you now, you treacherous bitch. You'll be out of the old man's favour at last. No hounds, no big know-all cousin now; you're on your own. Father said I was a fool when I told him you were a girl, but I'll be in his favour again now. I knew there was something not right about you and your cousin." Owain stepped forward, his face inches from Ealdgith's. "You've a lot to be sorry for, bitch. We're taking you to my father right now; but I'll have payment from you before my father has his say, as will Beli." His hands began to push underneath her cloak, groping. Ealdgith pushed backwards, straining against the person holding her; it must be Beli. That must be why they had both lagged behind when the men set off. She suddenly realised that their plan had been to attack Hravn and her.

Owain's touch repulsed her. If only she could free an arm, she would be able to draw the seax that was beneath her cloak; but she must do so before Owain's groping hands found it. She had seconds left in which to react. Ealdgith tensed and pushed herself hard backwards. Beli's footing slipped and he jerked back a hand's width before he recovered. It was enough. Ealdgith leant forward and slammed her right knee up into Owain's groin. He gasped and, as he doubled up, Ealdgith brought her head sharply forward onto his nose with a sharp crack. Owain staggered back, a bitter taste of blood in his mouth.

Ealdgith sensed rather than saw the grey thunderbolt that tore into Beli's right thigh just as her head snapped Owain's nose bone. Hati's jaws locked onto Beli's leg, ripping him away

212

from Ealdgith and sending him sprawling. Ealdgith fell backwards, twisted onto her knees and stood up drawing her short seax in a swift, fluid movement. "Guard, Hati! Guard!" she screamed at the hound just as it released Beli's leg and pounced towards his throat. She swung around, cat-like, to see where Owain was. She balanced on the balls of her feet, her seax held defensively in front of her with her right hand as she tightened the belt of her breeches with her left.

Beli screamed. As the shock of Hati's attack wore off, the pain from his ripped and twisted leg kicked in. Ealdgith glanced at him from the corner of her eye whilst she kept her gaze fixed on Owain. Beli lay on his back with his right leg twisted out unnaturally; the ground quickly absorbing the blood oozing from the deep gashes. Hati stood over him.

Owain drew himself up, spat blood from his mouth and slowly drew his long seax. "You're dead, bitch!" He spat again as he casually tossed his seax from hand to hand trying to intimidate Ealdgith. She held his gaze and read his eyes. She could see his uncertainty about her and his fear of Hati; she could see too the pain that his broken nose caused him. Ealdgith held her ground as Owain slowly moved towards her; she knew that she had to kill him; she also knew that Hravn would come.

Beli's scream echoed through the forest. Hravn's heart jumped. "Edie!" He snatched his spear from the holster by his saddle and ran to the forest, leaping across the stream and skidding on the dry dirt forest floor in his haste to reach Ealdgith. Sköll was already ahead of him. As he entered the clearing, Hravn saw Ealdgith; her back to him as she crouched facing Owain as he advanced gradually towards her. Hravn was over twenty paces from Owain, but the way was clear. He paused, aimed and threw the spear with one smooth arc of his arm. "Edie! No!"

Ealdgith could see that Owain was trying to use his size to intimidate her and force her back against the tree behind her. She decided to strike first by using his weight and movement against him, much as she had done in her sessions with Oswin. She measured the distance to the point at which she would strike under Owain's sword circle and held her ground, drawing him in. Ealdgith's move was fast. She dived forwards, twisting onto her left side and drove her seax into Owain's abdomen just as she heard Hravn's scream behind her.

Hravn's spear thrust into Owain's chest just as Ealdgith's seax slashed his abdomen. The impact threw Owain onto his back where he lay; legs apart, hands grasping at his stomach, eyes staring at the sky. Frothy blood gurgled from his mouth and chest. He was already near death.

Hravn reached Ealdgith almost as quickly as his spear point reached Owain. He helped her up gently then pulled her to him. She was shaking in reaction to the last five minutes. Hravn knew instinctively what Owain and Beli had intended. A further sharp cry from Beli drew his attention. "You'd best pray help comes soon, Beli. Come Edie, call Hati and we'll be gone. These bastards got all they deserve and we can't tarry."

Hravn was deliberately cold hearted. He wanted to get Ealdgith away as quickly as possible before a reaction set in. Their immediate flight was no longer an option; it was vital.

Hravn turned to retrieve his spear from Owain's corpse. His heart beat leapt.

"No!" Beli's screams must have been heard beyond the wood. Urien was running up the hill, thrashing though the undergrowth, his two men panting behind him.

"Edie, draw both your seaxes. We need to face them in open ground. Quick! Sköll! Hati! Heel!" They ran to the centre of the clearing. "Edie, keep the hounds either side of you and cover my back. Just remember our holmganga. Urien will be fired with revenge; use his anger against him."

Hravn braced himself and held his spear poised to throw; the iron head still wet with Owain's blood. As Urien burst into the clearing, he paused when he saw the two prone bodies. His shock turned to anger and exploded into a roar when he saw the cousins in the middle of the opening. He started to run. Hravn aimed and threw the spear; it sliced across the clearing in a low arc. Urien jerked to one side instinctively;

the spear caught him on the edge of his left cheek bone, sliced the flesh and tore through the lobe, shredding his ear. Urien staggered, clasped his hand to his ear and drew his sword. He didn't stop, the two men followed, drawing their seaxes.

Urien intended to drive straight at Hravn and use his size and weight to thrust him to the ground, but the sight of him standing resolute, flanked by the two hounds forced him to skid to a halt on the grass and loose earth. His two men joined him, panting heavily. They took up positions to either side of the cousins, edging their way behind Hravn to see if they could find a gap. Ealdgith made sure they didn't as she swivelled from left to right, blocking possible moves with a large seax in her right hand and the small one in her left. She felt far less confident than she looked, but the impression was all that mattered; she remembered Oswin's advice about winning the psychological battle. Sköll and Hati covered the gaps between Hravn and Ealdgith, snarling and straining forward whenever they saw a gap, although they too understood and respected the danger of the glistening blades.

Hravn's gaze held Urien's eyes rather than watching his sword tip; he wanted to read his intentions before he even started a move. They circled slowly; Urien kept edging to his right as he led with his sword hand.

"First blood to me, Urien" Hravn taunted him in Cumbric so that the other two men would understand too.   "It's but a wee scratch compared to what the hounds will do to you all. Just look at Beli, he'll never walk again, even if he lives."

Urien spat, "We'll take you both, you cock-sure brat. Two kids against three men; it'll be slow, painful. Remember the miller?"

Hravn shrugged without moving his eyes from Urien's, "Huh! In your dreams Urien." He then switched to Norse so that Ealdgith would understand as well as Urien. "Prepare to meet your family in Valhalla Urien; Owain's soul will be there by now, burning endlessly as he deserves; as you all deserve. I'll see all the Pendragons dead."

Hravn's taunt hit home.   Urien lunged thoughtlessly at Hravn's head. Hravn twisted, back-handing with his seax, the blade catching Urien hard on his wrist; only the leather of his gauntlet saved him from a cut. Hravn smiled mockingly and slowly shook his head; he was rattling Urien, turning his fury into anger and frustration, forcing mistakes.

Urien continued to circle to his right, forcing the cousins and the hounds to shift constantly to their left. He was trying to force an error, cause them to stumble or create an opening so that he could strike behind Hravn, but he didn't see the effect that this was having on his two men.   As they circled around, the two men were bunching closer together; the hounds snapping at their flanks tending to pen them. Ealdgith realised that, when she feinted with the large seax in her right hand, the man to her right would thrust his right sword-arm out to block her and in so doing he kept catching his partners left arm, obstructing him from moving against her. This was their weakness; she could use it against them.

Ealdgith feinted again with her right arm and the men's movement was the same. This was her chance. She would dive between them, twist and slash backwards with her long seax to cut the back of the legs of the man to her right. She couldn't risk holding her small seax in her left hand because she would have to fall on her left side; she would have to drop it as she dived. "Get ready, Hravn" she screamed in English, knowing the others wouldn't understand. "Now!"

Ealdgith crouched down and sprang headlong between the two men, twisting to the right, rolling and slashing at the back of the man's legs. She felt the broad blade sink into the unprotected flesh severing the tendons with a resounding crack. He screamed and fell, unable to stand, the severed Achilles' tendons unable to control his feet as he writhed in pain.

Sköll and Hati pounced, taking the other man by the throat and legs. He died quickly, choking on his own blood. Ealdgith rolled as she hit the ground and stood immediately, screaming at the hounds to leave the man's body; she feared their becoming addicted to human blood.

Urien froze, transfixed momentarily in horror at the sight of such sudden carnage behind Hravn. Hravn thrust forward. His large seax disembowelled Urien in one swift clean cut. As Urien slowly toppled forward Hravn swept his small seax across his throat. Urien fell, dead.

The cousins swung around, looking for each other, then stood staring at the bloody scene around them. Hravn held out his arms to Ealdgith and pulled her to him. "Oh God, Edie, are you alright?" She nodded without emotion.

Ealdgith longed to sit down and just think through all that had happened in the space of just a few minutes. It felt like half a lifetime ago that she and Hravn were preparing to flee from Urien and Owain, and now both were dead. Nudd! She realised with a jolt that, once Nudd found that Urien wasn't at the manor, he would know something was wrong and would come looking.

"Hravn! We have to go, now. Nudd will be upon us. I can't fight a third time."

"I know." He ran to recover his spear and then took Ealdgith's hand as they ran from the clearing without a backward look.

Hravn untied all the ponies. They would lead them away from the wood to help confound any chance of pursuit. He selected four of the pack ponies to come with them and tied their reins so that they could be led. They would transfer their saddlebags and other kit onto them later and reduce the burden on their own ponies.

"Urien? Beli? Where are….What the…?" Nudd's call and harsh exclamation resounded from the clearing. The cousins mounted and rode directly away from the wood towards the western fells. They crouched forward over their ponies, urging them faster and faster, with the desperate need to get clear of the last of the Pendragons. All the ponies followed in a ragged line and those that hadn't been secured, scattered gradually as they became aware that no one was driving them on.

Chapter 20

Hravn and Ealdgith rode hard, digging their heels into their ponies' flanks, urging them ever onward. Ealdgith lost count of the number of shallow valleys and hillcrests they crossed. The further they rode the more the shock of their escape eased. Where they could, they followed tracks, skirting around fields and catching strange glances from peasants starting to work in the early morning light.

Splashing through a shallow river, Hravn urged the pony to the top of a hill before finally calling a halt by the edge of a mature wood. The ponies were lathered and blowing heavily; they desperately needed the break.

"Edie, we've got to stop. We can't keep this up and I'm sure we have got clean away." Ealdgith nodded, too tired herself to speak. "Catch your breath whilst I climb up that tree and have a look back to see if we have been followed."

Hravn dismounted and pulled himself up into the higher branches of a large oak. It was easy climbing; the boughs were well spaced and he quickly got to a point where he could walk out on a broad bough, holding the branches above, and get a look back across the several valleys they had cut across. He could make out the broad valley bottom in which the Eden flowed

221

and thought that he could even see the wood from which they had fled. He stood watching for several minutes, but could see nothing, and then glanced down to see Ealdgith's troubled face, peering up. He gave a deliberate tap dance and faked a slip to make her gasp and then laugh and smile.

"It's all clear, Edie, not a sign and I can see all the way back to the wood. Why don't you water the ponies? There's a spring just yonder." He pointed a short way back down the hill.

"Will do," she called back, relieved at last to do something positive, and suddenly feeling much happier with the realisation that they were truly free.

Hravn clambered down and ran over to join Ealdgith at the spring. The hounds were as thirsty as the ponies and they jostled for a space to drink. Ealdgith waited until they had finished and let the water clear for a while before she filled their leather canteens. Hravn then used the spring water to clean their weapons, removing all sign of blood and gruesome reminders of that morning's fight. He slipped his arms around Ealdgith's waist and hugged her close. She was shaking slightly.

"We're free, Edie, we're free after all this time."

Ealdgith took a deep breath. "Thank God, truly. I knew in my heart, as soon as Oswin told us about the Pendragons, that one day we would have to fight. It was a devil I feared, but we've now laid it to rest. The way our times have changed, I know I may have to fight again but at least I know what I am facing now."

Hravn was quick to still Ealdgith's natural reaction to the killings. "Come, let's head around to the other side of the wood and rest. The day's still early but we need a good break."

Ealdgith nodded. "We'll finish the food we have and then move on and find somewhere for tonight." She sounded much more buoyant.

They led the ponies to a small clearing under an oak, overlooking the distant fells to the west. Whilst Ealdgith prepared a scratch meal Hravn started to repack their belongings into the panniers on the pack-ponies and then made a small fire. They didn't need the warmth or the light; it simply gave a focus for them to sit and look at as they relaxed and let the stress of the morning ease. They stared into the embers for quite some time.

"Hravn, I've been thinking," Ealdgith said slowly at last, speaking as much to herself as to Hravn. "It's time for me to be Ealdgith again. It's past mid sumor and I must be fifteen now. I can't carry on being a boy any more. Owain saw through me and others will too. I'll face life's challenges as a woman. I've proved to myself that I can hold my ground, not that I want to fight like that again, but I will if I need to."

Hravn grinned at her. "You're always my Edie, little Valkyrie." He pulled her to him playfully.

223

"You're right, we need to be ourselves now. The threat of the Pendragons has gone. They won't look for us now. Nudd will have enough of a problem getting Beli home, if he lives, that is."

"I know. I hate what we did; five lives taken or broken, but they left us no choice," she sighed. "I still can't believe we succeeded. It was all Oswin's teaching. I'll still wear men's clothes though, as long as we are living like this. It's the only practical thing to do and I will blend in more, but no more pretending."

"I've been thinking too, Edie," said Hravn hesitantly. "We know we lost your home and probably mine. From what we saw of the Normans, we almost certainly lost our families too. But your family still has the right to the lands at Hindrelag, whatever the Normans might do, Thor held the land in his own right. If you are the only one to survive, you are the rightful heir to the manor and to the title. Wherever we go, you can claim to be Lady Ealdgith of Hindrelag. It's the truth and we shouldn't hide it. Word might even spread to Gospatrick and cause him to wonder about his wider family. What do you think?"

Ealdgith continued staring at the fire, lost in thought about her family, about what they might have wanted her to do. It was a big thing to claim and something she had never considered possible, but Hravn was right. If all her family was dead, it was her birth right and she should claim it. Even when she married Hravn, it would still be hers, although she also feared that she would never see her land again and if she did, it would already have been taken by the Normans.

"I agree," Ealdgith said at last. "I had never thought of it but you are right."

"There is something else," Hravn added with a smile and a glint in his eye. "We should say that we are married too. We are of an age now and we have made promises to each other; it's just that we can't formalise it. There is no one to give you to me or to whom I can promise to care for you. No one should gain say us. I think it would give us proper status and it might make it easier for us to stay together, wherever we are. When we get to wherever Wyrd is taking us we will find someone to formalise it for us."

Ealdgith smiled and laid her head on Hravn's lap. "Yes, I will marry you, of course I will; but we already tell others that we are promised to each other don't we. We just haven't consummated it, and the time isn't right just yet, is it? Whatever we feel that is too much of a risk. But, yes, we will tell those whom we need to tell that we are married."

Hravn ran his fingers through her hair. "Your hair's growing again, Edie, you look like a lady already." He bent his head down and their lips met.

The warmth of the day started to soak into their bodies and the sound of bees in the clover lulled them into a deep and welcome sleep.

~~~

Ealdgith dreamed that she was washing her face in a deep pool of cool, clear water. The pool suddenly turned into the reflection of the face of a dog and she woke up coughing and flapping her hands in front of her "Hati, get off, you big fool!" She spluttered as Hati persisted in licking her nose. Ealdgith felt refreshed and, glancing at the sun, realised that it was just into the early afternoon. She went looking for Hravn and found him up another tree, spying out the land to their west.

"Wait there, I'm on my way down," he called as he descended in a furry of shaking leaves. "I know where we are Edie," he panted gleefully when he got to the bottom. "There's a village called Morlund at the bottom of the valley, I could just see it. I know it, or rather I have been to it. The Bear took me a few years ago after we went to Kircabi Stephan market. It was once the home of the Kings of Rheged, or so it is claimed. There is an amazing stone tower there too, built by Earl Siward of Northumberland after he fought the Scots and took control of Cumbraland. He died the year we were borne. I think The Bear said the tower is part church and part refuge and watch tower."

"If it's a refuge, mayhap we could stop there until we can come up with a new plan." Ealdgith embraced the suggestion, keen to meet people on her own terms again after months of pretence.

Men were working the long strip-fields on the lower slope of the hill as they dropped down to join a rutted cart track. Riding abreast and leading the pack ponies behind them, they wound their way along to the edge of the settlement.

"Look, Edie, on the side of the hill across the river." Ealdgith reined her pony to a halt and stared. "That's amazing! It's so tall and narrow, it's higher than the trees. How does it stand up?"

Hravn pursed his lips in thought. "I think they dig a big trench and build the walls into the ground to hold them in place. They are almost as thick as a man's arms' breadth, certainly at the bottom. It must have taken a lot of men a long time to build it."

Ealdgith was fired with enthusiasm. "Come on, let's see it; it's such a wonder."

The whole settlement was a wonder; certainly compared to Sedberge. The people smiled cheerfully at them as they rode between the thatched cottages and they waved back at children playing with the goats and chickens that scratted around the homesteads. They paused as they crossed a bridge of broad wooden planks across a shallow, fast flowing river above a waterfall. The cascade below them was driving a mill wheel. They could hear the millstones grinding above the sound of the water.

The tower was surrounded by a green sward on level ground, part way up the next hillside. A wooden longhouse projected from the east side of the tower, its roof steeply pitched and thatched with a small wooden cross standing proud of the gable end. The tower itself appeared to have two storeys. The ground floor had a very small window high up in the centre of each wall. Higher again in each wall was a large window with a clear all around view above the village rooftops. The flat top of the tower appeared to have a low wall around it and a flag flew from a central mast. Hravn didn't know the colours.

"Look at those walls, Edie, even an army couldn't get through those. What a building. It's like the old walls at Bogas and the towers by the old road over Stanmoir, but it's new. It shows what our people can do."

"Let's hobble the ponies on the sward and go inside. Sköll and Hati will make sure all is safe out here." Ealdgith led the way towards the church door. As they approached, a young man stepped out, paused as he rubbed his eyes to accustom them to the brighter light and then looked in surprise at the couple.

"Can I help you? I'm Brother Patrick, priest to our church of Saint Lawrence. We rarely see strangers here."

Hravn held out his hand in greeting. "I'm Hravn of Ravenstandale and Lady Ealdgith of Hindrelag is my wife." Hravn felt proud to introduce

Ealdgith as his wife, but it all seemed very strange too, as if they were stepping into a different world.

"Hindrelag? Is that not over the fells in Ghellinges-scir?"

"Indeed it is Brother Patrick," Ealdgith was quick to speak, sensing that the priest was more than a little sceptical. She wanted to grasp the initiative. Hravn and I were hunting on the high moor in Aefter Yule when the Normans attacked all the settlements across the shire. From afar, I saw my father's manor burn and all my people slain. I have the title to my father's lands, but I fear that they are now lost to the Normans."

Hravn took over their story. "We fled along Jorvale and over-wintered in the wild forest. Come Lencten, we crossed into Mallerstang intending to find our Uncle, Earl Gospatrick, at Carleol. However, we were taken by the Pendragons and held hostage. We were forced to work for them and have just escaped."

Ealdgith noticed Brother Patrick's eyebrows twitch at the mention of Gospatrick and sensed an underlying problem. Hravn continued, "As to Ravenstandale, I discovered whilst we were hostage that the Pendragons took the land at Ravenstandale from my family two generations ago. My grandmother was Cumbric, my father Norse."

Hravn paused and Ealdgith interjected quickly. "We ask for sanctuary and for forgiveness. Our escape was not without much violence and although it could not have been otherwise, I regret the lives we were forced to take with our own hands."

Brother Patrick looked at their faces, reading their eyes, seeing honesty, pain, and hope within them. "Come into my church, we will sit and talk. Your animals and belongings will be safe enough where they are. Come and be welcome."

Ealdgith thought that the priest was in his mid-twenties. He was obviously well educated and had probably been raised for the priesthood; his other-worldly, knowing and self-confident manner rather overawed her, just as much as it irritated Hravn. He was certainly very different to Brother Oswin. They talked more about their families, how they had lived and what they had lost. He knew of the Pendragons and was concerned to hear that they had started to raid into the Vale of the Eden again. Hravn reassured him that future raids were now very unlikely. Ealdgith and he had drawn their sting.

"You are, of course, welcome to take sanctuary in the tower. There is a little room in the basement and more if you venture up the ladder to the first floor; but would you not be better seeking shelter at the manor house? You, in particular, Lady Ealdgith, would be more comfortable there. Would it not better suit your status and needs?"

Ealdgith inferred from the priest's rather supercilious tone that he would prefer not to have a woman staying at his church, but she wasn't to be bullied. "No, Brother, I would be more than comfortable here. Indeed, it is a luxury compared to how we have lived these past months. We also need time to gather our thoughts and decide our future. I would rather meet the lord for a meal in a few days if you could arrange that, please? He will doubtless have sound advice that can help inform our plans once we decide."

"Very well, yes, but do keep the hounds from the body of the church. They may come and go through here for the only entrance to the tower is from inside."

"Don't worry, Brother, they are well trained and obedient, but thank you, you are most kind." Ealdgith quite enjoyed taking the upper hand. Hravn gave her a subtle, wry smile.

"I will seek out the lord, Gunnar, and see if he could host you the day after tomorrow."

Hravn was quick to seize the opportunity. "Yes, thank you, Brother, that would be much appreciated, if it is no inconvenience to you." Much as the priest irritated Hravn, he didn't want Ealdgith's teasing to alienate him. "We'll gather our belongings from the ponies and bring them inside if we may, then later perhaps we could ask for absolution."

~~~

Much later that evening, the cousins sat around a small outdoor hearth in a secluded corner at the back of the tower and finished eating a stew they had cooked in a pot. They had sorted through their bags, repacked and shaken some of the creases out of the dress that Rhiannon had made for Ealdgith. They agreed that it would be more appropriate for Ealdgith to dress as a lady when they paid their visit to Gunnar. Their meal over, they continued to sit in seclusion whilst Hravn slowly combed the many tangles from Ealdgith's hair, taking great care to avoid painful tugs and great joy in the quiet intimacy that it provided.

"You're so beautiful, Edie, I'm so used to seeing you dressed as a boy that I can't believe you are the same person. I will have difficulty fighting off all the envious glances that you will attract."

"I just hope Gunnar is a responsible host. We have had enough of fighting off more than just glances these past months." Ealdgith was flattered by the compliment, but very nervous about dressing as a woman. She had rarely done so and in the past, had always thought that others saw her as a girl rather than an adult. Her new status as a woman and a lady of position, even if she had no lands to underwrite that position, was not easy to adjust to.

The following day, Ealdgith reverted to wearing breeches and they took all the ponies to the blacksmith for re-shoeing. Then, having attended to their animals' needs, they attended to their own and went in search of a cobbler.

Hravn was struggling with his boots. His feet had grown so much in the six months since they fled Ghellinges-scir that his toes were rubbed constantly. Ealdgith's boots were worn out. Hravn had also grown too large for his cloak and he commissioned a seamstress to make him a new one in a similar green, russet and purple woollen pattern.

"I think we should talk to Gunnar about Gospatrick and where we might find him," Hravn suggested to Ealdgith as they walked back to the tower. "Yes, but did you notice Brother Patrick's reaction when we mentioned him? I have a hunch something isn't quite as it should be."

Hravn agreed. "I know, I don't particularly like Brother Patrick's manner, but I just think that he is more a man of books than of people; yet he was very understanding when we talked of killing Urien and Owain."

Brother Patrick was quick to find them when they arrived at the church. He had spoken with Gunnar who would very happily host them to the meal of the day at noon tomorrow.

~~~

Gunnar's manor was just beyond the western side of the settlement, towards the old military road that ran the length of the Vale; the one that Nudd had mentioned to Hravn. They chose to walk there rather than ride because Ealdgith would be unable to ride astride the pony if she was wearing a dress.

Hravn had made an effort to smarten himself up, having run the comb through his hair, shaved and brushed much of the grime off his breeches. Ealdgith, on the other hand, made a determined effort to look the 'Lady of the Manor'. She wore the pale green dress, cream over-mantle and wimple that Rhiannon had made for her. Her hair was once again just long enough for her to pull through a silver ring at the back of her head, to hold it in place underneath the wimple. She wore the decorated seax around her waist. The fine gold thread in the leather waist belt caught the sunlight and highlighted her slim waist. The key to the tower hung from the right side of her belt. It was another symbol of her status as a woman in her own right.

Before they left the tower, Hravn placed his hands gently on Ealdgith's shoulders and turned her towards him. "Edie, you are without doubt the most beautiful lady in the land. Rhiannon knew what she was about when she chose the cloth for your dress; it matches the green fleck in your eyes perfectly."

Ealdgith was speechless for a moment and, having thought about poking her tongue at him, instead lent forward raising her head to kiss him very delicately on his lips. "And you too, are the most wonderful man any woman could want, now come on before you get too soft in the head."

With that, she skipped down the path from the tower, pausing for Hravn and the hounds to catch up. Ealdgith felt very self-conscious as she walked through the village, though the feel of Hravn's hand in hers bolstered her confidence. Try as she might, she couldn't get used to wearing the wimple.

The manor was a Norse longhouse. They saw it from afar, where it dominated a low ridge that over looked the village. It was smaller than the longhouse in Mallerstang and differed in that the large roof beam extended beyond each end of the long roof and each end was carved to give the appearance of a large dragon's head staring down on those below. The two cross beams above the gabled entrance on the side of the longhouse were smaller, but similarly carved.

"By Thor!" Hravn exclaimed as he paused to look at the building. "That's impressive. I knew we Norse could build, but those dragon heads are truly impressive. Just look at the wood, it must be as old as Oswin!"

Ealdgith was less impressed, she thought the dragon heads were grimly intimidating; but she was quickly reassured by the sight of two laughing children who ran out of the gabled entrance down the path towards them.

The children, a boy and a girl, quickly introduced themselves as Tyr and Aebbe. Hravn wondered why the girl had a peculiarly Saxon name whereas her brother's name would pass in both Norse and Saxon communities. Their father was obviously Norse. The two chattering children led them by the hand to the longhouse. As they went, Ealdgith smiled to herself, thinking just how much their lives had changed in the past few days.

Chapter 21

Gunnar stepped out of the gabled entrance to greet them, beneath the carved dragons' heads, which glared down from the apex.

"Welcome, you must be Hravn and Lady Ealdgith?"

Hravn nodded and smiled, holding out his right hand. Gunnar grasped it, and placed his left hand over Hravn's wrist in a gesture of warm welcome. He then turned to Ealdgith, took her hand and, stooping, raised it to his lips. "My Lady, welcome too."

Ealdgith flushed with embarrassment. She said, "Edie, my Lord, please just call me Edie."

Gunnar stepped between them, turned, and placing a hand on each of their shoulders said, "and I am Gunnar. Come, take a seat on the bench by the light from the door."

Gunnar was stocky, blond and probably in his early thirties. Although no taller than Hravn, he was twice the width and undoubtedly immensely strong. He had a broad bearded face, receding hair, bright blue eyes and a wide smile; it was hard not to be captivated by his obvious natural good humour. Hravn was intrigued by Gunnar's jewellery. Each of his bare upper arms was bound by a mass of engraved gold and silver rings; some were undoubtedly old and very traditionally Norse and they contrasted markedly with the silver cross that hung from the lowest ring on his left bicep, making a very obvious mix of the old and new religions.

As the cousins stepped into the longhouse it took them a few seconds to accustom their eyes to the dark interior.

Inside, the longhouse was typical of many that Hravn had seen before, and not unlike his father's. Two rows of sturdy wooden posts ran along the inside of the walls and supported great roof beams. The steeply sloping roof extended out beyond the posts almost to ground level and allowed space for sturdy wooden benches to fit between the posts, helping to brace them in place. There was little furniture, other than the benches that doubled as places to sit, eat, work and sleep. Some of the benches had loose rugs and fabric covers piled on them; a trestle table stood length ways across the room with benches on either side. In the middle of the main room, a long narrow stone-lined fire pit provided heat and light and it appeared that there were other rooms partitioned off at either end. Several logs glowed in the fire pit, above which a cooking pot was suspended from an iron frame which also held a spit in place. A young man turned the spit, roasting a joint of meat; the smell from which wafted through the longhouse. Hravn immediately felt hungry and his tummy rumbled. Ealdgith kicked his ankle swiftly with a sideward tap of her boot. Hravn grinned sheepishly, but even as he started to apologise, Gunnar landed a playful slap on his shoulders and chuckled "There's Norse blood in you for sure, we'll eat soon."

There were no windows and the smoke drifted up into the roof space and out through a central covered chimney and a series of small covered smoke holes. The upper rafters were stained black with smoke and disappeared out of sight in the dark of the roof space. Light was limited, coming from the fire, through the smoke holes, the door and from several tallow candles that burned on sconces fixed to the posts. Although it was gloomy and filled with all the smells of close human living, the longhouse had a homely, cheery atmosphere.

Ealdgith jumped as a wolfhound lying in the shadow beyond the fire pit growled at Sköll and Hati. Gunnar's gruff curse nipped any chance of a dogfight in the bud and the hound lowered its head with a disgruntled sigh.

"Let me introduce my family." Gunnar looked around and ushered the children forward. "Tyr, my son, you have met. He is ten, but thinks he's older. Aebbe is but eight and will charm the birds from the trees if you let her." Gunnar gestured to a young woman who stood in the shadows holding a young baby in a shawl, "and this is Mildgyd, she is Magni's wet nurse. Her husband is Aleifr, my cook and houseman. We call Magni the 'bull calf', he certainly drinks like one."

Ealdgith was about to ask the very obvious question when Gunnar's expression changed and she thought she saw a tear in the corner of his eye. "Aelfgifu, my wife, died bearing Magni at Yuletide. He is all I have left of her now, and Tyr and Aebbe too, of course."

"I'm so sorry." Ealdgith instinctively put her hand out to touch Gunnar's arm.

"Thank you, Edie, that means a lot to me." Gunnar's thanks were heartfelt.

Hravn was intrigued and asked, almost rudely, "Was Aelfgifu Saxon? Is that why Aebbe has such a Saxon name too?"

"She was, and yes. Aebbe is the spit of her. I cannot look at Aebbe now without feeling the pain of what we have lost." Gunnar's sadness was very evident and Hravn and Ealdgith could tell that he was still affected greatly by his loss. Each warmed to him in a different way. Hravn was drawn by his strength and honest open nature; Gunnar was a natural leader of men. Ealdgith sensed something more; rare compassion and a respect for women; Gunnar must have been a good husband.

Their shared moment of retrospection was shattered by a sudden, loud bellow that reverberated through the longhouse. Everyone jumped! Gunnar laughed. "That's just the other Magni. He's my bull and lives in the stable at the far end of my house. He's my son's name sake too." He chuckled, "Tyr, go and feed him, but don't tarry. Aleifr will serve our meal soon." He then gestured to the trestle table. "Come, sit whilst we wait for Aleifr, he doesn't like to be rushed. The priest told me something of your story, but I'd like to hear it in person for I am sure that there is much to tell."

They sat and talked; Hravn and Ealdgith taking turns, starting with the failure of the autumn rising and their fear of Norman retribution. Gunnar's jaw dropped and his eyes widened as they told of the massacre of the villages and their flight into the forest. The gloom of the longhouse seemed to rap around them and accentuate the horrors that had befallen them.

Aleifr's cautious cough interrupted them and they paused whilst he served them with trenchers laden with boiled vegetable and roast mutton. Gunnar asked if they wanted mead or ale to drink, but both preferred clean spring water if he had it. Gunnar assured them that he did, there was a spring behind the manor, which was probably why the site was chosen many years ago. He made sure that the animals were kept well away from it so that it was always safe to drink.

The meal served, they reverted to telling their story. Gunnar laughed at their description of Brother Oswin. "He's my kind of priest; a warrior at heart and keeping himself quietly out of the way." He also applauded Ealdgith's decision to dress as a boy and to learn the arts of sword craft and self-defence. "You're a rare lass, Edie. One with great imagination and willpower, without a doubt."

Gunnar nodded soberly when they started to describe their entrapment by the Pendragons. "Uther's family have long terrorised the upper dale, though life has been quieter since Gospatrick reived them in return a few years back."

"Well, they won't be reiving again a while," Hravn muttered grimly. He related how they had been held ransom and forced to work for the Pendragons before taking advantage of the Aplebi raid to make their escape.

"Edie proved herself a true Valkyrie. She faced Beli and Owain alone, killed Owain and then protected my back against two men while I faced Urien."

Hravn was fulsome in his praise, "It was Edie's quick action and daring that saved the day. I was so focused on Urien that I failed to see the opportunities that we were creating. When she moves, she's faster than a cat and even more deadly, and she is courageous beyond measure."

Ealdgith sat up and turned to Hravn with a look of surprised delight. "It wasn't just me, you know that, it was these two too." She pointed to Sköll and Hati, who rolled their eyes up towards her in expectation. "We're a team of four and these two are worth at least ten men." Ealdgith paused. Gunnar and Hravn could see that she was mulling thoughts over in her head. "I've grown up a lot since Yuletide. If I'm honest with myself, I was too much a child until then. I was enjoying pretending that I could live a boy's life with Hravn, but at the back of my mind, I half expected my father to marry me off. I suppose it was his involvement with the rising against the King that distracted him. That all changed at Aefter Yule; and after we faced One Eye and Scar Face in the forest I feared that, one day, I would have to kill to protect myself. Once we were held hostage by Pendragon I knew that our escape might be violent. It was. When Owain and Beli took me, I knew that if I didn't kill them, I would be killed and I knew what would happen to me first. I've seen the worst of men this past half year, what they can do to others and to women in particular. I've seen the best of men too." She looked meaningfully at Gunnar and Hravn, "and I've grown into a woman."

Hravn put his hand over Ealdgith's, grasping it tight whilst giving her a big beaming smile. Gunnar banged the table with his open palm. "Well said, Edie, well said. Your people will need lasses like you to stand against those Norman bastards. I've heard what they are like." He paused, looking at them both. "But I'm ahead of myself. What are your plans?"

Hravn looked first at Ealdgith and turned back to Gunnar. "We would welcome your thoughts about that. Edie's cousin, or probably her third cousin, I think, is Earl Gospatrick. We planned to go to him."

Gunnar hesitated, suddenly more sombre. He looked from Hravn to Ealdgith, choosing his words. "Gospatrick is a strange man. He is a Prince of Cumbraland, certainly, and has a claim to Westmoringaland, but his interests are also in Northumberland. The two don't always sit easily together as they are in the gift of competing kings. Although Gospatrick's family long held all the North, Cnut gave the land to Siward the Dane and he held the North with the support of both kings until his death. It was Siward that built the tower here a generation ago. Gospatrick then held Northumberland above the Tees, and also Cumbraland, but the Normans have really changed matters for him now. The Norman King, William the Bastard as you call him, took Northumberland from Gospatrick after last year's rising but I hear he is now back in favour again and Bernician Northumberland has been restored to him. William has placed a firm grip on Yorkshire and Durham. I think Gospatrick and his Bernician Northumbrians are the piggy in the middle between the two kings. Malcolm of Scotland has Gospatrick on a string. It's rumoured that he sent men to raid into Bernicia late last year, when Gospatrick was out of favour, and that the consequent Bernician raids into the lower Eden around Carleol early this year were Gospatrick's revenge because Malcolm still claims Cumbraland. It's interesting that the Bernicians only stole from Church lands, not from the people."

Ealdgith was confused by mention of Bernicia and Hravn explained in an aside that

Northumbrian Bernicia was the remnant of the old kingdom of Bernicia that once covered all the lands, east and west, in the North twixt the Tees and the Tweed. Now it was just the eastern lands north of the Tyne.

"Your own people were once Bernicians, you know." Hravn teased her, knowing that Ealdgith would realise he was right if she thought about it.

"That sounds like Loki's work, what a messy situation. Where is Gospatrick now?" Hravn returned to the matter in hand and was far from reassured by the news, blaming the Norse god of mischief and trickery.

Gunnar thought for a minute. "I'd put money on him being at Bebbanburge, that's the seat of the Earls of Northumberland. If William wants him to hold the far North against the Scots, he'll have to be there."

Ealdgith sighed, "It's like a game of chess and we are the pawns; or rather Gospatrick is the pawn and we are just bystanders. This tells me two things. The first is that we shouldn't go to Carleol and claim to be kin of Gospatrick, certainly not yet a while. The other is that we've got Hel's own trip if we are to find my cousin in Bebbanburge."

Hravn nodded, rather lost for an idea.

Gunnar narrowed his eyes in thought. "Hravn, your family is Norse, is it not?"

"Yes, though my grandmother is Cumbric from Ravenstandale. We lived in an enclave of Norse manors in the vale of the Greta, over Stanmoir, beyond Bogas. My father, Ask, was known as 'The Bear' by our people. He holds, held, the manor of Raveneswet."

"Well," Gunnar continued slowly, still stringing his ideas together and choosing his words carefully so as not to startle Hravn. "I think that maybe, just maybe, The Bear stills holds sway in the lands around the Greta."

"What?!" Hravn leant forward, wide eyed, questioning. "We saw smoke from all the manors in the vale of the Greta when we fled and we saw the slaughter in the manors close to where we were."

Gunnar lent forward and placed his hand on Hravn's wrist to calm him down. "I said maybe. Don't build your hopes. I know The Bear. I met him at Kircabi Stephan two years back and I know how he leads his people and will bow to none. I've just made the connection but now I have, I see him in you."

Gunnar continued to grasp Hravn's wrist. "I had news of your people early this year. Two families fled here before moving further into Cumbraland. They told of the devastation of the manors. Much was destroyed, as you say, but there wasn't the slaughter that you saw, not everywhere. Many fled to try and find food and survive the winter. I fear many will still have perished in the cold, but The Bear did at least survive the harrying. They said that he had fled with several families into the Arkengarthdale Forest and swore to resist, stay free from the Normans, or die."

Hravn and Ealdgith sat speechless. Ealdgith placed her hand on Hravn's free one. "That sounds like your father. We must go and find him. That is what we must do."

Gunnar sat back and thumped the table with his fist. "That's right, Lady Edie! You must go to The Bear and help him fight for all you've lost. If all is lost, then follow the hills north and go to Gospatrick; but seek out The Bear first." He clicked his fingers to gain Aleifr's attention. "Bring mead for we must drink a toast, and I am sure Edie will enjoy its sweetness. Come, drink! To, The Bear."

"Gunnar?" Ealdgith asked with a coy smile, "We should leave for Arkengarthdale now and take advantage of the weather, but it is many months since I felt safe and at home anywhere, not since we said farewell to Brother Oswin. Haerfest is upon us. Can we stay with you a short while and help you bring the grain in? We can relax a little too, build our strength and really plan our journey. What say you too, Hravn? I don't want to keep you from finding The Bear."

Gunnar sat back with a broad smile. He waited for Hravn to answer. Hravn put his arm around Ealdgith and squeezed her shoulder "My thoughts too, we need time to be ourselves again and, if Gunnar doesn't mind, I can't think of a better place to be." Gunnar leant forward, taking one of their hands in each of his, "Welcome, stay as long as you need; the honour will be mine." He paused, adding with a chuckle, "a little help with haerfest wouldn't go amiss either."

~~~

Hravn and Ealdgith felt as if they were walking on air as they headed back to the tower to collect their belongings and bid farewell to the priest. Gunnar had lifted their spirits and they finally felt secure and confident that they had a plan, even if it was based upon the tenuous hope that The Bear was alive and risked the likelihood that they would live under Norman oppression. They had agreed with Gunnar that they would return before dusk.

"Brother Patrick," Hravn called to the priest just as he was entering the church, "We have come to bid you farewell and to thank you for your hospitality. Gunnar has asked us to stay and help with haerfest before we move on."

Brother Patrick's eyes widened as he saw Ealdgith in her dress. "My Lady'" he nodded courteously. "The pleasure was mine; and God's too," he added as an afterthought. "May I ask where you are moving on to?"

Hravn paused. "Can we talk inside?"

Brother Patrick opened the door to the church. "Of course, I am intrigued."

They sat on stools at the back of the church whilst Hravn explained that Gunnar had told them of the Bernician raids, that Earl Gospatrick was probably now at Bebbanburge and that he believed that Hravn's father was alive. They would return to Ghellinges-scir in the hope of finding his father and then, if needs be, they would go to Earl Gospatrick.

Brother Patrick said nothing for a few moments, studying them both with a fixed, thoughtful stare. "I try to keep apart from worldly matters for it is not a priest's role to become involved, but I do hear a great deal. There are those who still travel back and forth across the fells. Gunnar may well be right in thinking that your father is alive, Hravn. I have heard that the Normans are creating a stronghold in Ghellinges-scir and that many who survived the slaughter and the winter are now employed on building their castles there. There is one built from wood on a man-made hill at Ghellinges and I have heard of one called Richemund. It is being built from stone and is named 'strong hill' in the Norman language."

Ealdgith's jaw dropped and she looked from Hravn to the priest. "Brother, where is this Richemund? Is it at Hindrelag? My father's manor was built on a strong hill and it was burned before my eyes. Building a castle there would surely cow our people."

Brother Patrick paused, before saying very gently, "That I cannot say Lady Edie, but it may well be so. It is best that you are prepared for much change when you return there."

He studied them both for a moment, then added, "It would seem that some of your people have thrown in their lot with the Normans, work their manors hard and squeeze tax from their people for the benefit of the Normans whilst others have forfeited their estates. I've heard too that some still resist as best they can and at great risk to themselves."

Hravn took Ealdgith's hand. "Edie, we will find out. We know your lands will be forfeit now. The land we return to will be very different to that we fled, but family is more important than land and we will strive to find all the family that we have." Ealdgith fought back her tears and nodded, accepting.

The priest saw the watery glint in her eyes and continued gently, "Lady Edie, Hravn is right. If you find that you have no family in Ghellinges-scir, then do go to Bebbanburge, for I too have heard that your cousin is there. I know a little of the area having once helped with the rebuilding of the abbey at Hagustaldes-ham."

Hravn interrupted "Is there anything you can tell us of the way there?"

The priest nodded. "You have to be able to cross the Tyne and the other large rivers. The easiest route is along the old military road of

Dere Street. There are crossings over the main rivers, but the road will doubtless be used by the Normans. It may be your only route in winter. If the weather is better mayhap you should follow the high ridges until you can cross the Tyne, or come back this way and take the old road north from Kircabi Thore. That way, you would avoid Carleol. Then follow the north bank of the Tyne to the sea, before taking the coast up to Bebbanburge."

Ealdgith leant forward, taking the priest's hands in hers, confident that, despite his condescending manner, Brother Patrick had their best interests at heart. "Thank you Brother, we are very much in your debt for your kindness and advice. I now know what we must do and the challenges we must face. Mayhap we will meet you again one day."

Haerfest and Winter

Chapter 22

"Hah! Lady Edie, I can see why Hravn calls you his Valkyrie." Gunnar's laugh boomed through the dusk as Hravn and Ealdgith rode up the track, leading the pack ponies towards the longhouse stable. Ealdgith had changed from her dress into her men's clothes, with her seax at her waist and bow over her back. Gunnar's expression was one of amusement, amazement and considerable respect. "You are a rare and wonderful sight, Edie." He paused, "I just wish my Aelfgifu could have met you, you would surely have been friends."

Ealdgith flashed Gunnar a cheeky smile. "Greetings, my Lord Gunnar. Are those compliments just because you need a hand with the haerfest?" Gunnar just smiled. As they dismounted, he placed an arm around Hravn's shoulder, chuckling and whispered from the side of his mouth, "You've got your hands full there!" Hravn nodded, smiling, confident in the knowledge that in Gunnar, he had found a firm friend.

The ponies stabled, Gunnar welcomed them into the longhouse just as night fell. The flickering light from the tallow candles and the fire pit threw long shadows behind the broad roof posts. They sat at the trestle table as Gunnar poured them each a cup of watered ale. Hravn drank thirstily whilst Ealdgith sipped, amused. As Gunnar finished pouring his own ale he looked them each in the eye with a seriousness that immediately drew their attention.

"Now that you are to return to the wolves' lair, you need to be better protected. Any fight with a Norman will be unlike your experience with the Pendragons."

Ealdgith's light-heartedness disappeared. "Y..yes?" she said hesitantly.

Hravn nodded. "I was thinking the same. Do you have a leather worker here who could make us padded jerkins, and a weaver or seamstress who could perhaps replace the cloak I've grown out of?"

Gunnar laughed, relieved that Hravn had already anticipated the risks that lay ahead.

"You're a canny lad, Hravn, but better than that, Ulf, my smith, is my armourer and his wife is a seamstress. We'll see them in the morning." Gunnar interrupted Hravn and Ealdgith just as they started to offer their thanks. "Wait, there's more. Hravn, I have a mail shirt. It's old and has been in my family for more generations than I can say. It is small for an ox like me," he teased, spreading his arms and flexing his biceps. "But it should fit a young wolf hound like you, and it is serviceable and oiled. It's yours. Oh, and there's a helm to go with it," he added, almost as a teasing after thought.

Gunnar turned to Ealdgith whilst Hravn sat momentarily speechless with surprise, delight and more than a little pride at the prospect of dressing as a Norse warrior, even though he had lost his claim to title and land. "Now, Edie, how does a well-bred young lady dress to fight the Normans, I wonder?" Ealdgith smiled at Gunnar's teasing and cocked an eyebrow, prompting him to continue. "Mail would be too heavy for you and even if I had a shirt small enough, it would slow you down too. Your agility is your strength. The weight of an iron helm would hinder you too. I suggest that we use carefully shaped saddle leather, well-padded with sheepskin. That should be light but strong enough to protect against a glancing blow to the head should, Heaven forbid, you ever receive one. Combined with a padded jerkin and leather arm guards, these should give you protection without hindering you over much. What do you say?"

Ealdgith was almost as stunned as Hravn, then instinctively leant forward to kiss Gunnar's ruddy cheek through his thick and tickling beard.

"Thank you," they said together.

~~~

Ealdgith woke early, the birdsong from the dawn chorus rousing her. She and Hravn had bedded down on the benches near the fire pit and she lay for a moment with her eyes closed, listening to the reassuring sound of his rhythmic breathing. A faint cough in the otherwise still room caused Ealdgith to open her eyes quickly. Her mouth dropped, then turned into a warm smile as she saw Aebbe sitting cross-legged on the floor next to her, her chin resting on her hands. Aebbe sat back, worried that she had woken Ealdgith and might have upset her. Ealdgith's quick smile reassured her and she said "You look just like Moder when you sleep, watching you made me think she was here again."

Ealdgith sat up and opened her arms in an instinctive hug. As she held the little girl's head close to her breast, she stroked her hair whispering "I can't be your mother, Aebbe, but I can be your friend; would you like that?"

"Please," came Aebbe's muffled reply.

"Come then, why don't we leave Hravn and the others to sleep a while and you can show me around outside and I'll introduce you to our ponies, but quietly now." They rose and slipped silently, barefoot, through the ashes by the fire pit. Hati followed. The house cat, a mouser, slunk out of sight.

They returned to the longhouse a little while later, once they heard the sound of early morning activity. Gunnar grinned as they walked in through the door, hand in hand. Aebbe's beaming face told him that Ealdgith would have a young shadow for the rest of her stay and he wondered how Aebbe would feel when her new friend had to leave. He resolved to cross that bridge when he came to it. For now, he would enjoy the company of his new-found friends just as much as his daughter would.

The heather on the high fell tops to their east flowered in a great purple band and the sun dropped behind the western fells earlier every day, a sign that the year was passing. Days turned quickly into weeks as they settled into their new routine of helping with the haerfest and preparing for their return to Ghellinges-scir.

Most days, they toiled to dusk, scything wheat, barley and oats for threshing and long grass for hay. The men stood in line as they moved through the fields, cutting the crops down. Behind the men, the women and children were bent at the waist, bundling the harvest into sheaves that lay like bodies behind them. Later, the men would return and stack the sheaves into high ricks to dry. Ealdgith spent much of her time away from the fields, helping the older women prepare food, which she then delivered to the fields, driving an ox cart carrying fresh loaves, cheese and ale to the toiling workers. Aebbe was her constant help. Tyr worked in the fields alongside Gunnar and Hravn until his arms tired and he fell back to work with the women in the row behind.

Then, after the corn and barley were gathered, Ealdgith and Aebbe gathered forest fruits, carrying sacksful back to the manor for the women to conserve.

Hravn took time out to work with Ulf, who was a great help. When he wasn't repairing and sharpening all the haerfest tools, he dedicated himself to helping Hravn and Ealdgith prepare. Both were amazed at how quickly he could work metal. The links in Hravn's mail shirt were quickly adjusted so that it fitted neatly over a padded leather jerkin made by Ulf's wife. Both were designed carefully to allow for Hravn's continuing growth. His helmet was a near perfect fit; a little extra sheep skin padding was all that was needed for it to provide a firm, but not tight, hold on his head. Ulf added a new buckled chin strap and, with Hravn's agreement, added a nose guard. Ulf's advice that he'd seen too many broken noses from a quick head-butt was enough to persuade Hravn.

Ealdgith's helmet was a work of art. Ulf measured her head and, allowing for a sheepskin cap as a liner, fashioned a leather headband to which he fitted a leather cruciform shaped to the curve of her skull. Leather panels were then riveted to the cruciform cradle to provide all over protection; a leather nose and spectacled eye guard covered her upper face, and her cheeks were protected by flaps that buckled under her chin. Ulf chose the leather with care. The frame, nose and eye guards were a dark russet, whilst the panels and cheek shields were a lighter tan. The whole effect was quite intimidating. "If you weren't a shield-maiden before, you are now, my lady," Ulf complimented Ealdgith as much as himself as he stood back to look at her.

"By Freyja, Edie!" Hravn was stunned by the effect. "You look like a cat about to strike. All I can see is the green of your eyes surrounded by the red of the eye guards and the tan of the cheek shields. Oswin would certainly say that you have the psychological advantage. Thanks, Ulf, you're a wizard!"

Ulf added to Hravn's selection of spears providing a sheaf of lighter, throwing javelins and two heavier spears with large iron heads for stabbing, particularly when riding. He honed their seax blades to very fine cutting edges and suggested that Hravn might benefit from using a sword instead, thinking that he would find the extra length and protection of a hilt useful. Hravn agreed. He would switch his seax to his opposite hip, to fight with it in his left hand, so that its broader, double edged blade could be used to parry a sword thrust.

Finally, Hravn bought a sack of heavy arrow heads, some barbed, others with a bodkin point for piercing armour. Ulf shook his head slowly, "You've enough for a small war there, lad."

"I know." Hravn gave a wry smile. "I fear that is exactly where we are headed."

Later, Ulf spoke privately to Gunnar. That evening, Gunnar disappeared from the hearth where they were all sitting, watching the glowing embers, sipping ale and swapping tales. He returned moments later carrying a long object wrapped in cloth. Stopping by the hearth, he turned to Hravn. "Hravn, I have a special gift for you. Ulf tells me that you should carry a sword, and I agree. If you are to fight for the honour and protection of your people, our people, you will need all the power possible. This sword has been in my family for generations. It was crafted in the Norse-Irish lands before my people came here and is one of a pair; the other is mine. I had thought to give it to Tyr, but the need for it is now. He shall have mine in time. It is said to have a power of its own. Maybe it does, use it wisely and always prevail."

Hravn was speechless, momentarily. He stood, gracefully took the sword from Gunnar then, placing it carefully on the bench, he turned and embraced Gunnar like a brother. "Thank you, Gunnar, this means more than you will ever know. I will use it as you say and always for the protection and honour of our people."

Gunnar grinned, "It is called Nadr. Make sure you live up to its name and always strike with the speed and lethal intent of the adder." Hravn slid the sword from its scabbard of leather, bound with hard silver and bronze. The sword was long, light and perfectly balanced with the natural patterning of the beaten metal blade enhanced by an engraved lattice of serpent bodies and heads. Norse runes spelt its name on the centre of the blade; Nadr.

Some days later, Gunnar sat with Hravn and Ealdgith on the boulders by the entrance to the longhouse, watching the sun fall behind the western fells. Crimson clouds silhouetted the peaks contrasting with the dark grey above the vale. Bats flitted under the eaves. The men drank horns of Gunnar's best ale and Ealdgith sipped from a cup of mead, the taste of which she had developed a strong liking. They talked about their plans and how they would see what form the resistance, if there was one, was taking.

Ealdgith was captivated by the evening and in love with the vale. Its long horizons were bordered by the safe embrace of the fells that enclosed rolling, fertile fields and rivers. It was her ideal haven; a place of peace and prosperity. "I wonder, what is the history of the vale?" she asked, her question more to herself than to the two men. Gunnar looked at Hravn, raised an eye brow, and said, "I only know my people's history, but your birth line straddles both camps, it's your tale to tell."

Hravn chuckled, "Now that's a quick escape if ever I heard one! But, my grandmother made sure she taught me her people's story and The Bear made sure I knew ours." He glanced knowingly at Gunnar.

"Go on," Ealdgith encouraged, "it's such a special place, I need to know."

"Well..." Hravn paused. "My grandmother told me that Cumbraland and Westmoringaland were always the land of the Cumbri and part of a much bigger kingdom right across the North. The Romans came, and went, leaving their roads, their forts and their walls, but the kingdom remained. The Cumbri had remained great after the Romans. Their kingdom was called Rheged and under their leader, Urien, they fought the new people coming from the east. Those were your people, Edie." He paused, to give her a teasing frown, "but plague came and killed many Cumbri."

Ealdgith looked surprised. "Was there much fighting?"

Hravn shook his head. "No, I think that by then, the Cumbri were too weak from plague. Many villages had died out and the people had scattered. The newcomers, Edie's people, mainly settled peacefully and the valley prospered."

Gunnar took up the story. "That's much as Aelfgifu told it to me. My people came across the sea from lands their forefathers had settled in Ireland. Some sought booty and fame, but others came to farm the green and fertile valleys west of the fells. My people are farmers as well as warriors. We prospered and moved up the valleys, around the sides of the fells and up the vale from Carleol. There was land to spare and we made new settlements, mixing and marrying with those already here, just as I have done."

"But which king held your fealty?" Ealdgith was still unsure about who really controlled the Vale of Eden. Gunnar laughed. "You might well ask, many wonder at that. We've had various leaders, usually we unite and fight anyone from outside. The Cumbri and the Norse, and even your people from Bernicia, Edie, have all held sway at times. In the past, we fought Eric Blood Axe and the Danes from Euruic, beating them on Stanmoir and we've united with the Cumbri in Strathclyde, north of the Solway. The English king has attacked more than once. The last time was a hundred years ago when it was agreed to split the land north and south along the line of the Eamont and Ulueswater; that split Cumbraland from Westmoringaland."

Hravn interrupted. "They say the kings all met at Dunmallard, which is that low round hill there, at the foot of Ulueswater." He pointed towards the hill, its top just catching the last light from the setting sun. "It was once a fort of the old Cumbri, before the Romans."

Gunnar smiled and nodded, happy with the interruption. "Mmm, it makes sense, though I hadn't heard that. Anyway, at the moment, Gospatrick holds sway in Cumbraland and is liegeman to Malcolm of Scotland, but who knows....?" He shrugged his shoulders and looked skyward, "For now, I have no liege lord, but look to Gospatrick. I think it is all in the hands of Wyrd."

"Thank you..." Ealdgith was silent for a moment or two, lost in thought as she gazed down the valley at the silhouettes of the fells. "What's that fell called, the one on the eastern side that looms above all others?"

Gunnar followed her gaze. "That's Cross Fell, though others call it Fiend's Fell after the sound of the wind that can scream down its slopes. It is a fearsome sound and can be a fearsome wind, so much so that men cannot stand and birds cannot fly."

"I have heard of it, but never felt it, thank God," Hravn said. "They call it the Helm Wind, do they not?"

"Yes, the time to take shelter is when the cloud forms in a long bar-like cap along the summit and the wind starts to scream down from the north east."

"That's really terrifying. I thought it looked such a protective mountain," said Ealdgith, concerned and disappointed.

"Ah, but you're right, it is protective," Gunnar reassured her. "Its great shoulders block all routes from the east other than the old high pass at Stanmoir." Gunnar paused for a moment, chuckled, and added, "The same happens along the tops above Mallerstang at times, maybe that explains the fiends that live there?"

"Well, fiends or not, I think it is a beautiful valley. It's so peaceful and fertile and," she paused, "safe…I can see why it is called Eden."

~~~

Early the next morning, Gunnar clapped Hravn and Ealdgith on the backs of their shoulders as they sat at the trestle table breakfasting on oat cakes and milk. "Well, young warriors, I know you practise sword play and combat daily but if you're to be real thorns in the side of the Normans, I think you need to practise wearing your armour."

Hravn laughed, spluttering oak cake. "You're always a step ahead of me, Gunnar. I was just thinking the same. The jerkin will constrain me and the weight of the mail will certainly tire me more quickly. I do need to get used to them."

Ealdgith pushed her stool back and turned to them both, rubbing her hands enthusiastically. "A holmganga, my lords?"

Gunnar laughed, impressed that she knew the term "You are without doubt a Valkyrie."

Ealdgith pursed her lips as if in deep thought. "Give us two days to practise and then I'll wager my money on Hravn against you; though don't bet on me. I'll practise with you, Gunnar, but I won't compete with you…I couldn't bear to hurt you." She teased, poking her tongue at him.

Hravn shook his head slowly. "Why do I feel as if I've been stitched up again?

Gunnar beamed. "It'll be my pleasure, my Lady."

Ealdgith kicked Hravn's ankle. "Don't dally then, I'll be your squire and get you dressed. That mail shirt will take some getting used to."

Aebbe followed Ealdgith as she and Hravn went to change into their armour. Aebbe was captivated by Hravn's mail shirt and helmet as she had never seen her father wear his. Ealdgith was amazed at how flexible the mail was. Although it was heavy to lift, Hravn said that the weight was less than he had imagined when it was spread over his shoulders. Ealdgith pulled her padded leather waistcoat on, buckled it and slipped the leather helmet over her head before turning and springing cat-like in front of Aebbe. The girl froze, screamed and fled. Ealdgith pulled her helmet off and ran after her. "Aebbe, Aebbe...don't run, come back, I only meant to tease you, not scare you. Come, let me explain."

Hravn practised moving with his sword, feeling the weight and pull of the leather and mail on his torso. Ealdgith sat and reassured Aebbe.

"Hravn and I are returning to our lands on the other side of the high fells. There has been fighting and bad people have taken over our manors and are harming the people whom we must look after."

Aebbe nodded, worried, listening.

"Your father is a good Lord, he cares for his people and they look up to him. That is how it should be, but it is no longer like that in our lands. That is why we must go back and see how we can help our people. Hravn must be prepared to fight and I must fight with him, to protect his back and to keep him safe."

Aebbe nodded again, her eyes and mouth wide in surprise and admiration. "But you're a lady. Moder didn't know how to fight."

Ealdgith smiled and took Aebbe's hand. "Yes, but I was taught by a very special soldier, one who once served our king and who now serves God. He taught us both that it was right to fight to protect the lives of our people, and what he taught me has already saved our lives. Watch us practise and you will see how; and later, I will tell you some of the tales of my people, our people, for they are your moder's people's stories too."

Hravn and Ealdgith practised between themselves for the next three days. Ealdgith was reassured that the jerkin and leather helmet didn't slow her much and they gave her confidence when she threw herself at Hravn's legs to unbalance him. She also welcomed the anonymity that the helmet gave her; she could watch Hravn and read his intentions without giving her own away. She pushed herself harder and closer to Hravn's sword line than she would have risked in the past and several times felt the thump of the wooden hilt on her back or head. They were blows that would have hurt or stunned her if she hadn't worn the armour. Ealdgith sensed that her skills were returning to a level that Oswin would be proud of and, at last, she was ready to take on Gunnar. His bulk and strength intimidated her, but she also knew that she could turn these advantages against him.

Hravn found that the mail and helm took a lot of getting used to. Their protection reassured him, but he felt more detached from the fight and at first, his reactions were slow. With constant wear, the leather jerkin became more flexible and as he became more accustomed to the weight and movement of the mail, his confidence began to grow. He reasoned that although the armour might slow him, any armoured Norman soldier would be similarly encumbered.

That evening, as Hravn sat rubbing lanolin into the leather of the waistcoat in order to improve its suppleness and help the chain mail slide over it smoothly without rubbing, he felt as if he was massaging his new outer skin. It was a strange feeling as he suddenly realised how important his armour was and how it was going to become very much a part of his body. He felt that he was changing from boyhood, to manhood, to warrior-hood all too quickly. The smell of the lanolin and the leather mingled with the wood smoke from the hearth, adding a new smell to the many that permeated the longhouse. Ealdgith sat with Aebbe, snuggled on a pile of fleeces in the corner of a bench-back, the bright firelight reflecting as red glints in her green eyes as she recounted the stories of her people's heroic past. Tyr squatted by the hearth and looked in awe at Hravn, and wondered about the life of a warrior.   In his mind's eye, he saw Hravn as the hero of the tales.

Ealdgith told how many hundreds of years ago, her people had lived on the other side of the wide Northern sea, where there had been many kingdoms along the frontiers of the lands of the Romans.   She concentrated on those stories where ladies had fought alongside men or worn armour to protect themselves in a violent world.

Ealdgith finished with the story of Waldere and Hildegyth; the boy and girl who had been sent as hostages by their fathers to grow up in the court of the fearsome Attila the Hun.   Attila had demanded that all the kings that he controlled must send him their male heirs as hostages for their loyalty.   Hildegyth's brother was only a young child and would never have survived the journey to the distant land of the Huns and, although she was only Aebbe's age, she offered to go in his place, pretending to be a boy. Hildegyth trained as a warrior, met Waldere and, as they grew to adulthood, they fell in love.

They knew they must escape and return to their own people before Hildegyth was discovered and forced to marry, and so they fled taking a hoard of Attila's gold in two large chests carried by their horses.   Theirs was a long journey, over high mountains and through forests along the great German rivers.   They were discovered whilst travelling through the lands of an enemy of Waldere's people and they were hunted down by greedy King Gudhere who wanted their gold.

They fought many battles, with Hyldegyth always fighting at Waldere's back, protecting him whilst he slew their foes. In the end, only King Gudhere was left standing. Waldere was hurt badly and Hyldegyth saved him by agreeing to show Gudhere the gold; but she was cunning. She showed King Gudhere only one of the two hidden chests. He took it and ran. Waldere felt that he had failed Hyldegyth, but she told him not to worry for they would never be troubled by King Gudhere again. She had given him a chest full of gold trinkets and jewellery that belonged to Attila himself and had kept the chest full of Roman coins well hidden. She knew that once King Gudhere started to display all of Attila's stolen trinkets, his spies would hear and that Attila would destroy King Gudhere and his people.

Aebbe was thrilled. Her eyes never left Ealdgith's face as she told the tale. When Ealdgith finished, she giggled. "That sounds just like you and Hravn," before adding, more seriously, "now I know why you must dress and fight like a warrior."

At last, they each felt confident to face Gunnar's ox-like strength. Tyr helped his father dress in his mail shirt and helmet. "Fader, have you ever had to fight as a warrior?" Gunnar could sense the concern in his son's voice.

"No, Tyr, thankfully in my lifetime we've seen peace in the vale, but I could always be called upon by our liege-lord."

"But who is our liege-lord?" Gunnar laughed. "You might well ask; as I said to Hravn, I look to Gospatrick, but really this land south of the Eamont falls to the English king. God forbid he comes calling and so I look to Gospatrick and he looks to the Scots. We all keep our heads down and trust in Wyrd."

Tyr wasn't impressed by the politics, but he was impressed by his father's warrior-like appearance, and he carried his steel helm with pride as they walked out to meet Hravn by the rocks at the entrance to the longhouse.

Gunnar lifted the wooden practice sword, shifting it from hand to hand. "Well, I've never cleaved a man's skull with one of these before!" He chuckled, as he brandished it above his head.

Aebbe screamed as she ran at him. "No, Fader, you can't! I won't let you!" He spun around and scooped her up. "Neither will I, my angel. I tease to unsettle my challenger, but I will never hurt my dearest friends; you know that. Come, watch with Edie."

The holmganga followed the pattern of their contest with Oswin. Gunnar lacked Oswin's skill and guile, but he was powerful. Hravn found that he had to let his sword arm roll with the force of Gunnar's blows, but what he lacked in strength, he made up for with agility and speed. He danced around Gunnar, tiring the larger man, taking blows onto his mail that sent him staggering until he sensed the time was right to break into Gunnar's sword circle. He parried Gunnar's sword with his seax and, ducking under the sword with his own wooden Nadr, he caught Gunnar with a swift strike to the leg that would have been crippling had the blades been steel.

Gunnar flinched and stepped back, holding up his hand in a salute. "I concede, Hravn, you're as good as I ever was. No, you are better. You've mastered wearing armour and can certainly handle that long seax and a sword. The Normans should fear you."

Hravn tapped him on the shoulder with his wooden blade, "Thanks, Gunnar, that's praise indeed. Now, let's see how Edie fares."

Ealdgith squeezed Aebbe's hand, bade Sköll and Hati to stay and stepped forward, tightening her helmet chin strap.

"Now, remember Gunnar," she cautioned, "this is just a practice, not a contest."

He chuckled, "Are they not always one and the same? But I will spare your bruises."

Ealdgith faced him, just outside his sword circle, swaying slowly from side to side. She held her long practice seax in her right hand and a shorter wooden seax in her left. Her green eyes were fixed on Gunnar's as he shifted his sword from hand to hand. Gunnar teased her at first, pulling his blows, but Ealdgith always danced sideways or backwards, spinning and twisting, avoiding the swing and thrust of his sword. Gunnar began to appreciate the challenge she posed and he became more focussed and assertive. Ealdgith kept moving, always facing Gunnar, encouraging him to waste energy by swinging at her constantly moving body.

Ealdgith began to read and anticipate Gunnar's intentions and observed that he never aimed below the bottom of her padded jerkin. She knew that she was being unfair, but she sensed that she could use Gunnar's chivalry against him. Using the experience of her previous fights, she deliberately feinted to her right. As Gunnar responded with a hard blow to his left to counter her, she stepped back to give herself space and then dived under his sword and flung her weight into his knees, wrapping her arms around his ankles and twisting onto her back. It was the last thing Gunnar expected.

The weight of his mailed body added to his momentum and he fell heavily into the empty space in front of him. Ealdgith rolled and leapt onto the back of his prostrate body, pressing the wooden blade of her practice seax against Gunnar's neck. She stood up to claim victory as Gunnar rolled slowly onto his back and roared with laughter, before sitting up and rubbing his bruised knees.

Ealdgith gave a low bow. "I fear that the bruises are yours, my lord Gunnar. Do I pass?" He nodded, still winded.

Aebbe flew to Ealdgith, awe-struck, and reached up to give her a kiss before taking pity on her father and jumped into his lap, winding him further.

~~~

As haerfest came to an end, they each spent more time with Tyr and Aebbe; as they both put off the day when they must take their leave. Both children were very taken by Hravn's horn and he spent time teaching them all his hunting calls. Tyr had a musical ear and quickly copied all Hravn played; Aebbe struggled and Ealdgith was note perfect herself by the time Aebbe had mastered the haunting notes of The Bear's personal call. "You've a lot to answer for there," Gunnar teased. "They'll want one apiece once you leave. They'll never share. I'll never know peace again."

Neither wanted to be the first to talk of setting a day to begin their journey home, as each felt that home was Gunnar's manor. The period of daylight was already shorter than the length of the night when a sudden sharp frost changed everything. Almost overnight, the oak and ash leaves were tinged with growing patches of red and orange. Hravn squeezed Ealdgith's hand. "It's time," he said, resignedly.

The eve of their day of departure came at last. They packed as much dry, smoked and salted food as possible into the space left in their saddle bags and filled their water sacks from the spring. Gunnar threw a feast in their honour

273

and it was well into the afternoon before they sat to eat; Aleifr having sweated over a roasting lamb most of the day. Mildgyd joined them, as did Ulf and his wife. Mildgyd covered Magni carefully with her shawl as he suckled at her breast. Gunnar poured cups of mead and ale and, thumping the table with his fist, proposed a toast to a successful reunion with The Bear and revenge upon the Normans.

Hravn laughed, rose, thanked Gunnar for all his hospitality and then paused before adding, "I think revenge is a lot to hope for my Lord. Survival might be all we can ask under the Normans, but I have a mind that we can perhaps make life a little more difficult for them."

"Well said, Hravn, well said!" Gunnar cheered enthusiastically and then presented Hravn with a Thor's hammer on a neck chain, quipping that he was "a true Viking at last."

Hravn looked serious. "My Lord, we have no gifts for you in return, save our heartfelt and life-long thanks and friendship; but we do have a little something for two very special young people."

With that, Ealdgith swung her hands from behind her back and presented Tyr with a small bone-handled seax, its blade engraved with a raven, its wings outspread. "The raven is Hravn's namesake, for you to remember him by; and for you, my very special friend I have a new friend for you."

Ealdgith turned to Aebbe and flourished a small leather collar and leash. "If you run to the stable, you will find a brindled collie pup that I just happened to find in the village. She is yours to name as you please." Aebbe looked from Ealdgith to the stable door, ran to kiss Ealdgith, then almost fell over her skirt as she dashed from the room, returning moments later with a mewing puppy in her arms. "She's to be called Edie," Aebbe said, with a cheeky smile.

"Thank you, my friends, those are all the gifts I could ever want." Gunnar's appreciation was heartfelt as he knew Aebbe's heart would not now be broken by Ealdgith's departure.

Later, the children having fallen asleep and the servants having departed, Gunnar leant forward across the table towards Hravn and Ealdgith, his chin resting on his giant fists, his bright blue eyes catching their gaze. "I know this may be the ale talking," he paused, "but take this as the advice of an uncle, for that is how it is meant. You are both young and the future is not known. Do not rush to have a family. One day, you will be the best of parents, I can see that, but that time is not now. If you fulfil your love for each other, there will be consequences, there always are, so be prepared and plan. If you have a child, you must be able to care and provide and that may be difficult if you are living in the forest and fighting the Normans. Life can be cruel too, as it was for me. After we had Tyr and Aebbe, Aelfgifu fell with child three more times and each was still-born. The pain of those losses nearly broke our hearts. We were over joyed when Magni was borne with a healthy scream, but moments later, Aelfgifu began to bleed and it could not be stopped.

Bide your time. Edie, when you find The Bear, seek out the birthing women and ask for their guidance as to which herbs to use to lessen the chance of conceiving. I know the church does not favour such actions, but it can help save you both from much distress..." He stopped, a distant, sad, look in his eyes.

They looked at each other and at Gunnar's sad and serious face. The fun had gone from the evening, but Gunnar's openness pulled them both closer to him. Ealdgith spoke for them both. "Gunnar, we understand, for we have spoken of it already. You are right. I am sure too that you have a mindfulness of a woman's situation that few men have. We already plan to do as you say...but thank you." Ealdgith leant forward, grasped Gunnar's big fists in her hands and kissed his cheek.

Chapter 23

Two strings, each of three ponies, splashed through the shallow ford, kicking up fountains of glistening droplets that dissuaded the panting children from running after them any further. Hravn gave a whoop and a wave urging his line of ponies up the far bank. Ealdgith turned one last time, called "Farewell, Aebbe, look after Edie 'til we return," and blew a kiss towards the breathless children.

"Come on, Edie, we need to cross the Eden at Aplebi and be well along the east fellside before we find a camp for tonight." Hravn was keen to put several leagues behind them and make a good start to their return. He sensed that they would both find the journey more difficult if they tarried over long in the comfort of Eden's vale and Gunnar's lands. They crossed the wooden bridge at Aplebi without pausing to water the ponies, both wanting to be across the broad river and clear of the manor where they had fought the Pendragons for their freedom. They could see the wood where they had killed Urien and Owain in the distance on the skyline above the small town. It looked very different now; a cheerful blaze of yellow and orange leaves belying the horror that they had experienced there.

Men who were working nearby, repairing the low lynchet banks that formed the boundaries between narrow strips of fields that bordered the Eden did not look up as the ponies passed along the narrow tracks between the fields. Ealdgith was relieved. It was a sign that their presence didn't attract unnatural interest and, with luck, they would be taken for merchants travelling between markets. She wondered if it would be the same once they were east of the Pennines. Sköll and Hati ran ahead, constantly glancing back to check that the ponies were following. They had learnt from bitter experience to avoid the fell ponies' quick hooves.

It was a day of broken cloud and sunshine and Hravn was unsure how the weather would develop. He didn't want to face the gloom of a wet night on the Pennines' east fellside, exposed to the winds that could whip in from the Cumbraland fells behind them to the west. Shielding his eyes with his seax hand, he peered into the sun light ahead. He called back to Ealdgith, who was leading the second string of pack ponies. "There, Edie, beyond yon strip of wood, you can see the line of the old road, it'll give us easy going onto the tops."

Ealdgith replied, shouting ahead, her voice almost drowned by the birdsong that carried on the breeze. "We'll pause when we get there. The ponies need a breather, as do I. I'm too long out of the saddle."

The late-haerfest sun was already following a more southerly track these days. As he reached the old road, Hravn paused, allowing Ealdgith to catch up alongside him. Just then the sun broke through the clouds, throwing a bright shaft of light onto the bold flat-topped fell across the valley to their right.

"Look, Edie!" Hravn was almost ecstatic. "That could be a sign from Wyrd. See how the light hits Boar Fell and Ravenstandale and highlights the gloom of Mallerstang behind. Mayhap that promises good will overcome evil. We beat the evil of the Pendragons and we can beat the evil of the Normans too."

Ealdgith smiled, but said nothing. She had no illusions about the difficulties ahead. The beauty of the scene impressed her though and, as she looked from the little cameo of light playing against dark and gazed across the width of the vale of Eden to the Cumbraland fells beyond, she suddenly felt a pang of leaving; of leaving a place that she could perhaps call her home.

After a long look, Ealdgith tore her eyes away. "Come on then, show me this road you've told me so much about." She immediately understood why Hravn was so keen to take advantage of the old road. The road led the way up the dale, deviating only slightly to avoid craggy outcrops. The width of a manor house in places, it was firm underfoot with great blocks of stone knit together, the gaps filled with coarse packed gravel. Its great age was obvious. Where it ran across areas of bog, stretches of the stone paving had sunk, and water seeped through forming small mossy pools. In other places, reeds and thistles had taken hold and were forcing the stones further apart. She had seen a road like this before. It was similar to the one that crossed the river Swale beyond Hindrelag, linking Euruic to the lands further north; but, like Hravn, she was always impressed by the skill of the people of old and she wondered how much else they had done that was now forgotten.

The old road was deserted, just as Brother Patrick had said it would be. "I remember this stretch from one of my trips with The Bear, but it was certainly busier then. Where are the merchants and market traders?"

"It's not a good sign; it certainly shows how life in Ghellinges-scir must have changed." Ealdgith was quite circumspect. "At least the quieter the better for us right now."

Hravn glanced up at the sun to gain a feel for the time "I reckon we could do another couple of leagues at least and we can travel more quickly now. I think we should find a camp by the foot of the saddle in the fells ahead, before the ground climbs more steeply. Then tomorrow, we will head south over the tops."

Ealdgith nodded agreement. "I think you're right. Much as I would like to follow the road and take the easy route, I fear that once we cross the border between Westmoringaland and Ghellinges-scir, and get near to Bogas, we will risk meeting a Norman patrol. I am sure that they will guard this route, they have to."

"I'm afraid so, Edie. If we are to head home by the Swale, we have to cross the high ground to the right of the road and head south for several leagues. That's tomorrow's journey, and it will be slow going."

The clouds gradually cleared away to the east and the day became increasingly warm and humid. Hravn began to sweat under the padded jerkin and mail shirt that he had worn, rather than pack. He could feel sweat trickling down between his shoulder blades and pooling in the small of his back, his breeches grew clammy. He rather regretted his decision to wear his armour, but he knew that he had to get used to its weight and limitations, as would his pony; and he now understood why Oswin had been so keen on bathing. Ealdgith laughed; after all, she had told him so.

The upper stretches of the valley were quite heavily wooded with mixed hazel, birch and oak. Stumpy, jagged peaks lined the ridge to their left; it was a forbidding, yet protective, barrier. They made good time. The ponies trotting sure-footedly along the paved surface whilst Hravn and Ealdgith became lost in their own thoughts as they watched the buzzards circle on the wind above the fell sides. The silence was broken only by the strike of hooves on stone, the rustle of drying leaves in the wind and the haunting mewing of the buzzards' calls. Ealdgith felt as if they were making a journey through a no-man's land; from the safety of the vale to the unseen danger in the hidden valleys beyond the horizon.

Hravn's mind focused on their more immediate needs. "There we are, Edie! That'll do for us. Look!" He reined the pony to a halt and called back, pointing to a stand of junipers at the base of a limestone crag by a beck with a small waterfall. "The ground looks to be dry and flat, and the trees will give us some cover from wind and view." He mused to himself as he dismounted and led the ponies forward that it was rare to find juniper so high, maybe it was another good omen? As he got closer to the waterfall he was seized with the desire to cool off; and shouted "Tether the ponies, Edie, I'm for a quick dip!"

Ealdgith laughed, calling back, "You'll regret it, you're no Oswin." Hravn cursed as he fumbled to unbuckle the mail shirt and drew it slowly over his head before quickly stripping off his remaining clothes and jumping from the low grassy bank into the deep, clear, peaty black pool at the foot of the waterfall.

"By Hodr, that's cold!" His voice was an octave higher than normal as he called to Ealdgith. "Can I entice you in?" She laughed and shook her head, by which time Hravn was already hauling himself onto the grass bank to dry off in the sun. Ealdgith turned to busy herself tethering the ponies and gather kindling and wood. A loud smack and muttered curse caused her to turn back to Hravn. He was sitting up, smacking his naked torso with one hand whilst the other scratched his tussled, wet hair.

"Let me guess. Midges, perhaps?" Ealdgith teased him and, smiling, said "I told you that you'd regret it." She threw him a blanket to dry himself. "Get dressed whilst I get a fire going, the smoke will clear them," and then added with a sideways smile, "at least your ardour is cooler now; best to make yourself useful." Hravn laughed, remembering wistfully how he had felt the last time they had both bathed.

After watering the ponies at the pool and feeding the dogs on dry meat and bone meal, they ate a simple meal of hard cheese and oat cakes. Whilst in Morlund Hravn had bought an expensive wool blanket made from thick Herdwick fleece. It had been shrunk to tighten the weave and then rubbed in lanolin to enhance its already good waterproofing. He placed it on the ground in the lee of a large juniper bush and then pulled a softer blanket over them. "That should at least keep the damp from our bones. I wish we had had it when we were first in the forest." He leant over and kissed Ealdgith. She snuggled backwards into him, already half asleep. Hati stretched out on her other side, and yawned.

The night changed around them. Stars gradually disappeared as the clouds lowered onto the high fell tops and, as first light broke in a dull gloom, a sudden wind blew down the fell-side. Hravn woke with a jump, felt the first damp breath of mist on his cheeks and cursed.

This was not the weather he wanted. Heavy black cloud hung over the valley head and long strands of white mist draped over the crag sides. It wasn't raining, but he instinctively knew that it soon would. He nudged Ealdgith in the small of her back and rather brusquely muttered, "Come on Edie, we're going to have to move." Ealdgith was about to chide him for being ill tempered, but when she opened her eyes she knew he was right.

Hravn's mood brightened. "I know, there is an old stone tower by the road, just over this first coll. The ancients built it, probably the Romans, because the walls are of the same hard stone as the collapsed fort at Bogas. It will give us some shelter. When The Bear and I were last there, an inner floor was still in place and gave some cover from the rain."

Within minutes, they had broken camp, stowed the blankets, placed packs on the ponies' backs and were leading them towards the old road. The hounds stood for a moment, scowling at the mass of cloud that swirled all around; a wet day loomed.

The mist was almost down to the road by the time they reached it. "There is no way we could risk crossing the tops in this; at least with the road we can keep to safe ground and maintain our direction." Hravn nodded in agreement with Ealdgith's statement of the obvious.

White tentacles of cloud surrounded them. Ealdgith felt as if she was being sucked into a damp and gloomy nether-world. Everything was grey. Even the grass and heather of the high moorland was coated in clinging grey droplets. She worried that they would never find the tower and end up walking straight into the arms of the Normans. The hounds sensed her trepidation and stayed close, casting wary eyes around them.

Hravn was a lot more confident. He had travelled this way with The Bear and experienced the dense hill fog of the high moors before. "Don't worry, Edie, the tower is four or five furlongs further on. We'll see it to the left of the road, there's a faint track that leads to it and peaty ground just before. I'll find it;" and find it he did.

"Hravn, you're my hero! How do you do it?" Ealdgith was incredulous and very relieved. He laughed, "I've told you. I'm hefted to all these fells, just like my people's sheep are. It must be my Cumbric blood. After all, we have been here longer than anyone else."

The tower loomed out of the mist. Its walls were a darker grey than the clouds and Hravn sensed rather than saw it at first. The hounds' hackles rose as they sniffed the air trying to work out what it was. A faint track did indeed lead through the scrub and heather. It was as if nothing could grow on ground that had been trodden on by the warriors of old.

The track led across a ditch and through a low earth bank towards an entrance gaping in the south side of the moss-covered stones that formed a squat square tower. It looked old and foreboding, but at least it was a shelter from the rain that was now increasingly blowing in from the west.

Leaving the ponies outside for the moment, Hravn led Ealdgith inside. It was surprisingly still and dry, but dark. Hravn felt around the inner walls until he found what he sought, some dry wood from the fallen roof timbers that he remembered had been piled in a corner. Two years ago, he had helped The Bear throw them down from the upper storeys for use in just such an eventuality. He scraped away earth from the central floor to reveal stone flags and then, taking some kindling from his pouch, he struck sparks from his flint and steel to ignite the kindling, blowing gently until the dry wood caught alight.

"Edie, The Bear always set a small fire here. If we keep it low and away from the rafters, we should be alright." As the flames grew Ealdgith could see that there was a ceiling a man's height above them, but it was much lower than the walls outside. Hravn said, "There is another floor above this one, but the ladders have long since collapsed. I dare say we could both get up there if we tried, but I don't know how strong the ceiling is. The upper roof has fallen in, but the floor above was still dry when I was here two sumors past. I might climb up later and see if there is more dry timber to hand. For now, we'll get the packs inside and hobble the ponies in the ditch. They'll have some shelter there and should be happy to graze."

They lugged the packs inside, saw to the ponies' needs and built a larger fire that lit the room all-round. Smoke billowed under the ceiling and then found its own way out through the gaping doorway and also through the hatch in the ceiling into the upper room. Ealdgith was surprised at how big the room was; a large group of warriors could certainly have lived there. Hravn spread the Herdwick rug on top of the stone flags and left Ealdgith to prepare a rudimentary meal. Taking a water sack, he went in search of a spring that he knew was a half furlong or so down the slope to the west. Sköll followed, keeping very close; he was far from confident in the mist.

The rain persisted. It wasn't heavy but it was constant and wind driven. The ponies moved their way around to the shelter of the earth bank and eastern ditch and Hravn left them there. He was sure that they would prefer to be in the open in their natural element than forced into cover in the smoky tower.

The day dragged on. There was nothing that they could do until the cloud lifted and allowed them to see their way clearly across the tops to the south. Hravn kept checking on the ponies and Ealdgith kept the fire going. Later, when it became obvious that they would have to stay overnight, Hravn tied a damp cloth over his mouth and swung his way up into the smoky room above. Ealdgith passed him a lit torch and he groped around to find more wood, much of it bits of old furniture that he threw back down the hatchway before lowering himself down, coughing and red eyed from smoke. Ealdgith laughed at him and pushed him towards the entrance "Ugh! you poor thing, you smell and look like a kipper. You'd best go outside and clear your eyes and chest. Thank you for the wood, at least it should last us 'til dawn."

The gloom faded into an early dusk; the low fire's flickering flame light reflected back from the entrails of grey mist that crept around the doorway. Hravn and Ealdgith huddled with the hounds under a blanket, and talked through their plans. Hravn was adamant that, although the old road was the easiest route, it was too open and they could be seen and intercepted by a Norman patrol. He assumed that the border would be watched and neither of them wanted to take that risk; their pack-ponies and the armour and weapons they carried would raise immediate suspicion and questions. Hravn favoured a route south from the Stanmoir summit, following the broad, rolling ridge lines until they descended to the Norse settlement at Kelda. It would be a slow rough route over harsh high moorland, without any cover and skirting wet peat bogs, but he was confident that they would not be observed and that they could do it in one day. He hoped that, at Kelda, they would find out more about conditions lower down Swaledale and could then work out the next stage in their route.

It was a long, cold night and Ealdgith struggled to sleep. She could hear water dripping on the floor around them and she dreaded what they would find in the morning. Try as she might, she could not get thoughts of what the Normans were building at Richemund out of her mind. She had a nagging worry that Richemund was her home at Hindrelag. It was the only strong defensible hill she could think of; but if they were building a military camp there, what did that mean for her people? Her thoughts were becoming a nagging worry. Hravn had said, "We'll cross that ford when we get to it", but she knew that he too was concerned.

Ealdgith finally slipped into a deep sleep sometime before dawn and was woken by Hravn shaking her shoulder enthusiastically. "Come on, Edie, its stopped raining and the clouds have lifted a bit. Here, have an oatcake and then we can get going."

Ealdgith, still groggy after the fitful night, rubbed sleep from her eyes and propped herself up on her elbows. She wasn't inspired by Hravn's enthusiasm. Although the rain had stopped, she could see through the open doorway that heavy grey clouds hovered just above the fell tops. As she chewed the oatcake and drank from the water sack, she mused about just how wet underfoot it was going to be, but it would certainly be better than another day imprisoned in the wet and smoky tower.

Chapter 24

The journey over the top of the moors was as slow and hard-going as Ealdgith had feared. Quaking mossy bogs repeatedly blocked their way, and they were forced to dismount and explore alternative ways around the treacherous ground, leading the strings of ponies by hand. Hravn again wore all his armour and its added weight slowed him down as he sank to his ankles in the clinging peat. Eventually, he let Ealdgith take over. He maintained their general direction across the featureless tops whilst Ealdgith concentrated on the detail of how they would cover the next half furlong.

Fortunately, the mist lifted gradually and by late afternoon, a weak sun broke through and warmed their backs as they crested the edge of the dale high above the little settlement of Kelda. Thin columns of blue wood-smoke rose from several of the small, turf-roofed buildings that clustered on a platform of flat land above the steep, rocky sides of the River Swale's gorge.

Hravn knew that they would be spotted well before they had made their way down the fellside and, as the steep slope started to level out, they were met by several young children running towards them, calling a welcome in a broad Norse dialect similar to that of the Norse of the vale of Eden. The children, who were all barefoot and wore ragged clothes, clustered around the ponies wanting to know who they were, where they were from and why they were visiting their village – because no one ever visited. Hravn reined the ponies to a halt, jumped down and grasped the outstretched hands smiling. "Whoa, too many questions, give me a chance."

"I'm Hravn of Ravenstandale," he said in Norse. Before Hravn could introduce Ealdgith, a fair-haired boy interrupted. "Are you a warrior?" Hravn paused, smiling. He looked at Ealdgith then, ruffling the boy on the head, answered "Yes I am, and may I also introduce my wife, Lady Ealdgith of Hindrelag."

The children all gasped and turned to stare at Ealdgith, a mixture of surprise, awe and admiration on their faces – a 'lady' had never been to their village. "Are you a warrior too?" a small girl asked hesitantly. Her accent was difficult for Ealdgith to understand. She slid off her pony, unbuckled her helmet, placed her hand on the hilt of her seax, tugged the bow that was slung over her shoulder and laughed with a wide smile. "Yes, I suppose I am, when I need to be."

The girl continued to stare at Ealdgith. "I have never seen a lady, or a warrior…" It was a simple statement and the girl was lost for words. Ealdgith crouched down, took her hand and said, "Why don't you walk with us and take me to your village. You can introduce me to your parents." The girl grinned and ran alongside Ealdgith, holding her hand. Two of the older boys ran ahead to tell the village headman that they had special guests.

Kelda was small; barely a dozen low-roofed small longhouses clustered on or around the level ground. Some were linked together, as if the longhouses had grown over the years as the families within had expanded. A group of men were gathering outside the largest house as the children led Hravn and Ealdgith down the fellside. As they neared the group, the girl let go of Ealdgith's hand and ran to a stocky, balding man standing in the centre, his hands on his hips. "Fader, Fader, this is Lady Ealdgith. She is a warrior."

The men were little better clothed than the children and, as Hravn looked around, he could see that the houses were all in need of some repair. It was a village that teetered on the edge of survival. Hravn led the way and held out his hand to the girl's father, introducing themselves.

He responded, "I'm Frode. Headman. What is your business here? Few visit so you must have good reason."

Hravn understood Frode's suspicion. Frode listened and the men around him nodded glumly as Hravn quickly summarised their Aefter Yule story. Frode spat and cursed at mention of Pendragon. "He has caused us grief in the past, anyone who has brought him harm is a friend of ours." When Hravn described their escape and how Ealdgith and he had killed Urien, Owain and their men, she saw the men's looks of wry amusement at her dress and weapons change to one of surprise and admiration. In their society, a warrior was always respected, regardless of their sex.

Frode needed no more convincing. "Hravn, Lady Ealdgith, welcome. Come, stay with my family tonight and tomorrow we will have a feast in your honour. As you see, we are not a rich village…," he paused and looked around for effect, "but your visit honours us and your fight with Pendragon is a joy to hear. We must talk of the Normans too, for they are a grave threat to us all." He turned to his daughter. "Agata, run and tell your moder that we have guests."

The next day's feast was, indeed, a real honour. The people of Kelda had already started to slaughter animals for the winter and Hravn knew that by feasting now, they risked going hungry later in the season. He knew that he could not refuse such generosity, but was well aware that those who give the most often own the least. He must find a way to leave some payment with Frode when they left. He also realised the benefit of having the loyalty and support of the remoter dales' communities. This could be invaluable in the days to come.

The feast was held in the middle of the day. Villagers busied themselves carrying trestle tables and benches from their houses to a central area amidst the clustered houses. The younger wives tended a pig that they turned on a spit over an open fire, whilst Frode presided over the feast. He claimed the top table that was set slightly higher than the others. Hravn sat to his right and Ealdgith to his left. Frode's wife, Edda, sat on Ealdgith's left whilst an older man, Alfr, sat with Hravn.

The younger men and elder girls served the meat on large wooden platters, placing it in front of Frode where he could place meat onto his guests' wooden plates. There was also salted trout and goat and plenty of fresh bread; and, for dessert, sweet freshly-harvested apples from the trees that grew along the river bank and a little honey on buttered bread. There was plenty of local beer and more than enough mead made from heather honey. The villagers' generosity was overwhelming and Ealdgith said as much to Frode.

"The honour really is ours." Frode was emphatic. "Pendragon has long plagued our lives. We mine lead here that we send to Penrith and Carleol. It is an easier market to serve than using the route down the dale to Gellinghes, but Pendragon's men too often ambush our ponies and demand a costly tribute that we can't afford. From what you say, we are less likely to be threatened in future, although I fear that the Dark Lord will be a curse on us all so long as he lives."

Hravn interrupted to ask about lead mining and Frode leant across to introduce him to Alfr who was the oldest of their miners.

As Ealdgith's conversation with Frode ended, Edda turned to her. "Lady Edie, we have never had anyone of your status here, and rarely have we seen a warrior. Now you come as a lady and a warrior. How so, for I cannot see how it is possible to be both, let alone for one so young?"

Edda was very forthright, but Ealdgith could see that her blunt, matter of fact, approach was simply her nature; for Edda's character was naturally warm and friendly, almost motherly. Whilst Edda's accent was stronger than Ealdgith was used to, she could understand it. She was aware that the women of the small Dales' settlements rarely travelled more than a few miles in their lives and that village dialects varied considerably.

Ealdgith nodded her head slowly, smiling, "It is something I wonder about myself. It is Wryd's way for me, I suppose." She paused to gather her thoughts and then told Edda more about her family, the Aefter Yule destruction of her people's way of life, her escape with Hravn and the need to pose as a boy.

Edda was just asking, "But why a warrior?" when Ealdgith told her about meeting Brother Oswin and their realisation that they would one day need to fight to protect themselves. "It was probably then that I realised that Hravn and I could always be together. Until then, I was destined to be married for my family's benefit, to some lord with land, but the one good thing to come from all this suffering is that Hravn and

I are now sworn to each other. It is as if we are two sides of the same coin. Together, we are much stronger than either us would be by ourselves."

Edda interrupted, placing her hand on Ealdgith's arm. "Lady Edie, I must say you are truly rare and gifted. Your family is connected to some of the most powerful, yet you happily live as one of us. You are as much at home with the Norse and the Cumbri as you are with your own people, and you have the skill and strength of mind to face a man in a fight. That is rare indeed."

Ealdgith blushed. She was truly touched. "Thank you, Edda, I think you know me better than I do myself. We promised Brother Oswin that we would only use the skills he taught us for self-defence and the protection of others. It is a promise I mean to keep. I hope we can use our skills for our people in Gellinghes-scir or in the service of my cousin, Earl Gospatrick, but I am sure that too is in the hands of Wyrd." She paused to take a sip of mead. "I am saddened by the loss of my family, but not distraught. At first, I just felt numb, but no more. If I am honest, Hravn's family have always been closer than kin to me and it is their loss that I fear. That, and the suffering of all the families on our manors. They always welcomed me as one of their own and, though I was but a child, they always asked what I thought. They are my people." Ealdgith paused, her eyes unfocused, thinking of her people and turned to Edda again.

"I have rarely talked to another woman all year, there is much I want to ask you…"

They put their heads together and talked as sisters or best friends do.

Hravn spent much of the feast learning about lead mining and smelting. He knew how lead was used, but not how it was extracted and processed. He was fascinated and was sure that there was scope for the little villages to prosper, if only the lead could be taken to a proper market. Hravn realised too that Frode and Alfr were very worried about what would happen if the Normans discovered the potential riches under the ground. He was sure they would soon find out.

Frode advised Hravn not to follow the river-side track down the dale. "The Bastard's men slaughtered all at Rie. I was there in early sumor. There was naught but skeletons and the black stumps of the wall-posts of the houses." Frode spat as a he cursed the name of the King William and then sat staring, lost for a while in the memory of Rie, and the horror of what could befall them all.

"I fear that the small Norse villages between us and Rie may be next," Alfr added, "and I doubt the Normans realised they were there when they burnt Rie, but I am sure they will find them soon enough."

"Aye," Frode said eventually. "It's best you take the fell-top route over the ridges to Langethwait in Arkengarthdale. I hear Langethwait escaped too, but not for long, I fear."

~~~

Hravn and Ealdgith stayed at Kelda for another day before moving on. In truth, Hravn had rather a heavy head on the morning after the feast. Ealdgith had drunk more water than mead and mischievously teased Hravn as he screwed up his eyes to keep out the daylight and cursed the very thought of ale. "We can't make our way over the tops whilst I feel like this," he moaned. "I hope Frode will host us for another day?"

"He will if you spend the morning chopping logs. Edda's already agreed," Ealdgith added, after a pause to let the notion of chopping logs sink in. "You'll feel better for some exercise."

The day of their departure was clear and bright, though a cold nip in the wind heralded the start of winter. They crossed the Swale over a narrow wooden bridge below some waterfalls and then made their way slowly up the steep side of the gorge, fording another river that plummeted into the Swale in a series of rocky tumbles. The fellside was too steep for them to ride the laden ponies and they zig-zagged up slowly, to gain height, until they finally felt the gradient ease and they could see the rounded top of the ridge line in front. Hravn called a halt; his lungs felt as if they were bursting from the effort of climbing whilst wearing mail. The ponies were winded too, and they stood together in a small group, panting.

Having regained their breath, they mounted and quickly rode the final half furlong to the top. "Look, Edie," Hravn was enthusiastic. "See how Swaledale winds its way towards the east and the ridge line follows a couple of leagues to the north, skirting around the tops of the valleys that feed into the dale."

Ealdgith's eyes followed the line of the ridge route. "It seems to merge into high ground in yon blue haze. How far do you reckon it is?"

"No more than four or five leagues. We'll stop just beyond that high ground. Arkengarthdale is the other side. We'll camp above the dale tonight and then cross at Langethwait at first light."

The ground was firmer than the high moors a few days earlier and they made good time. Steep, heavily wooded valleys fell away to their right. Hravn found a track that Frode had told him about and it helped them make their way more quickly through the low scrub, heather and coarse grass.

"We should remember this way, Hravn, in case we need it in the future. It is certainly a quick way out over the tops." Ealdgith was quick to appreciate the value of the almost secret route.

The track led them to the top of the fell that Ealdgith had seen earlier as a mass of blue haze. She halted just over the crest, aware that they did not want to be silhouetted on the sky-line should anyone be watching from the valley below. Hravn rode up next to Ealdgith as she said, almost wistfully, "It's beautiful, so calm and peaceful and we're almost home."

The sun was sinking towards the fells behind them, casting low purple-grey shadows over the orange and brown colours of the broad wooded vale of Arkengarthdale. They could see Langethwait almost directly below, a small cluster of square thatched houses in the centre of strips of fields, wrapped in the security of the forest. Smoke curled upwards from a couple of the cottages.

"I wonder if it is really as peaceful as it looks?" Hravn said quietly, doubt in his tone.

Chapter 25

"Good morning! Wait! I would speak with you...please?" Hravn shouted across the clearing towards the back of an elderly man who was scurrying back from his early morning visit to the communal cess pit behind the cluster of small wattle and daub cottages that formed Langethwait. The man stopped and turned, peering towards the two riders and string of ponies that loomed from the half-light of dawn.

Hravn reined to a halt and slid off his pony as Ealdgith called Sköll and Hati to heel. The man was obviously nervous enough and she did not want the wolfhounds to panic him.

"Wh..who are you?" The man stuttered. "Armed and dressed in mail, but one of us by your voice?" It was more a question than a statement. He was stooped, balding with long greying hair to his shoulders and as thin as the thread-bare clothes he wore.

Hravn strode towards him and held out his hand in greeting. "I'm Hravn, son of The Bear, Lord of Raveneswet, or at least, he was. We fled at Aefter Yule and have returned. I heard my father has survived. Do you know what has happened to him...to my family?"

The man stared at Hravn. His jaw sagged open, eyes wide, hands starting to shake. "Go! You must go, now! Your father is at Hyrst; but go before they come."

Hravn was taken aback by the man's fear. "Who are 'they'?"

The old man almost shouted in his panic to send Hravn away. "They are coming this morning, now, at dawn; Count Alan's men, to take the tax that we must pay after the haerfest. They will take our grain and select cattle and swine to kill and take...we will doubtless starve this winter. His Reeve's men will come first and an ox cart will follow on. If they find you here, armed as you are, they will kill you, and kill us for aiding you...Now go!"

Hravn grasped the old man's hand in thanks, turned and ran back to his pony, shouting to Ealdgith to follow. They led the ponies at a gallop, past the cottages where doors were opening and dogs barking at the commotion; down towards the ford, across the river beyond the village. A distant shout followed by the sudden call of a horn shattered what was left of the peace of the early dawn.

Hravn turned in his saddle. "We're in trouble, Edie. The old man was right. Look! Four of them, three furlongs away; they've turned this way." The first rays of the rising sun suddenly lit the valley, side-lighting the four horsemen, throwing their shadows in long, menacing shapes across the ground at the top of the rise beyond the fields.

"Can we out run them? I'll unleash the ponies; they'll do better free running behind us."

"Yes, do that. If we follow this track into the forest on the hillside, there is a cleft in the cliff above it that we can take. It's steep, but the ponies should make it."

The four horsemen, seeing a string of ponies fleeing the village and assuming that the harvest was being hidden before their arrival, turned and charged down towards the Arkle beck. They intended to cut across the line that Hravn was following into the forest. Three of them wore chain mail, were helmeted and carried spears, but no shields. The fourth was the Reeve's man. He rode without mail, but carried a sword. Their horses moved swiftly over the harvested fields, covering ground far more quickly than the laden ponies that were now beginning to labour as they galloped up the steep track towards the trees.

The Reeve's man led the race, his horse benefitting by not carrying the weight of the armoured soldiers. The fast-flowing Arkle beck cut its way through a narrow, rocky gorge at the bottom of the fields. The Reeve's man urged his horse at the gap and jumped, clearing it easily. The next two horses, less well balanced under the weight of the armoured soldiers, were wrong-footed and just cleared the gorge, their hooves skittering on the rocky ledge, striking sparks on the stone and dislodging loose dirt and pebbles into the wild water below. The fourth horse shied at the last moment, panicked by the sight of the sparking hooves and white water on rocks below. It twisted sideways, halting on the edge, as momentum threw the rider bodily into the rocky side of the gorge. His short scream was cut short as his head cracked open against the cliff.

The Reeve's man wheeled at the sound of the scream, cursed and shouted at the other two soldiers to follow. There was no point in wasting time over a dead comrade.

Hravn saw what had happened and knew that it gave them the time they needed to reach the cleft in the cliff, but only just. Wyrd was kind to him. He knew they couldn't risk being chased up the steep, rocky passage; the soldiers could pick them off from behind. There was only one choice; he thought quickly and shouted his plan to Ealdgith as the ideas formed in his mind.

"Edie! We are going to have to stand and fight. The entrance to the cleft is the best place. Once we get there, push the ponies ahead and get your helmet on. Climb up onto the edge of the cleft, there are ledges on both sides, and take your bow and as many arrows as you can. The entrance is barely the width of two men. I can hold it and take them one by one. Sköll can guard my back and Hati yours. Hit the one with no mail first, then take your time and go for the eyes of the others, hunting arrows won't pierce their mail or leather."

The initial nausea that had seized Ealdgith's stomach when the soldiers gave chase ceased at the realisation that Hravn's plan could work. They had fought and killed and won before. They would do it again. The plan focused her mind and gave her confidence; the confidence that she would need to keep cool and controlled in the fight ahead.

As soon as they reached the forest, Hravn slewed to the left of the track and urged his pony up through the thickets of birch and oak. The pack ponies followed with Ealdgith urging them on from behind. Hravn hoped that the pursuing soldiers might lose them in the close cover of the trees, but he knew that it was no more than a slim hope. The soldiers continued to follow, but the move did buy them more time. The sure-footed fell ponies were at home on the rough terrain and were small enough to zig-zag under and around the low, stubby trees. The horses did not like the close, dense woodland and they struggled on the loose, rough ground; and their riders hugged the necks of their mounts, to avoid low hanging branches. Hravn smiled as he remembered Nudd's comment about horses and why they weren't suited to the high fells. He was right in that at least.

Hravn knew the hillside well from his days hunting with The Bear. He was on home ground. They burst out of the woodland just below a long, high limestone cliff, an impassable barrier. A dark cleft split the cliff in half. Shouts, curses and the sound of heavy bodies thrashing through the wood warned them that the soldiers were close behind.

"Quick! Edie, push the ponies through into the cleft. It opens up to a small grass patch before it goes higher, they will be fine there. See that ledge? You can scramble up to it from the grass patch."

Ealdgith pulled her helmet on quickly, her fingers fumbling in haste with the buckle, and then slung two quivers of arrows and her bow over her shoulder and ran to where the ledge started. Hati circled back and forth below her, confused about what was happening. Ealdgith called down to reassure him, as she crawled carefully to a position twenty feet above the entrance to the cleft. Although the ledge led to the cliff face, Ealdgith was loathe to crawl that far; she would be too exposed to a well thrown spear. She called down to Hravn, "I can cover you from here and see everything to our front and right. I would need to crawl back and move across to the opposite ledge to cover the left."

Hravn glanced up and smiled. Ealdgith's green eyes peering through the face guards on her helmet and her stance on the ledge gave her a cat-like beauty. He raised his left thumb in approval; his right hand was already grasping the hilt of his sword.

Whilst Ealdgith made her way along the ledge, Hravn had fitted his helmet and positioned his spears along the edge of the cliff inside the cleft. He would throw them from within the cover of the cleft, before taking position at the entrance, with Sköll at his back, to guard against any attempt to cut behind him. He was confident that they were as ready as they could be, but they were just in time. He could tell by the crashing in the forest that he had maybe a minute to get ready.

"Edie, stand by, don't move, get in the aim and freeze. Hopefully, they won't notice you." Ealdgith smiled, but didn't waste time with an answer. She was already in the aim with three more arrows laid in front of her. Hravn hefted his heaviest spear in his right hand, judging weight, balance and the distance to the point, over to his right, from which he anticipated the men would emerge from the forest. He knew that creating surprise and shock was the key to victory. With skill, and luck, he might take one of the soldiers down before they even saw him.

The Reeve's man burst from the forest and paused, panting, stooped forward with his hands on his thighs as he drew breath. His horse's reins were grasped in his right hand. Hravn stepped from the cleft and threw his spear in a clean, swift motion, ducking back to watch its flight from the cover of the cleft. The Reeve's man screamed and spun to his left, grasping his left shoulder as he staggered into the soldier behind. Hravn could tell that his spear had found its mark, but whether it had caused a flesh wound or something more serious, he could not see. He grabbed a second spear and stepped forward into the aim just as the first soldier hurled his own spear directly at him.

Hravn's next move was instinctive. He dropped to his knees and spun backwards into the cleft as the spear struck the rock above his head, to bounce back outside the cleft.

The two soldiers separated. The larger one, who had thrown the spear and appeared to be in charge, ran across to Hravn's left and then turned to face him, ten paces away from the cleft. The second approached slowly from Hravn's right, his spear held over arm, ready to throw. Hravn waited. He held Nadr in his right hand and the long seax in his left. He talked softly to Sköll, controlling him, keeping him just behind and to his right. He knew their next move would be a spear thrown from his right and a rush from his left; it was just a matter of when. Hravn watched the spearman from the corner of his right eye. The first move would come from him. It did. Just as the soldier's arm tensed to thrust the spear, Hravn stepped back behind the line of the cleft edge and braced himself, sword forward, for the assault from his left. The spear flashed past his face and slammed into the rock to his left, then skittered down the inside of the cleft. The assault didn't come; both soldiers had seen Sköll and were suddenly wary of engaging too closely.

"You deal with the hound whilst I take the bastard," the larger soldier barked.

"Now, let's have you, English filth. I want you alive; Count Alan will have you talking soon enough."

Hravn was puzzled. He understood the soldier, who was speaking in a rough Cumbric dialect, but why? He held the soldier's gaze, moving the tip of his sword slowly to distract his attention and holding his seax across his body to block a thrust towards him. Hravn let the man come closer, then spat and spoke quietly but forcefully. "You may want me alive, but I'll have you dead soon enough. Come, come closer, my hound wants to taste your throat."

The man hesitated, thrown momentarily by Hravn's use of his own language, Bretton. The second soldier picked up the spent spear and pointed it at Sköll as he cautiously closed the gap between them. He paused. "You're a cocky sod, how come you speak Bretton? You..." His words choked in his throat as he collapsed backwards, his arms wide apart. An arrow had pierced his left eye, into his brain.

"Sweet mother of Jesus!" The larger soldier glanced up, saw Ealdgith string a second arrow onto her bow and flung himself to his right, out of her line of sight. "Mihael! Get here now and guard that sodding hound; and keep clear of that frigging cat-archer on the cliff!"

The Reeve's man ran forward, letting go of the half-tied strip of undershirt that he was trying to bind around the gash in his upper arm. He grabbed the fallen spear and crouched behind the soldier, his spear point jabbing at Sköll's throat. Sköll leapt forward, but fell back with a yelp as the spear tore across his chest. The gash was minor, but it was enough to stop him from leaping at the man again. "Steady, boy," Hravn reassured him. He glanced at Mihail, whose blood was soaking quickly through his upper clothes. He would soon tire from blood loss. The soldier was the threat now.

Ealdgith cursed. She could see Hravn and Sköll below her, but the edge of the cliff hid the two men. She glanced to her right, but the gap to the parallel ledge, across the cleft, was too wide for her to jump. She wriggled backwards and retreated to the start of the ledge, and then crawled quickly along the second one, spare arrows clenched between her teeth. She could hear the clash of metal as Hravn held the soldier at bay in the entrance. Would she be in time?

The soldier, angry at the death of his comrade, battered his way forward. He grasped his sword with both hands and used the advantage of height and weight to rain blows repeatedly upon Hravn's sword and seax. Hravn countered well, moving constantly and deflecting his opponent's sword so that much of its momentum was wasted. His wrists ached from the heavy blows; his left wrist in particular was weakening and he knew that he couldn't retain its strength much longer.

Hravn stepped to his left to use the side of the cliff as a shield and then pulled backwards to draw the soldier forward. The ruse worked. The soldier lunged with a heavy thrust at Hravn's right shoulder. Hravn twisted under and thrust upwards with his seax. The blade stabbed into the soldier's arm pit, but caught on the chain mail links and barely penetrated. The soldier pulled his arm down sharply in pain and self-defence, catching Hravn's helmet heavily with his sword hilt. Hravn pitched forward, stunned.

The soldier kicked Hravn over onto his back. Hravn's eyes were open but unfocused, his face ashen and his breath shallow. "Keep that hound where it is whilst I bind him; then we'll catch the cat."

The soldier knelt and used his knees to pinion Hravn's arms to the ground. The scrape of falling pebbles caused him to look up at the hitherto empty ledge. The last thing he saw was the green flash of Ealdgith's eyes behind the arrow that tore into his eye. The soldier collapsed twitching, instantly lifeless.

"No!" Mihael's scream died as Sköll's teeth tore into his throat.

Ealdgith almost fell from the ledge in her hurry to reach Hravn. He was half raised on his elbows, shaking his head and mumbling as Ealdgith got to him; Hati close on her heels. She unbuckled Hravn's helmet and eased it over his head, cradling his head in her lap. The sword hilt had dented the metal but the thick padded cap underneath had protected the skin and bone of his skull. Ealdgith stroked Hravn's cheek as his eyes slowly refocused on her. Sköll came forward slowly, whining. She hadn't the heart to push him away as he gently licked his master's face.

311

"Hravn, can you move?" Ealdgith asked tenderly. He nodded. "These men are all dead. We can't stay here."

Hravn smiled up at her. "Edie, you did it. You won the fight, my Valkyrie." He raised his hand to wipe away her tears. "Yes, I can move, I'm just very dazed." He pushed himself up slowly and stood, wavering slightly. "Help me onto my pony and I will be alright. We'll take it slowly up the cleft. There is a cave in a craggy outcrop just beyond the top. We can shelter there awhile."

Ealdgith supported Hravn's weight with her shoulder as she led him into the cleft, leaving behind the three bodies and their deserted horses.

Chapter 26

Hravn rode slowly as he led the way up the steep gully. Ealdgith rode close behind and the pack-ponies followed in their own time. Hravn felt nauseous and dizzy. Sweat trickled down his back, but he felt cold. As they came to the top, the ground levelled out and he could see the craggy outcrop and the hill-top forest beyond. "There, Edie, Hyrst is in the forest, two, maybe three, leagues away." He turned to look back to her and as he did so, he tumbled from the pony.

"Hravn!" Ealdgith screamed and jumped down. Hravn was conscious, but muttering incoherently. Ealdgith eased him onto the heather and pulled a blanket from a saddlebag to wrap around him. Strangely, she felt in control. She didn't panic and surprised herself by knowing instinctively what she had to do next. She had seen the effect of delayed concussion once before.

The ponies gathered together and she hobbled them where they stood, to prevent them from straying. Then, bidding Sköll to stay with his master, she unslung the hunting horn from around Hravn's neck and ran with Hati to the outcrop of rock, and scrambled to the top from where she had a view over the forest that cloaked the tops of the hills. Thanking God that, due to Aebbe's fascination with Hravn's horn she was now note perfect in The Bear's hunting call, she placed the horn to her lips and blew, and blew. The notes echoed across the trees in the still, early-winter, morning. The air was crisp and cool and the notes carried. At the back of her mind she worried that Normans might hear, but she was high up on the tops and the gentle, westerly breeze should, she hoped, carry the sound to Hyrst and beyond, but away from the villages in the lower Swale and Arkengarthdale valleys from which they had fled so frantically.

After blowing the call several times, Ealdgith paused to gather her breath and to listen. Silence. She blew again and paused. Nothing. She had to get help; what else could she do? Ealdgith kept blowing the haunting notes of The Bear's call and then pausing to listen. She had lost track of how many times she blew the horn when, suddenly, the call came back to her in a faint echo. She blew again and this time, the returning call was louder. Hati joined in, his own yowl piercing the morning air. Ealdgith relaxed and, leaving Hati to yowl, she ran back to Hravn. He smiled weakly at her and, when she tried to talk to him, she could tell that he was lapsing in and out of lucidity.

Hati's yowl turned to a rapid bark. Ealdgith looked up to see four riders, galloping on ponies along the tree line towards her. They had to be friends; she waved. They closed in quickly and then suddenly reined to a halt. Two of them drew their seaxes and circled slowly. Ealdgith gasped in sudden fear and then relaxed, realising that, still wearing her helmet and with her bow on her back and seax at her hip, she posed a less than friendly sight. She raised her hand. "Sorry! Just let me get this off," she called, unbuckling her helmet and shaking her long, fair hair free.

"I'm Ealdgith, from Hindrelag and this is Hravn, The Bear's son. We fled the..." Ealdgith stopped in mid-sentence. One of the riders crossed himself, two others looked frozen with fear. The fourth, a young man slightly older than Hravn, dismounted slowly and looked carefully before cautiously walking forward. "Ealdgith? But you're dead, surely?"

Ealdgith smiled thinly and shook her head, "I'm not; we're not. We fled the killings at Aefter Yule and have returned from sanctuary in Westmoringaland." She paused, "I know you. You're..."

"Yes, I'm Orme. I served your father..." Orme stumbled on his words. "I found your father's body, after... and your family...I thought you had perished too...yours was the only body we didn't find. We, I, thought you had perished in the flames." Ealdgith stepped forward, held out her hand and pulled Orme to her in an embrace. "Say no more, Orme. You have told me all I need to know. I long thought all my family had perished. We've returned to seek Hravn's family for we heard that The Bear had survived."

"Indeed he has. I serve him now and he sent us when he heard his call."

Ealdgith turned to the others who were now visibly relaxed "Come quickly! We fought and killed three Normans at the foot of the gully. Hravn has a blow to the head and is concussed. We need to get him to The Bear to be cared for until he recovers."

Orme glanced at the others "What would you have us do?"

It was clear to Ealdgith that Orme spoke for the men. They were lads really, for all were of a similar age, but he wasn't their natural leader.

Ealdgith took charge. "Can one of you take us to The Bear? Orme, can you take the other two and find the men we killed. We can't leave them to be found. That will lead the Normans back here, and to you and The Bear. Strip them of their mail and weapons, find their horses and bring all the weapons and armour that you can back here. Pull the bodies into the cleft and bury them with boulders. Unless the stink of decay gives them away, that should hide them."

Orme nodded, impressed by Ealdgith's cool logic and authority. "I can do that."

Ealdgith looked directly at Orme. "There is another task. The soldiers were the Reeve's men, who were due to take payment today from the villagers at Langethwait, but gave chase to us instead. We heard that an ox-cart was due later to collect the payment. Can you get to the village and tell the Headman that he must say that the Reeve's men did not arrive and have not been seen. A fourth was killed jumping the Arkle beck, the villagers will have seen that. Tell them to pile boulders on the body and hide the horse. There can be no trace of the Reeve's men having ever got to Langethwait if the village is to be safe." She paused to let her orders sink in. "I may have only just returned, but I think I read the situation correctly; is that right?" All four nodded.

Orme leant forward and took Ealdgith's hand. "Ealdgith, my lady, I served your father and you are now all that is left of the family. I think I should serve you now."

Ealdgith was taken aback, but smiled. "Orme, thank you, but let us all meet The Bear. We will talk about the future then, for much has changed for all of us. Now, what are your friends called?"

Before they left, Orme and the others helped Ealdgith remove Hravn's mail and weapons. They tied these to the pack-ponies and then helped a very shaky Hravn to mount his pony. A lad called Ulf stayed with Ealdgith and led the ponies slowly onto a narrow track that wound through the woods and around the tops of the ridges that formed part of a network of almost hidden upland valleys. The journey seemed to take for ever and Ealdgith kept calling a halt to check that Hravn was managing to stay upright in his saddle. Both hounds kept very close to his pony, staying as close to their master as they could.

The sun was climbing towards the noon-day zenith when they spotted a thin column of smoke rising from a clearing ahead. Ulf turned back towards them. "Welcome home," was all he said, then spurred forward into the clearing.

Hravn gave Ealdgith a dazed smile, pulled himself as upright in the saddle as he could, and then rode steadily into the clearing. Ealdgith rode beside him and the hounds ran at either flank, their ears pricked and wary. A small group stood by a fire at the edge of the clearing. As Ealdgith's eyes adjusted to the brighter light in the clearing, she saw that it was ringed with small huts and roughly built shelters. They were made from logs of green timber and woven branches, with rough roofs of turf, thatched reeds, bracken or coarse grass. It was a very rudimentary settlement, but blended very well into the woodland behind.

A tall, thickset man stepped forward from the group. His face was gaunt and his long hair was grey. It took a few moments for Ealdgith to realise that he was The Bear. He had aged considerably. The woman whose hand he held had aged too. Freya was petite with the same black eyes and hair as her son. Her hair was now greying like her husband's.

Hravn slipped carefully from his pony and, still light headed, walked slowly towards his parents. As Hravn walked towards his father, Ealdgith realised just how much he had grown in the last year; he really was the image of The Bear as a

318

younger man. Now tall and muscular, he would soon catch up with his father's height and stature. Ask strode to him, arms outstretched wide, and gathered him in a tight embrace before he paused and, still holding Hravn, pulled Freya and Ealdgith to him too. Ealdgith felt his tears fall onto her face to mingle with her own that flowed freely; she breathed deeply and sighed, confident that, for the moment at least, their journey was over.

Ask stood back and looked at them both. He grinned that warm reassuring smile that Ealdgith loved so much. "Well, you've both grown, I have to say. Hravn, you're a man, and more of a warrior than me by all accounts. Edie, well?" He shook his head. "I don't quite know what to say. That boyish girl has certainly gone. A warrior princess to rival Brunhilda has returned."

"Come. My warrior son and his shield maiden."

With an arm around each of their shoulders, The Bear walked them slowly to the fire and sat them on one of the logs that enclosed it.

~~~

There was much to say and The Bear insisted that they took their time to tell their story. He wanted to hear their news before he told them his. Ealdgith spoke for them both, Hravn listened, still dazed and only interrupted to emphasise just how courageous and skilful she was in combat. At times, she flushed with embarrassment, but she was secretly pleased at the awed looks of those around her.

As soon as she heard that her son had mild concussion, Freya had made an infusion of mint and insisted that Hravn sat by the fire to drink it. As he sipped it he felt his nausea slipping away and the dull ache in his head start to ease. Freya sat behind Hravn and slowly rubbed his back; and Ealdgith felt strangely detached. She realised that now they were reunited with Hravn's family she might just have to share him with them.

Some of the other women in the camp fussed around bringing freshly baked unleavened bread and hard cheese for them to eat. Hravn only nibbled, but Ealdgith was ravenous and ate enthusiastically, talking and eating at the same time until she realised that others weren't eating. She was suddenly aware that perhaps food was very limited.

Just as she drew their tale to a close with a description of that morning's fight and her urgent call for help, Orme rode back into the clearing leading the three Norman horses laden with arms. All about them gasped and The Bear was momentarily speechless as Orme jumped down from his pony and, with a flourish, presented Ealdgith with the two arrows she had used to kill the soldiers. "Yours, my lady. I cut them from their heads," he said with a cheeky smile of admiration, adding, "The horses are yours too, they have your father's brand on them. Oh, and I have been to Langethwait. They know what to say and not to say."

Hravn stood slowly and held out his hand to Orme. "Thank you, Orme, your action just now saved us both, it certainly saved me. Join us."

The Bear smiled, laughed, slapped Orme on his back and said, "Well done, lad, something tells me you have a new future ahead of you. Now join us whilst I tell my son and daughter what has happened here." He put his arm around Ealdgith's shoulder, knowing that he need say no more about what she meant to him.

Hravn and Ealdgith listened intently as The Bear recounted the Aefter Yule massacre. It was much as they had supposed. Parties of Norman soldiers had worked their way methodically along the valleys of the Jor and Swale, killing, raping, burning and destroying all the livestock and crops. "I was wrong to think that our smaller valleys north of the Swale would be safe; they weren't and were harried too" he admitted.

The Bear continued to explain that, in some villages including his own, the Normans simply killed the livestock and burnt the crops whilst in others, such as Hindreslag, they had killed all who were there and destroyed everything. It was as if they were working to a plan. That plan was now evident. All the lands of Ghellinges-scir had been given to Count Alan of Brittany, a relative and supporter of the King. Hindrelag was now being rebuilt as an armed camp and all the people in the shire had been grouped into the villages in the fertile, lower Swale and Jor valleys where they could be controlled and provide food, revenue and labour for the Normans. The remoter villages had mostly been wrecked, or their cattle and crops destroyed and the people left to starve over the winter. "If you go there now," Ask told them, "you will find bodies picked clean and their bones scattered or left lying in buildings." Large tracts of land were simply dead.

"Raveneswet was one of the villages allowed to survive, as was Ghellinges itself, but the cruellest blow was that Count Alan then turned Englishman against Englishman. If a Thegn swore him loyalty, a loyalty that meant working his people to the bone to raise the taxes he demanded, then they could keep their land. Otherwise, he took the land and gave it to one of his own, Bretons mainly, or to others who would swear the loyalty he demanded."

Hravn nodded, interrupting, "And, of course, you wouldn't swear loyalty."

"I would not swear!" Ask almost spat the word loyalty, before continuing. "But Thorfinnr did, and that bastard drove out those who would not submit. We fled here, to the forest. The Normans didn't touch Hyrst, it's hidden by the hills and valleys within the forest and they didn't know of it, they still don't. We haven't moved to the village though, instead we survive in the forest with their help. The winter was hard, many died. Hild was one."

He looked at Ealdgith. "I am sorry, Edie, but your aunt wasn't strong enough and..." Ask choked on his words. "She lost the will to live when our daughters were killed in the massacre."

Hravn knew not to ask if they had been raped. He feared that he knew, but he would hear the answer in his own good time. He knew too that he would take revenge.

Ask took Ealdgith's hand in his. "Your family too, Edie, they all perished. That is another reason why Hild forsook this world. With all her family gone, she had nothing to live for."

Ask paused, the tone of his voiced changed. "Save for your uncle, that is. Gospatrick chose to keep his lands and swear fealty to the Count. That finally broke Hild's heart. Your father's lands were taken too and given to a Breton called Enisant, and a real tyrant he is, by all accounts. The whole of the plateau where your manor was, has been cleared and surrounded by a wooden palisade. He's built a hall there and is now starting to build one in stone; a castle I've heard it called; some sort of fort I think. They've even renamed the manor as Richemund, it's at the centre of the armed camp."

"So we heard when we were at Morlund." Hravn confirmed that, although the news was bad, it wasn't unexpected. "We suspected the land was forfeit, but Edie's going to claim the tittle herself anyway."

Ask guffawed, "Quite right too, it's your birth right, Edie, sorry; Lady Ealdgith."

"What of Bron?" The question was Ealdgith's rather than Hravn's.

Freya answered. "She survives, but is very frail. The people of Hyrst have taken her in as I fear she may not survive the winter."

"We must see her," Ealdgith said, turning to Hravn, "to tell her of Rhiannon and, after today, I want to learn all she knows about medicinal herbs and healing. She has a rare skill and, if we are to survive, I need to master it."

Both Hravn and The Bear looked surprised, but Hravn nodded with a grin, "You're right, Edie, that you must."

"How do you survive here?" Hravn asked the question that was already forming on Ealdgith's lips.

Ask answered. "We have built a small community here, as you see. There is still much to do, but there is shelter enough to see us into the winter that is almost upon us. We live in the forest, and from it. There are deer and hares a plenty, and nuts and wild fruit that we trade for grain with the people of Hyrst. There are a handful of small groups like this in the remote parts of the forest and a few in small clearings where we keep swine and goats. My people are spread throughout the forest; and so, if one group is found by the Normans, then I hope the others will survive. We've got skills too, from all the villages, including a charcoal burner, and a smith with a forge. It has been a hard year, but we have scavenged what is left in the villages and claimed clothes and tools, enough to see us through so far."

Freya took over. "And men and women need each other. Most families were broken up by the massacres, wives left without husbands, husbands with no one to look after children, so we've bonded together anew, just as your father and I are now properly together, many other families have started afresh." Hravn and Ealdgith smiled at her. It was the only way forward for them all.

Ask continued. "We all have a role to play. I suppose you are wondering about Orme and the lads?" Hravn nodded. "They work for me, they watch the approaches to the forest to warn me of unwanted interest, they run messages from one small group to another within the forest; they are my eyes and ears and now know the tracks and glades as well as you ever did."

Hravn glanced across to Orme and grinned; a plan already half formed in his mind. Orme grinned back. As Ealdgith watched, she knew that the two young men would be friends. She remembered Orme and was sure that his earlier offer of fealty had been heartfelt. She knew that he would be part of their plans for resistance and revenge.

"What of the Normans, though?" Hravn was unsure how such a community could be allowed to survive.

Ask took his time before answering. "That is something that is also on my mind. They have yet to find us, but when they do, I fear that we will be forced to submit, or ..." He left the thought hanging.

Suddenly serious, Hravn turned to The Bear. "Father, we have heard of a resistance, is that true?"

Ask paused before replying "Yes, there are groups across the North who rebel. Some fight the Normans and perish, others seek revenge against those who have turned against our own. Mainly though, these are acts of defiance, destroying granaries and the like. There is great risk and no mercy for those who are caught. The Normans won't tolerate dissent and are swift to put it down. We won't see another uprising, that is for sure. I haven't become involved because my duty is to my people here in the forest; but I have helped those who do resist." He paused again and lowered his voice, leaning forward so that only Hravn and Ealdgith could hear. "Earl Gospatrick is involved now that he has bought his way back into the King's favour."

Ask looked intently at Hravn and then Ealdgith. "The Earl will be here within a few days. He is to call on Count Alan and is playing him with one hand whilst he pulls the strings of resistance with the other. I have received a message from him to say that he wants to meet you both if you are here. I know not why, nor do I know how, he has heard of you, but the messenger said that the Earl has heard of your exploits against the Pendragons."

Ealdgith said simply "Brother Patrick!" Hravn nodded, catching her eyes with his. "I think we have a job to do, Valkyrie."

******

Hravn and Ealdgith will return in 'Resistance and Revenge'; a tale of the year 1071.

Glossary

Aefter Yule. After Yule. January; the month after the Yuletide festival that became Christmas.

Burh. A Saxon fortified settlement. Typically a timber-faced bank and ditch with a palisade on top, enclosing a manor house and settlement.

Castle. A European innovation, castles originated in the 9th and 10th centuries. Many castles were originally built from earth and timber, but had their defences replaced later by stone. The motte and bailey castle was introduced to England by the Normans. It consisted of a circular moat surrounding an earth mound (Motte) upon which a wooden keep (Tower) was built. The Baily was a wooden palisade inside the moat encompassing the motte and flat land upon which the castle's domestic buildings were built.

Cell. A cell is a small room used by a hermit, monk, anchorite or nun to live, and as a devotional space.

Churl. The lowest rank of English freemen.

Dale. Old English and Norse for a valley.

Earl. An Earl is a member of the nobility. The title is Anglo-Saxon, akin to the Scandinavian form jarl.

Fader. Father.

Fell. Norse for a high hill, mountain or high moorland.

Freyja. Norse. Goddess of love, fertility, and battle.

Furlong. Old English. An eighth of a mile or 200 metres.

Haerfest. Harvest.

Hall. Old English: Heall, a large house.

Hefted. The instinctive ability of some breeds of sheep, including Cumbrian herdwicks, to know intimately the land they live on.

Hel. Queen of Helheim, the Norse underworld.

Hide. An area of land capable of supporting an extended family of up to 50 people.

Holmganga. Norse: "going to an island", a special place for a duel governed by rules of combat.

Hundred. Most of the English shires were divided into 'Hundreds;' groups of 100 'Hides'.

League. A league is a classical unit of length. The word originally meant the distance a person could walk in an hour. Its distance has been defined variously as between one and a half and three miles. I have used the Roman league which is 7,500 feet or one and half miles.

Lencten. Spring.

Longhouse. A Viking equivalent of the English manor house, typically 5 to 7 metres wide and anywhere from 15 to 75 metres long, depending on the wealth and social position of the owner.

Manor. An estate of land. The manor is often described as the basic feudal unit of tenure. A manor was akin to the modern firm or business. It was a productive unit, which required physical capital, in the form of land, buildings, equipment and draught animals such as ploughing oxen and labour in the form of direction, day-to-day management and a workforce. Its ownership could be transferred, by the overlord, In many cases this was ultimately the King.

Moder. Mother.

Ratch. Yorkshire slang. To rummage.

Reeve. An administrative officer who generally ranked lower than the ealdorman or earl. Different types of reeves were attested, including high-reeve, town-reeve, port-reeve, shire-reeve (predecessor to the sheriff), reeve of the hundred, and the reeve of a manor.

Seax. The seax is a type of sword or dagger typical of the Germanic peoples of the Early Middle Ages, especially the Saxons. The smallest were knives, the longest would have a blade over 50 cm long.

Shire. Groups of hundreds were combined to form shires, with each shire under the control of an earl.

Sumor. Summer.

Thegn. A member of several Norse and Saxon aristocratic classes of men, ranking between earls and ordinary freemen, and granted lands by the king, or by lords, for military service. The minimum qualifying holding of land was five Hides.

Wapentake. An administrative area. The Dane-law equivalent of an Anglo-Saxon Hundred.

Warg. In Norse mythology, a warg is a wolf and in particular refers to the wolf Fenrir and his sons Sköll and Hati.

Yule. The two months of the bleak midwinter. Aere Yule ('Ere Yule or Before Yule) is our December and Aefter Yule (After Yule) is our January.

Historical Note

The pre-Norman conquest population of the north and north east of England can be described as "Anglo-Scandinavian". It was a mix of Viking (Danish) and Angle people and traditions. The various dialects of English spoken in Yorkshire and the north east would have been almost unintelligible to people from the Saxon south of England. The Yorkshire aristocracy was primarily Danish in origin whereas that of Northumberland was Angle (Germanic), albeit generally subservient to Danish rule from York.

Communications between the north and south of England were difficult due to the terrain, the poor state of the roads and the large tracts of marshland that formed the southern border of the pre-Danish kingdom of Northumbria along the rivers Aire, Ouse, Trent and Humber. The more popular route between York and the south was by sea. In 962, King Edgar had granted legal autonomy to the northern earls of the Danelaw in return for their loyalty, thereby limiting the powers of future Saxon kings north of the Humber.

In north west England, the borders of the old Romano-British kingdom of Rheged expanded and shrank regularly. In time, Rheged became the kingdoms of Cumberland, the land of the

Cumbri, and Strathclyde. At one time, the kingdom possibly stretched from the Clyde all the way to Chester – mostly down the west coast of Britain.

In the ninth century, Norse-Irish Vikings started to raid and settle in Cumberland. They also started to make incursions over the Pennines into English Northumberland and Yorkshire. Alliances changed continually and the kingdoms of the Cumbrian / Norse and Danish / Angles fought each other for dominance. The kings of Cumbria had eventually to give their allegiance to the Saxon English king Edgar at Chester in 973 and, in doing so, acknowledge the line of the River Eamont as the boundary between England and Cumberland / Strathclyde.

After the defeat of the English army and death of King Harold at the Battle of Hastings in 1066, English resistance to the conquest was centered on Edgar Ætheling, the grandson of Edmund Ironside. Edmund Ironside was half-brother to King Harold's predecessor, Edward the Confessor, and son of King Ethelred 2nd ('The Unready', or poorly counselled).

In late 1067, Oswulf, the Earl of Northumbria, was assassinated. Gospatrick who had a claim to the earldom as grandson of Earl Uhtred, offered William the Conqueror a large amount of money to be given the Earldom of Bernica (Northumberland). The King, who was in the process of raising heavy taxes, accepted.

In early 1068, Gospatrick joined with Edgar Atheling, Edwin Earl of Mercia and Earl Morcar his brother, in an uprising against King William. They lost and Gospatrick was stripped of the earldom.

King William replaced Gospatrick as earl with a Fleming called Robert de Comines. The appointment was very unpopular and led to another rising in the North, with the support of the Danish King Swein. Gospatrick joined this too.

The Harrying of the North was a series of campaigns waged by King William in the winter of 1069–70 to subjugate northern England.

King William paid the Danes to go home, but the remaining rebels refused to meet him in battle, and he decided to starve them out by laying waste to the northern shires, before installing a Norman aristocracy throughout the region.

Contemporary chronicles record vividly the savagery of the campaign, the huge scale of the destruction and the widespread famine caused by looting, burning and slaughter. But some scholars doubt whether King William could have assembled enough troops to inflict so much damage, and the records are believed to have been partly misinterpreted.

King William's strategy has been described by some modern historians as an act of genocide. Contemporary biographers of William also considered it to be his cruelest act. Writing about the Harrying, over fifty years later, the Anglo-Norman chronicler, Orderic Vitalis, said: "The King stopped at nothing to hunt his enemies. He cut down many people and destroyed homes and land. Nowhere else had he shown such cruelty. This made a real change. To his shame, William made no effort to control his fury, punishing the innocent with the guilty. He ordered that crops and herds, tools and food be burned to ashes. More than 100,000 people perished of starvation. I have often praised William but I can say nothing good about this brutal slaughter. God will punish him."

The land was ravaged on either side of King William's route north from the River Aire. His army destroyed crops and settlements and forced rebels into hiding. In the New Year of 1070, he split his army into smaller units and sent them out to burn, loot, and terrify. Florence of Worcester, a contemporary monk, said that from the Humber to the Tees, William's men burnt whole villages and slaughtered the inhabitants. Food stores and livestock were destroyed so that anyone surviving the initial massacre would succumb to starvation over the winter. Some survivors were reduced to cannibalism. Refugees from the harrying are mentioned as far away as Worcestershire in the Evesham Abbey chronicle.

Gospatrick survived the Harrying of the North. In early 1070, he submitted himself to King William, who, interestingly, re-granted him the earldom. He remained earl until 1072 when

William took the earldom away once more and gave it to Waltheof, Danish Earl Siward's son.

The Doomsday Book, which was compiled in 1086, records that in Yorkshire, 60% of all estates were waste, only 25% of the original population and plough teams remained, and there were 80,000 oxen and 150,000 fewer people.

Archaeological evidence supports reports of wide-spread destruction and displacement of people and subsequent restructuring and rebuilding of villages in a more standardised style. However, some historians have argued that it was not possible for William's relatively small army to be responsible for devastation on such a wide scale in the depths of winter, and that later raids by Danes or Scots may have contributed to some of the destruction. It has also been argued that the term 'waste' might signify manorial re-organisation, some form of tax break, or merely the inability of the Domesday commissioners to determine details of population and other manorial resources.

It was evident, from chroniclers, that King William did harry the north. But, as Paul Dalton argued in 2002, the bulk of William's troops were guarding castles in southern England and Wales, and as William was only in the north for a maximum of three months, the amount of damage he could do was limited.

Other historians have questioned the figures reported by Orderic Vitalis, who was born in

1075 and would have been writing his Ecclesiastical History around 55 years after the event. The figure of 100,000 deaths was perhaps used in a rhetorical sense. The estimated population of England, based on the 1086 Domesday returns, is difficult to calculate precisely, but is probably 1.25 to 2.25 million. Thus, a figure of 100,000 represents approximately 5% to 8% of the national population.

If the productivity of the manors recorded in the Doomsday Book is transferred onto a map of Richmondshire, it can be seen that the valleys of the River Swale below Richmond, and the River Ure below Leyburn, generated as much tax in 1086 as they had done before 1070. The regions to the north and south of the river valleys, the higher land in between and the valleys above Richmond and Leyburn are all recorded as waste. The fact that these waste-lands are recorded as belonging to new gentry implies that they had a significance and may well have had a residual, limited and unproductive population. Never-the-less, the Harrying was a cruel, vicious act that impoverished the people of the North, and terrorised them into near slavery for at least a generation. It is probable that the Harrying caused immediate winter starvation, the loss of grain and life stock with which to regenerate communities and the consequent total dislocation of the economy, thereby rendering the smaller communities unsustainable.

The Normans chose Richmond as the focus for a military camp from which they could dominate the North. It is highly unlikely that they wantonly destroyed the local population because they would need them to farm in order to sustain the garrison and to provide the labour to build castles.

I have drawn upon the Doomsday Book, using the names of those who held the respective manors at the time of the Harrying. Gospatrick was a family name. There were Gospatricks other than the earl and several of the local manors were held by a Thegn called Gospatrick. I have chosen to include him within Ealdgith's family.

The Normans did not intrude across the Pennines into Cumbria until the 1090s.

Pendragon Castle in the upper Eden valley of Mallerstang has long been associated with Arthurian legend in that it is claimed that it was built by Uther Pendragon, the father of King Arthur. Cumbria has a strong claim to many of the Arthurian legends, most notably through Urien, the Romano-British king of Rheged, a post-Roman Kingdom in Cumbria. Mallerstang would have been an ideal valley for a renegade British warlord to thrive; though the Pendragons are purely fictional.

65388023R00212

Made in the USA
Charleston, SC
23 December 2016